THE
SOUTHAMPTON
CHRONICLE

A NOVEL

also by

RICHARD
MASSEY

The Gascony Letters

Municipal Tilt

THE
SOUTHAMPTON
CHRONICLE

A NOVEL

RICHARD
MASSEY

TIREE
PRESS

an imprint of
OGHMA CREATIVE MEDIA

OGHMA
CREATIVE MEDIA

Tiree Press
An imprint of Oghma Creative Media, Inc.
2401 Beth Lane, Bentonville, Arkansas 72712

Library of Congress Cataloging-in-Publication Data

Names: Massey, Richard, author.
Title: The Southampton Chronicle/Richard Massey | Gregory of Bordeaux #1
Description: Second Edition. | Bentonville: Tiree, 2018.
Identifiers: LCCN: 2018944185 | ISBN: 978-1-63373-446-3 (hardcover) |
ISBN: 978-1-63373-473-9 (trade paperback) | ISBN: 978-1-63373-086-1 (eBook)
Subjects: BISAC: FICTION/Historical/Medieval |
FICTION/Historical/Renaissance | FICTION / Action & Adventure
LC record available at: https://lccn.loc.gov/2018944185

Tiree Press trade paperback edition October, 2018

Cover & Interior Design by Casey W. Cowan
Editing by Staci Troilo

 would like to thank the following people for helping me with this book: Albert Del Page, Gregory Crofton, Staci Troilo, Amylou Wilson, Serenah McKay Coleman, Casey Cowan, Richard Howk, and Gil Miller.

This book is for my mother, Mary Rensalear McClure Massey,
and my dear friend, the late Daniel L. Foster.

"The City of London shall enjoy all its ancient liberties and free customs, both by land and by water. We also will and grant that all other cities, boroughs, towns, and ports shall enjoy all their liberties and free customs."

Magna Carta 1215, Clause No. 13

A BEAVER SKIN HAT

AND A SPANISH FILLY

Gregory watched the kitchener hang. Dangling, gurgling for breath, his face a ripened gourd of anguish as the boisterous crowd at Smithfield jeered. His feet twitched. Spittle dripped from his chin. He swung with the last angry convulsions of life as he struggled against his fate.

Gregory poured another cup of wine, leaned against the merchant's stall, and took a long drink. Yes, this man deserved to hang. He'd raped a nun, slit her throat, and blamed an innocent man. Those are the kinds of crimes that merit a date at the gallows. And in London, where justice often fluttered away on swift wings, it pleased Gregory to see the right man in the noose.

He had led the inquest proving the innocence of the man first charged with the crime, a gifted goldsmith who'd just produced his masterpiece. In turn, he had built the case against the real culprit, a lay brother who worked as a kitchener at Greyfriars. During the inquest, Gregory discovered that the kitchener had been expelled from Norfolk for an assortment of trespasses.

He only found shelter in London after his noble family had made a large donation to the friary. When this came out in court, the kitchener spit and hissed, and when the judge sentenced him to death, he damned Gregory to the dripping cave of hell.

Indeed, Gregory didn't like executions and rarely attended them, but on this wet and windy day at Smithfield, he enjoyed the vindication.

"Look at him, Gregory," Stephen said. "He longs for the life he never should have had."

Gregory lifted his cup and agreed with his friend. "The goldsmiths cannot withstand any taint on their reputation, especially if the taint is untrue. And just as important, the nun needed to be avenged."

"You delivered justice, my dear friend," Stephen said.

The case became a source of gossip and crude humor at the taverns and markets. The denizens of London fancied the chance to rehash and embellish a tale of murder involving a goldsmith, a lay brother at Greyfriars, and a nun with a checkered past. The matter was even discussed in the halls of the great townhomes along Fleet Street. In no time, attention turned to Gregory himself. People wondered about that lanky, stylish fellow who unearthed the nasty truth. Word spread he was from the great wine city on the River Garonne, and if you wanted a fine Malbec from Cahors or a sweet Sauternes, then you should visit his shop down on the waterfront.

It was 1296, and from then on he was known by the title he'd earned— Gregory of Bordeaux.

Gregory lived in a timbered merchant house tucked in a tight row of merchant houses on Royal Street in the Vintry. His house had a workshop and storefront, a cozy hall with a hearth in back, and a bedroom on the second floor, all over a vaulted cellar stacked with great barrels of Gascon wine. Gregory's cousin, Jean du Mont, managed the family's winery from the storefront. Gregory liked to sit at a desk off to the side and work on his documents as Jean du Mont haggled with buyers and sellers. A lawyer and man of letters, Gregory stayed busy reviewing, writing, or witnessing a contract. He wrote wills and public notices, and if someone needed a poem or sonnet, Gregory would put quill to parchment and compose a few simple verses. He took dictation and translated French and Latin into vernacular English. He kept an active correspondence with associates from across the realm, and he maintained correspondences for others, too. All manner of merchants and craftsmen came and went, but none left Gregory's house without handing over a few coins, a raw material, or a finished good of some sort. Indeed, he was happiest when at his desk, making profit as the wine flowed.

On one such day, a dusty and road-worn messenger arrived. Jean du Mont brokered an export shipment of grain, so Gregory rose from his desk and greeted the newcomer. As the rider wrapped the horse's reins around the post, he said, "I'm looking for Gregory of Bordeaux."

"It is I. And whom may I ask has come calling?"

"The Earl of Southampton is requesting your services."

"Please, come inside so we can discuss the matter."

The two of them went back to the hall and sat at the trestle table. The apprentice hung the rider's cloak and hat on a peg. He stoked the embers in the hearth and set the table with fresh bread, hard white cheese, and a flagon of Gregory's best wine, a Moissac. The rider took a quaff, gave a nod of approval, and as he sliced a hunk of cheese and tore at the loaf, explained the reason for his arrival.

"I'm Robert, a member of the Earl of Southampton's household," he said. "He will arrive in London in two days and would like to meet with you to discuss a proposal."

"What kind of proposal?" Gregory asked. He took a sip of wine.

"My lord is aware of your work at court, in particular, your handling of the case involving the goldsmith." He wiped his chin with the back of his hand. "He wants to employ you."

"For legal services?"

"Perhaps," he said. "But what you need to know about the earl is he is fond of manuscripts. He trades them, collects them, and is now, God willing, trying to read them. You are a man of letters. He wants you, Master Gregory, to write a chronicle."

"The offer is flattering, I assure you," Gregory said. "But I'm a lawyer, not a chronicler. And besides, I do quite well at court and here at my shop."

Robert seemed to savor the wine while he looked around the hall. Gregory followed his gaze over the plush embroidered wall hangings, ornate hutch, carved oak table, and the fine worsted wool of Gregory's clothing. All served as ample proof of his standing.

Robert nodded in agreement. "Yes, Master Gregory, you have done well for yourself. In time I'm sure you will become a merchant prince."

Gregory detected a subtle but unmistakable note of sarcasm in Robert's voice when he'd uttered the words "merchant prince." Gregory was unaccustomed to being insulted by middling noblemen, especially in his own hall. He rose from the table, walked over to the hearth, and stoked the embers in an exaggerated show of displeasure. He looked over his shoulder at his guest. "Robert, from what I understand, Southampton is but a boy and is not as secure in his earldom as he'd like to think. Perhaps he should pull his head away from his manuscripts and do what a lord is supposed to do—fight and fornicate for his title!"

Robert slapped his knee and erupted with laughter. "It seems I have offended you."

"It is impossible for you to offend me, for you are but a hearth knight," he said. "No, it is Southampton who has scratched me in the wrong place. If this chronicle is so important, perhaps he should have come himself."

"Or perhaps he should hire someone else." Robert stood and made as if to leave.

"Where are you going?" Gregory said.

"Back to the earl to tell him you have rejected his offer."

"But I have not!"

"Oh, but you have." He smiled. "My only hope is you regret the decision."

"Wait," he said as Robert put on his cloak and hat. "Tell Southampton I'd be glad to speak with him in person."

Robert grinned widely as he positioned his plumed hat just so and secured his cloak with a ruby brooch. In ceremonious fashion, he pulled a gold signet ring from a pouch at his belt and slid it onto his left pinky. Gregory noticed the silver necklace, the Merino wool, the kid leather, and the silk and fur trappings. The sword pummel sticking up from his hip glowed with a deep patina. Robert no longer had the dull look of a common rider but shone bright with twinkling eyes. Here was a man who had come of age on the battlements, a man who hawked, hunted, and feasted, and who spurred his horse until it galloped with the wind. Gregory guessed he also had a small but growing library in a great chamber at his castle on the south coast, and he needed a chronicler. Gregory took a quick, worried breath and put a hand to his mouth. He felt a flush of embarrassment and a tremor of fear, and he dared not speak as the man in his hall blossomed with the dreadful glamour of a lord. He was confused as to what was about to happen, but even as panic bubbled, one thing was certain—there stood Richard Beaufort, the Earl of Southampton.

"Master Gregory, you can sit here and count your pennies and argue over shit versus shit at court, and you will grow rich in so doing," he said. "Or you can venture into the realm and write the history of our times. Your name will stand even when we are all but dust and bones. My offer is good until tomorrow at this hour. Otherwise, Gregory of Bordeaux, I will employ a Greyfriar who will be more than willing to do what I asked of you."

Speechless and ashamed, Gregory hurried after Southampton to the door. What he saw when he reached the storefront astonished him—a dozen of Southampton's men, on horseback and knee to knee, waiting in the street for the young baron. Their presence caused a major stir on Royal Street as merchants, buyers, and porters craned their necks to see what happened at Gregory's otherwise quiet and respectable wine shop. Southampton pulled himself into the saddle. "My townhome tomorrow at this time, Bordeaux." He and his men wheeled their horses and left.

Jean du Mont turned to Gregory and with a puzzled look, said, "Who was that and what did he want?"

"That," Gregory said with a note of disbelief, "was the Earl of Southampton, and he wants me to write a chronicle."

He and Jean looked at one another for a long while, reading one another's eyes. They shared a grin as the enormity of what had just happened settled in. Gregory would go to Southampton the next day and accept the commission. With his talent and ambition, it could be no other way. Gregory, who just a few years ago was a starving student and heir to a declining wine business, was now Gregory of Bordeaux, and he was going to work for a powerful earl. Jean opened up his arms and Gregory stepped into them for a long embrace.

"Dear cousin, you will run the shop as I travel across the land?" Gregory said.

"Of course, and drive harder bargains than I ever have before," Jean said and laughed. "And whenever you return, we will eat and drink and sing and dance and count our coins as you regale us with your tales of adventure."

Gregory washed down the last bite of spiced pork gelatin with a sip of red wine and settled into his place at the long table at the center of Southampton's hall on Fleet Street. He sat at one end and the earl at the other. Just the two of them in the dim candlelight, Gregory trying to glimpse into the heart of his host, searching for hints and clues as to why he was really there, and trying in silence to determine if the earl was his friend or foe.

Gregory had never been in the presence of an earl before Southampton's visit the day before. He had only seen them parading through the streets on their glistening steeds, in the train of large, armored retinues, jolly and confident in their power to do as they pleased. Gregory was always one of the many who watched the high nobles come and go, and perhaps who smiled and bowed in deference, but otherwise said not a word.

Taught from an early age to respect his elders and those in higher stations, Gregory had honored that convention throughout his life. But here in this hall loomed a new kind of business, and as it involved a chronicle, it only made sense that Gregory should speak about it. He didn't know what he'd say, but he took another quaff of wine, hoping the words would come to him. The earl outranked him by many degrees, but Gregory was the older of the two. When he could take the silence no longer, he decided to split the difference, and in what he considered the biggest risk he'd taken in years, ventured to speak first.

"So why did you choose me?" he said. "Surely you know people who are more accomplished with their quills?"

"Perhaps," the earl said. "But it is not just quality I desire."

"But in a chronicle, my lord, quality is what you must have, or else it is forgotten as soon as it is read," Gregory said.

"The goldsmiths," he said. "They have done much work for me and my family. When the apprentice found himself in trouble, I took more than a passing interest in the outcome of his ordeal. And then you came along. You gained a royal writ to transfer the case into King's Bench."

"And the guild paid dearly for it, too," he said. "Had the kitchener not been such a beast, I doubt I would have succeeded. But the Greyfriars were eager to wash their hands of him."

"I know, but what kind of man takes such a risk for the fate of an apprentice goldsmith?"

"I serve the law, and I serve the guilds, my lord, and perhaps I am zealous when I do both at the same time."

The earl laughed. "And what if you served me? Would I be entitled to your zealous loyalty?"

"Yes, but before we talk of service, what is it exactly that you want of me?" he said. "You mentioned a chronicle, but you must be more specific."

"I want you to ride out into the realm, Gregory of Bordeaux, and I want you to write down all of what you see and know and make for me a rare manuscript. I am not interested in the lives of saints and the stories of kings. I already know all of that. I want to know what is really out there, and I want you, a man of the world—not some poor and obnoxious friar—to tell the story."

In a burst of energy, the earl rose from his seat and guzzled a cup of wine. Despite the decorum by which a nobleman must comport himself, he paced back and forth across the hall. Gregory did not budge. He remained stern and upright in his chair, put a hand to his chin, and pondered the proposition. He would have to leave his beloved London and its maze of leaning half-timbered houses and shanties, its hodgepodge of mansions, barns, churches, and priories, and its soggy stench of commerce. He would miss the soaring spire of St. Paul's and its nave of stained glass, rainy afternoons with friends at the Purple Pot Tavern, standing at the edge of the pier when his laden wine ship arrived, and the assorted sundries that comprise a fruitful life. He had never considered doing something like this, leaving the certainty of London for the vague promise of a chronicle. His first impulse was to tell himself he was not up to the task. But his second emotion, the one that reached down and stirred the very marrow of his soul, suggested otherwise. He looked at Southampton, still a teen growing into his noble bones, and saw in him a rare and wonderful opportunity.

"You do know I have bought and sold wine all my life, don't you?"

"Yes," the earl replied. "But what does that mean?"

"It means I will do your chronicle," he said, raising an index finger for emphasis, "but the price, my lord, the price must be right."

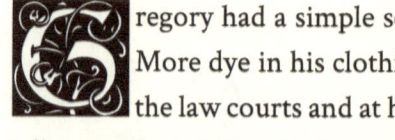regory had a simple sense of fashion—the more color the better. More dye in his clothing proved to the public how well he did at the law courts and at his wine shop. Let them see red, blue, green, yellow, and a bright jay's feather sprouting from his cap. Let them see the twinkling of a jewel on his wrist and the shine on the buckle of his belt. Let them be envious and whisper amongst themselves, "Gregory must be break-ing the law, for every time I see him he seems dressed for the royal hall."

There in front of him was all of it, the finest silk and wool trappings from Flanders, displayed on racks and there for the taking while he shopped on the earl's lavish account. As much as he wanted to splurge on a check-ered hood, a mantle of satin and a deer pelt, and as much as the shopkeeper implored him to do so, Gregory denied temptation and kept walking down the long clutter of stalls. He finally stopped in front of a merchant who of-fered a different brand of clothing, a kind Gregory had never worn. These clothes looked and smelled different. Triple stitching at the seams and heavy selvage—browns, blacks and greys, not the rainbow of the peacock but the somber hues of the carrion birds. Gregory had an intriguing thought, and when the merchant caught his eye, he flashed a smile and said to him, "What is your wish, fine sir?"

"I will be traveling far and wide and wish not to fall apart along the way," Gregory said. "I wish to be windproof, waterproof, and fireproof. And when I arrive in a town where nobody knows my name, I want them to think twice before asking of me my business."

The shopkeeper rubbed the back of his neck and looked Gregory up and down. As he squinted, a keen crease showed in his brow and he nodded in a slow and thoughtful way. "You have come to the right place."

he shopkeeper had done well. In exchange for a handful of sil-ver coins, he furnished Gregory with a matching set of cordovan gloves and boots, nub spurs, a thick leather belt, a black robe, and a black cloak lined with felted beaver fur. He gave Gregory a curious kind of black beaver skin hat with a deep crown lined with red silk and a brim large enough to keep out the sun, the rain, and the snow. He turned the hat in his hand before putting it on. The shopkeeper handed him a polished plate of silver and Gregory looked at his reflection. He made a sour face. The hat looked as if it had devoured his head, and if he were to wear this hat to court, or at his winery, he would surely be the butt of jokes.

"This hat is ridiculous," he said, and took it off.

"You say so now, but when the winter wind is calling, and when the road in front of you is long, you will think differently," the shopkeeper said.

Gregory thought about that for a while.

"The winter always comes, doesn't it?" he said, and the shopkeeper gave the nod of a sage.

A fortnight came and went in which Gregory organized his affairs. Everyone knew he readied to leave, and in those final days before the journey started, he enjoyed the heightened status of being an associate of an earl. While Gregory had always had a place of privilege in London society, Southampton's direct and open patronage had elevated him to the top rung of the merchant class. He knew he could wield his rank, but he also knew even the sharpest sword went dull if used for the wrong reasons. With that in mind, he remained humble and steady in his preparations, and said his good-byes, not really knowing if he would ever return. When the day of departure dawned, he was surprised to see a large crowd gathered in front of the winery. His cousin Jean du Mont, Alan Spicer, Joan the Widow, the four Williams—William Purchase, William Pepper, William Stokes, and William Hawkins—and many other familiar faces, all there to see him off and to grant him Godspeed. Though touched by their support, deep inside he knew a few people in the crowd came for just one reason—they wanted to see him try and mount the horse given to him by Southampton.

The earl had handpicked a silvery Spanish filly with a white mane, four white socks, and a rambunctious disposition, and she had a tug to her Gregory had never felt in the tame rounceys he usually rode. And talk was made of Gregory's first attempt to ride her, when she lurched and nearly threw him. Gregory named her Moonbeam, and though she was a lord's horse of racing and of war, he wanted to become her merchant master.

Attired in his dour black garb and his big beaver skin hat, Gregory knew he would make a fine fool of himself if Moonbeam bucked and tossed him to the ground. Aware that at least a few people wanted to see exactly that, he summoned the gumption to grab the pummel, plant his foot into the stirrup, and pull himself up into the saddle. And when he did, Moonbeam reared, kicking out her hooves and sounding a boisterous neigh. But Gregory held on tight, and as she snorted and flinched and trotted in a circle, he managed to bring her under control.

"Hold London dear to your hearts, my friends," he said, "for I should like to return to what I now leave."

Out through Newgate he went. When London was just a dark spot on the horizon, he wheeled his horse around and took one last look. He vowed to return, but not until he had seen enough to write an astounding chronicle for his earl. He slapped the reins. Moonbeam barged into a full gallop, charging west through the morning drizzle and mist to the tournament at Oxford.

PEPPER, CAPONS AND EELS

The trumpets blared at Northgate. With last night's wine still heavy in his head, Gregory pulled on his boots, cinched his cloak with a silver brooch, and dashed out the door. He stopped briefly for a beef pie and devoured it as he made his way through the meandering streets toward the central market at Carfax. It didn't matter that a proper sun hadn't shown in Oxford in a week and the city lay mired in mud. People of all walks came in droves and headed to the great procession. Walter of Helmsley, an obscure lord from Yorkshire, had arrived, and all of Oxford wanted to see the spectacle.

The young knight Helmsley came to Oxford for the chance of a lifetime. King Edward, to the surprise of the court, had chosen him from among the hundreds who'd sought the appointment to a vacant estate on the Welsh Marches—the Lordship of Laugharne. Edward needed a man from among the English baronage, one who would live in Wales, and live the right way, out of fear he would jeopardize his holdings back in England. He also needed a man of modest means, one who owed all his good fortune to the king and to no other. Helmsley was that man.

The church, however, had other ideas. A grand coalition within the Archdiocese of Canterbury had sponsored a rival appointee, Eustace of Dover, the second son of a magnate in Kent. The church threatened King Edward with ecclesiastical retribution, perhaps from the Pope himself, if Dover was not appointed to Laugharne. To defy the church outright, or to buckle under its pressure, would have been foolish. Instead, King Edward proposed a compromise. Helmsley and the church's candidate, Dover, would meet at Oxford for hand-to-hand combat, a horse race, and a joust. To the winner went the grim, dank castle of Laugharne perched on the windswept coast of south Wales.

Once at market, Gregory shouldered his way through the crowd to the workhouse of John, a friend and wine merchant with whom he had traded for years. He stepped inside and pulled the hood from his head.

"I see you've made it." John clapped Gregory over the shoulder. "After last night, I figured you'd sleep until the return of Christ."

Gregory swallowed his last morsel of beef pie, grinned, and motioned to the apprentice for a cup of watered wine.

"What, and miss all this?" He gestured toward the teeming street. "Surely you will close your shop this day and spend time with your friend."

"Yes," John said, "but I will not drink with him like I did last night."

The two of them climbed a steep stairwell to the third floor. From there, Gregory saw all of Oxford and the pious stonework of its holy orders, its squalid student quarter, the pits and wheels and smoke of its industry, and the suburbs sprawling out from the city wall. The tower at St. Martin's, its bells ringing, loomed over the urban panoply. Gregory looked down at the convulsions taking place in Carfax. Sentries cleared the street of the throng of peasants gathered for the procession. Beating them back with clubs and thongs, the sentries cursed and threatened the peasants with all manner of harm if they did not make way for Walter of Helmsley.

The apprentice arrived with a jug of wine and poured cups for Gregory and John.

"To your health," John said.

"And to yours," Gregory replied, who winced with the day's first drink.

He craned his neck for a glimpse of Helmsley and his retinue. A surge of excitement gripped Gregory as they slowly rounded the bend on Northgate. Amid the furls of his green and gold banners, Helmsley sat tall and proud on his prancing charger. As he made his way into the din of Carfax, with flowers tossed his way by shop girls, he looked this way and that from beneath the raised visor of his plumed helm. Within the folds of his jupon shone his armor of plate and mail, and from his hip hung a great sword. A shield emblazoned with the face of a boar hung over his back. Fastened to his boots were long, gilded trowel spurs. The crowd, loud with cheers and singing, gawked at this rugged man of the north who glittered in martial finery. Followed by his liveried household, Helmsley looked like the kind of young lord who could not be denied. But Gregory knew this was all part of the show.

"He looks so self-assured," Gregory said. "And perhaps he is. But from what I hear, he borrowed a year's income for this. If he wins, then he'll be fine. But if he loses, he'll most certainly be ruined. He's deep in debt to the mercers of York."

Gregory and John smiled when Helmsley tossed a few of his borrowed farthings to the boys who'd followed him from Northgate.

"What are his chances?" John asked.

"Oh, they're good," Gregory said, who took another sip of wine. "I've been told he's campaigned in Scotland, Ireland, and across the channel in Flanders. And he was raised in the Earl of Northumberland's household. If he has a weapon in his hand or is on his horse and tilting, then he has a chance."

"And what of his rival, this Eustace of Dover?" John asked.

"He's a bastard, whelped on a young milkmaid," Gregory said. "He has neither talent nor ambition. His only qualification is that he is the son of Lord Chatham, who has endowed two abbeys in Kent. If somehow he wins, he will be the Lord of Laugharne in name only. He will do the bidding of the abbots."

The crowd primed its gullet and grew exuberant with ale and wine, roasted pork and beef, and the antics of minstrels and acrobats. Lords and ladies in silk and fur, and the mass of commoners in linen and rough wool, pressed into the market for a glimpse of the combatants. Students sang lewd songs as their masters shuddered and looked away. As all manner of society gambled on such events, the haggling over bets and the pledging of coinage, clothing, food, and tools was heavy.

Though Gregory was no slave to the wheel of fortune, he did like to wager on the tournaments. On this day, when one of King Edward's men faced off against a representative of the church, Gregory had no shortage of takers. But instead of betting on Helmsley, the favorite, Gregory wagered on Dover, from the settled county of Kent. Corpulent and reputedly fond of little more than women and wine, few gave him a chance against Helmsley, a budding warlord shaped by the stone, wind, and wilds of the north. Gregory figured the reward far outweighed the risk, and with the Earl of Southampton's pennies heavy in his pouch, he had set a series of bets the day before with an assortment of merchants.

"You do know I stand to win a pot of pepper, and much more besides, if Dover is victorious, don't you?" Gregory said.

"And if he wins, and if that pepper becomes yours, I am having you over for capons and eels," John said.

Helmsley and his retainers continued onward in orderly fashion to their final destination, the castle on the west side of town. As Helmsley faded down Bailey Street, more trumpets sounded, this time from Eastgate. Eustace of Dover had arrived. Gregory and John turned and looked at one another with raised eyebrows. A gang of cutthroats pushed through the crowd, a rhythmic taunt sounded, and people booed and whistled with derision. The mood of the crowd became hot with menace, and in the faces where Gregory had just seen frivolity, he now saw malice. The apprentice poured more wine. Gregory and John took their sips to fortify themselves for what was to come.

"I do believe the people are supporting the king's candidate," John said.

"Indeed." Gregory raised his cup. He and John drank again.

And then came a stanza of violent, alarming noises from down High Street. Gregory craned his neck, and through the narrow opening between the houses leaning out over the street, he saw mass confusion at the east end of the city. The cutthroats pushed against a detachment of soldiers as they tried to pull Dover from his mount. His white horse, startled by the sudden rush of assailants, whinnied and reared as Dover struggled to remain in the saddle. Gobs of mud and offal lobbed through the air, landing on the young knight and his bucking steed. Shrill cries and harangues, the glint of swords, the gush of blood, and the push and pull of the scrum—Dover had been welcomed to Oxford.

When the crowd parted, Dover spurred his steed forward. Chamber pots emptied on him as he careened down High Street to safety. Gregory, eyes wide and mouth agape, watched the soiled and unpopular lord gallop by in a blur of ignominy.

"Yes," John said with a wide smile of sarcasm. "Pepper, capons, and eels."

n the aftermath of Dover's infamous entry into Oxford, a peculiar thing happened. Despite his purported love of women and wine, Dover swore off his vices and grew pious. In the week leading up to his competition with Helmsley, he'd spent his days and nights praying in the chapel at Greyfriars. He even took communion at St. Martin's with the mayor and his many bailiffs.

While Dover prayed, Helmsley drank. He and a group of young nobles visited the taverns and brothels each night. Rumors ran rampant about Helmsley getting blind inebriated and boasting of being the king's chosen man, stating he would destroy Dover and be the new Lord of Laugharne.

Those rumors must have been true, because at the first competition— hand-to-hand combat with blunted weapons, Helmsley arrived drunk, disheveled, and slow on his feet. After feeling one another out, Dover felled a stumbling Helmsley with a terrific ax blow and pinned him to the ground. For the horse race the next day, Helmsley appeared in much better form. Mounted on a splendid, high-stepping shire colt, he bolted from the start and never trailed.

The crowd, and indeed, King Edward's representatives, erupted with joy when Helmsley crossed the finish line in a splash and spray of mud.

It was then Gregory felt sure he would not win his pot of pepper and his other prizes. But the unthinkable happened. Helmsley arrived for the third and deciding event, the joust, drunker than he'd arrived for the first. As he took a final, sloppy swig of ale and mounted his charger, Dover finished a prayer. Then the men sat motionless, facing each other from opposite ends of the tilt, Helmsley in his green and gold and Dover in his blue and grey, their steel glinting in the pale afternoon light. The wind died down and the crowd grew silent. Horsetails twitched in anticipation. Then their mounts lurched forward, plumes dipped and lances descended for the strike. Faster and faster the horses hurtled toward the moment of truth, the moment when one man became a lord in Wales and the other a lord in ruin.

In the final moment before impact, Helmsley flinched, his lance going wide of the mark. Dover leaned in, stepped into his stirrups, and planted his lance squarely on Helmsley's shield. A flush thud sounded, and the lance bent like a bow and snapped. The jolt tossed Helmsley to the turf in a heap of clanking armor. Dover curbed his horse to a dramatic halt, pushed up his helm's visor and bellowed in triumph, "Behold the Lord of Laugharne!"

The crowd groaned. Gregory, wine in hand and watching from his perch in the timber grandstands, took a look over at the box where the King's men sat. Red-faced and holding out their hands in astonishment, the king's distraught nobles tried to console themselves while their ladies fanned their faces with exaggerated gestures of sorrow. At the other end of the royal box, the bishops, abbots, and friars failed to be discreet as they hugged and kissed each other's cheeks.

Gregory and John looked at one another and shared a laugh.

"Master John, what was it you said a few days ago?" Gregory said. "Was it something about pepper, capons, and eels?"

Gregory could hardly contain his smile when he arrived at the grocer's storefront a few days later to collect his spoils. He waited politely as the merchants attended to their customers. He was sure they took their time with the hopes he would turn, leave, and not return. But of all the things Gregory could do on that day, none was sweeter than taking possession of what he'd won at the tournament. So he waited, and when the time came to belly up to the various stalls and take what was rightfully his, he did so with relish.

"I believe a certain Eustace of Dover was victorious in what might become known as the best tournament in the history of Oxford," he said to the spicer. "And I believe victory is worth a pot of pepper to me."

"To the dogs with you," the spicer said. "How did you know the whoreson would win? And how can you collect on such a debt from me, a poor spicer who can barely feed his wife and kids?"

"Come now," Gregory said. "I've seen you at the Guildhall in London in a silk hat and a fur-lined cape. You only have yourself to blame."

The spicer, shaking his head and sighing, dug into his chest of treasures and pulled out a pot of pepper. Gregory took it in hand, bent into a mocking bow, and left. He made his way through the market, and by the time he finished, he had that pot of pepper, two pelts of rabbit fur, an extra vial of iron gall ink and quills, an ell of goatskin leather, dried cod and almonds, a razor—because he had forgotten his in London—and a comb, because he had forgotten that, too.

Gregory remained in Oxford for another week and wrote his account of the tournament.

Helmsley is the drunken lord of ale who found his title at the bottom of a barrel, whereas Dover is the lord of luck who found his floating at the top. When competing at a tournament for an important reward, it is better to drink the blood of Christ than it is to drink the Devil's brew.

Gregory and John feasted on capons and eels and had their long and rollicking bout of wine in front of the fire at John's hall. Even though the students rioted over an increase in rents and the quality of bread, Oxford was pleasant enough. With chilly autumn winds whipping up from the River Thames, Gregory knew it would be easy to explain if he were to stay for a while. But he already had the fever, an unshakeable longing for the road and its promise of knowledge and adventure. So on a dark and frosty dawn, he pulled on his black beaver and wool, mounted silvery Moonbeam, and clattered through West Gate toward Sudeley Castle in Gloucestershire, where awaited a condemned man of words.

THE GREAT
WHORESON
OF NOAH'S ARK

G regory leaned into the slanting October drizzle as Moonbeam made her way down the potted, muddy road. He'd likely spend this night as he'd spent the last—damp and miserable beneath a leaking, drafty tent.

He glanced up from beneath the sagging brim of his hat expecting to see nothing but the dying light of the day, but to his relief saw the silhouette of a castle along the twilight horizon.

Finally—Sudeley.

He coaxed his horse into a gallop, and Moonbeam splashed through the town and up the winding ascent to the castle gates.

"I am Gregory of Bordeaux and I am in the service of the Earl of Southampton," he called to the guard. "I am here to pay my respects to Lord Sudeley and to speak with his fool, Simon le Clerk."

The gates creaked open.

ne of the first people Gregory thought about when commissioned to write the chronicle was Simon le Clerk. Having risen to fame with the stroke of his poisonous quill, he was somewhat of a hero to people like Gregory, who found much fault in the great hierarchy of the world.

When Le Clerk was anonymous and unknown to the public, he had written an allegory based on a conversation between a swan from the village and an owl from the city. Known as The Swan, the Owl, and the Finch, it was the prized, secret treasure of readers across the realm, and particularly in London, where copies of it were stashed in trunks and cupboards, and hidden under floorboards and behind false walls, from Aldgate to Newgate. Pulled out in the wee hours, sitting by the fire with trusted company, The Swan, the Owl, and the Finch appealed to those who thought more of the future than they did of the past. And Gregory knew most of it by heart.

"... I like the village," the swan said. "The fertility of the fields, the wholesome communities, and the cleanliness of the air and waterways make it much better than the filthy city, home to crooks and knaves and little else."

"But you are a savage whose only pleasure is fornicating with your sister," the owl said. "In the city we have Oriental spices, silk from Lucca, and the races at Smithfield. Unlike you, we are aware of the world beyond the bend."

"Do not pretend you are keener than we, you of the city, for without the toil of the country, you would have no food for your bloated bellies," said the swan.

"It is true you feed us, but we give you coin for your trouble," said the owl. "It is best that way for we have better things to do than to wallow in the mud."

The birds glared at one another and arrayed their plumage. The swan honked and beat his great wings, and the owl, his talons coiled, swooped down from his perch in the bell tower. Before the birds collided, a crested red finch, sitting dandy on a bough of oak, intervened.

"Swan, what don't you like about the village?" the finch said in his lyrical, piping voice.

"I do not like black dogs," said the swan. "They claim the best land and eat the best food, all while telling the ploughmen it's a fair price for guarding their fields, livestock, and homes."

The owl banked out of his attack and returned to his perch.

"I can say the same of the grey dogs of the city," he said. "They live in packs near the market, and when they are not given the finest cuts of meat, they howl until the rest of us go mad."

"As long as the dogs sniff each other's asses and lick their privates, then they are good to have around," the swan said.

"But when they gnash their teeth at not getting what they want, and when they demand barrels of fish and sides of bacon in exchange for barking at intruders, they go too far," the owl said.

"We need dogs," said the swan.

"But mankind would be much better off if both the black and grey dogs remembered they were servants and not masters," the owl said.

The finch, proud at having brought the swan and the owl to agreement, splayed his splendid crimson crest and sang high and long. ...

Gregory knew the grey dogs represented the Franciscan friars and the black dogs the Dominican friars. While Gregory did not agree with everything in the poem, he cherished its voice of reasoned defiance and periodic passages of vulgarity and sarcasm. And so did many others. Minstrels recited it at noble feasts and banquets while merchants and peasants sang the bawdier verses during gatherings at the ale house. This was a source of great embarrassment for the friars, who for all their claims of sanctity and service, couldn't tolerate a firm poke in the ribs. They resolved to find the author and drag him before the courts. Try as they did, they failed to determine the identity of the author and therefore could not stop him. Each time King Edward convened with his lords for parliament, a new verse would appear on the streets of London, and by the time the friars arrived for the otherwise solemn and dignified meeting of Westminster, they were already the butt of many stinging jokes.

At last, Gregory would meet le Clerk, the person who deigned to challenge such powerful men, and who had given thought and laughter to those not courageous enough to pick that fight. The guard lowered the drawbridge and Gregory rode into the bailey. A groom led his horse to the stable while a servant boy took Gregory to the guest hall. Many people crowded around a roaring fire in the central hearth. They all turned as Gregory, soaking wet and with chattering teeth, entered the hall. The firelight cast shadows across their faces and reflected in the bellies of their pewter cups.

A man with a forked beard stood. "Who is this half-drowned rat who has arrived late and dour to our hour of revelry?"

Gregory pulled back the hood of his cloak, peeled off his beaver skin hat, and cleared his throat. "Gregory of Bordeaux, and I am in need of dry robes and a flagon of spiced wine."

"I received your letter, scribe, and have awaited your arrival, so you shall have both in short order," the man said. "And on the morrow you shall have your chance to console our great Lord Sudeley, who lies on his deathbed, and to meet his powerful friends. But tonight you will drink with the little people in this little hall next to this little fire and listen to our little stories of love, life, and death."

"After the road I have just traveled, nothing could be better," he said.

Gregory changed into warm robes and joined the company around the fire. Someone shoved a cup of wine into his hand, and someone else handed him a garlic-roasted drumstick. He took a bite and took a drink.

"To whom do I owe thanks for this hospitality?" he said.

The man with the forked beard picked up a lute from the table, strummed a few off-key notes, and let loose with a drunken yodel. The young nobles sitting around the fire burst into laughter.

"I, Master Gregory, am the getter of the goat, the sinker of the boat, and the cat who chases the dog. I am a frog, and I am a hog, and I am the eagle that soars at dawn. They call me a fool and feed me crumbs, but I have chapped the asses of all the friars in Christendom. I love my lord, and for him

I'll slay hordes with a fife I wield like a sword. Music is life and songs are the soul, but words can also be work. I, Master Gregory, am Simon le Clerk."

The nobles erupted with guffaws.

As their mirth subsided, Gregory knew he must respond in kind to this grand introduction. "And to think, for all these years I knew you as a swan, an owl, and a finch," said Gregory. "Now that I know you include cat, frog, hog, and eagle in your lineage, I know the truth about you. You are the great whoreson of Noah's Ark."

The nobles, some of them frowning, all of them speechless, looked to le Clerk, who himself seemed blindsided by the cutting reply. He set the lute back on the table and picked up his cup of wine. He took a long drink and licked his lips.

"The great whoreson of Noah's Ark," he said and smiled. "Master Gregory, that is brilliant." He leaned back and laughed so hard wine sloshed from his cup. As the bard collected himself and replenished his drink, Gregory thought about the long sash of humor this man had given to the people of London.

One year before parliament, the owl told of how he followed a grey dog as it traveled from Exeter to London, a journey of five days.

Each evening before hiking his leg, relieving his bowels, and going to sleep, the dog dug a hole and buried a large bone made of gold. In so doing, this dog, as fat as a pig and as sly as a fox, would always be near his treasure upon his return trip home.

A clear reference to Friar Nicholas of Exeter—notorious for his love of luxury—who flew into a rotten rage when greeted with the verse. Another year before parliament, the swan said he watched two black dogs breeding near the River Ribble.

When the puppy slid from the womb, it suckled at three teats, for it had three heads and three tails. It has grown into a spoiled and greedy mastiff that lives in a great hall made of stone.

One could not read the verse and help but think of Friar Henry, who had reputedly sired three bastards by three different mistresses at his fortified manor in Lancashire. And so it went, year after year, and verse after verse, until The Swan, the Owl, and the Finch had grown into a sprawling, comprehensive rebuke of the Franciscan and Dominican orders.

Two of the squires locked arms and danced around the fire as le Clerk strummed on his lute. Another squire beat haphazardly on a drum, while the rest of them lilted through a soggy rendition of a song much beloved in Gloucestershire, "The Old Money Bag." Despite the frivolity unfolding around him, and despite his boisterous participation, Gregory brooded over the implications of The Swan, the Owl, and the Finch. Meant as a piece of satire, even as an agent of change, the poem had turned down the wrong road, and in one year, had inspired more than laughter.

Incensed and encouraged by the criticisms of the swan and the owl, vagrants assaulted Friar Nicholas and his associates as they entered the city at Ludgate. During the attack, one of the friars was stabbed to death. The suspects fled, never to be found. Friar Nicholas reasoned if the actual murderers could not be brought to justice, then punishment should fall to the person who had written the poem. He managed to collect an original manuscript and all the addendums and made an official presentation to King Edward. The king consented to an inquest and ordered his agents to find the author and arrest him on a charge of murder.

That the king's men found the author surprised no one. They went to every manor and every castle, plying any and all with threats and bribes. What became the talk of choice throughout the realm was the author's identity— Simon le Clerk, jester to Lord Giles of Sudeley for thirty years. Had le Clerk been under the protection of any other lord, he would have been dragged to London, given a show trial, and promptly hanged. But Sudeley remained one of the king's most trusted allies. He'd stood beside him during rebellion, crusade, and throughout his reign. Instead of a swift implementation of justice against le Clerk, the king did Sudeley a favor. He forced Sudeley to renew his oath of loyalty and swear on holy relics he did not know le Clerk had authored The Swan, the Owl, and the Finch. In exchange, Edward decreed that for as long as Sudeley lived, he and his retainers remained under the king's peace while within the boundaries of the Sudeley estate. Upon Sudeley's death, any and all protections for retainers were forfeit. Albeit deferred in its enforcement, the king's decree was a death sentence for le Clerk.

Gregory hadn't meant to stay up so late the night before or to drink so much wine. Le Clerk entertained the knights and squires of the lords who had come to visit Sudeley, and Gregory wasn't about to choose sleep over joining the raucous affair. What he witnessed amazed him. Le Clerk, a short, barrel-chested man with silvery cropped hair and his absurd forked beard, performed with skill and stamina until the hour of Lauds. At one moment he played the lute and in the next a fife, a drum, a fiddle, or bagpipes. He veered from the sweetest of love songs to the bawdiest of poems about cuckolds and concubines. He somehow recalled the name of everyone around the fire and dropped their names into the narrative for poignancy. His stories took listeners to everyday places like the kitchen and the latrine as well as to great and distant cities out in the dreamscape. One story in particular touched Gregory in the dreary little corner of his heart that was always sad and lonely.

The ship sailed over the ocean blue, into the horizon bursting with the glorious, vermillion light of the sun. The lovesick Prince Gregory, who traded away all his riches for his chance to claim the hand of Lady Christine, stood at the stern. Search for her he did, through the broiling heat of summer and the biting cold of winter, in the burgs and in the country, in castles and palaces from France to Great Turkey. Everywhere he went he inquired of her.

"She is the tranquility of dawn, the fragrant kiss of spring rain, and the butterfly perched on the petal," he said to all he encountered.

So long was his quest, and so fruitless were his efforts, Prince Gregory lost heart. At the very moment when he thought it all lost, a shepherd told him that across the valley and over the mountains lived a maid as fair and kind as the one he sought. On aching feet and with an empty stomach, he raced over the bottoms and climbed through the steeps. On the other side, he saw a great city of walls and spires, of silver domes and golden towers. He arrived at the court of the potentate who ruled this city and was given a hearing.

"I have come for the hand of Lady Christine," Prince Gregory said. "Is she here?"

"Why, yes," said the potentate. "But she is a concubine who has shared her pleasures with me and a hundred men besides. Do you love her now?"

At the sight of Prince Gregory's disappointment, the potentate laughed. His nose was so big he could smell a pig sty from one thousand miles away, and his belly so fat he hadn't seen his feet in years. A hideous heap of a man, the potentate gorged on the misfortune of others. He looked at Prince Gregory, and after his laughter faded, said, "Your clothes are rags, your beard is shaggy, and there are no rings and rubies on your fingers. Even as a concubine, Lady Christine would never consent to entertain the likes of you."

"But I sold everything to pay for my travel, to be right here, right now, to profess my undying love," the prince replied. "Since I saw her years ago in London, my heart has beaten for no other."

"But she is my property," said the potentate. "I am sorry you have traveled all this way for nothing, but sometimes in life we are not equal to our dreams."

Enraged, Prince Gregory pulled a knife from his boot and lunged at the potentate, but his guards seized the prince and wrestled him to the ground. They cast him out of the city before he ever set eyes on Lady Christine. Three years later he arrived home, penniless and brokenhearted, no longer a prince but a pauper. The peasants who once feared him paid him no mind, and the new lord of the manor told him he was not welcome there. Unable to escape his misery, Prince Gregory went to London, climbed to the top of the spire at St. Paul's, and leapt to his death.

What Prince Gregory didn't know was Lady Christine, released from the potentate's bondage, had arrived in London a month earlier. She sat by the fire and waited for him at her house in Bread Street.

Le Clerk spoke every word with conviction, for he had lived the width and breadth of his tales. Whenever it seemed his audience's attention waned, he performed an astounding act of physical prowess. He juggled ten knives, swallowed fire, and put his foot behind his head. He leapt from the shoulders of one of the knights and turned a flip before landing one footed on the table. He stood on one hand while he said his name backwards five times. Finally too drunk to perform, he declared the show over. Before retiring to his quarters, he looked at Gregory.

"Remember what you saw and heard tonight, scribe, and be sure to put it in your chronicle."

Cold beneath his blanket, Gregory awoke to a shard of light stabbing through a shuttered window. He stoked the embers in the hearth and threw on another piece of fuel. As a flame curled from the coals, he looked around to find the hall empty. This surprised Gregory, who just a few hours ago had sat at this hearth with a dozen singing knights and squires. He figured at least a few would be like him, rising late with the night's wine still heavy in his head. Instead? Emptiness and silence. He then heard the sound of alarmed voices from outside in the bailey and a feeling of dread seized him. He put on his cloak and ran outside. To shield his eyes from the bleak morning light and a flurry of snow, he pulled down the brim of his hat. Gazing out across the enclosure, he saw teary-eyed townspeople crowd around something on the far end of the bailey he had not noticed the prior evening when he'd arrived drenched, freezing, and in the darkened haze of dusk.

The gallows.

"What in heaven's name is about to happen?" he asked.

"Simon le Clerk is to be hanged this morning," a townsman sighed.

"But what of Lord Sudeley?"

"You did not hear?" the townsman said. "He died in the night. Le Clerk's accusers arrived a week ago to prepare for this very moment."

Gregory shifted through the crowd until he stood up front, face to face with the cordon of troops surrounding the gibbet. They were the very same knights and squires who had celebrated with le Clerk the night before. Gregory looked long and hard at one of them, and as they made eye contact, he remembered his name. Pierre D'Iberville.

"Tell me, Pierre, did you know you'd be doing this today?" he asked.

"We all did, Master Gregory, including le Clerk," he said. "You were the only one who drank in ignorance."

"How can you sit and laugh with him at one instant, and in the next, stand guard at his execution?" he said.

"I am a squire who takes orders, and if I take enough of them and see them through, then one day I will live in a castle such as this one," he said. "Le Clerk was a talented fool, true enough, but a fool nonetheless. He lived not on his own largesse, but on the largesse of Lord Sudeley. Power is not in the word, Master Gregory, but in the cross and the sword."

Shaking his head with dismay, Gregory turned and threw up his hand. As he walked away, D'Iberville called his name. He turned and said with scorn, "What is it, you dimwit?"

"It's no secret you sent a letter ahead of your arrival requesting an audience with le Clerk," D'Iberville said. "And it's also no secret you wish to write a chronicle of the things you see."

"Yes, and it's no secret I am in the employ of the Earl of Southampton."

"Look over there and tell me what you see." D'Iberville nodded over his right shoulder. Gregory looked in that direction and saw a group of Franciscans, clad in their rustic grey robes, warming themselves at a large brazier. One of them wore a cross of gold plate around his neck and a gold signet ring encrusted with emeralds. While he wore a belt of rope like the others, his contained ostentatious threads of gold. He shared a casual laugh with an armed man who Gregory identified as the Sheriff of Gloucestershire. The friar glanced up from his conversation and through the swirling snow caught Gregory's eye. A dark smile crossed his face and his head dipped with a chilling nod before returning his attention to the sheriff.

"I'm sure it's all clear to you now," D'Iberville said. "That is Friar Nicholas of Exeter, and he is having his revenge a full five years after le Clerk last insulted him. He has your letter in his possession. In the days before your arrival he asked about you, and even wondered if you collaborated with le Clerk in writing The Swan, the Owl, and the Finch. If you are here on the morrow, you will have to answer to him, Master Gregory."

"Why are you telling me this?"

"Because I am not as cruel as you think. And I like you," he said. "If you care about your chronicle, and perhaps even your life, I'd leave soon and ride hard."

"May God bless you, Pierre," Gregory said.

He worked his way through the sullen crowd back to the guest hall. He collected his possessions and went to the stables. When he saw Moonbeam, rested and well fed, standing in her stall, relief washed over him. Gregory handed the stable boy a few farthings and together they dressed the filly with tack and saddle. Gregory mounted, leaned over Moonbeam's neck, and rubbed her nose.

"Today, my lady, we will ride," he whispered.

As Moonbeam sprinted toward the drawbridge, Gregory heard the collective gasp of the crowd as le Clerk was hoisted up by the noose. Gregory looked over his shoulder and caught a glimpse of the old jester, swinging from the rope, a hood over his head and his hands tied behind his back. Gregory turned his attention to the snow-covered road curling out in front of him. He slapped the reins and urged Moonbeam onward, and as the spurs bit, she galloped faster and faster.

Later he would have time to sit and record the events that transpired at Sudeley Castle. But as he rode north into a biting wind, all he did was think. He found grim pleasure in what came to mind.

The swan still glides across the water, the owl is yet perched in the belfry, and the finch speaks many languages. If the black dogs and the grey dogs think they have won, perhaps they should remember they will always be infested with fleas.

A CONTESTED
WEDDING
AT LICHFIELD

e took a squalid room in the cellar of the inn at Evesham. He ate cold victuals, drank a pot of ale, and before retiring to his quarters, reread a letter he received while in Oxford. It was from his friend, Thomas, the cellarer at Canwell Priory.

There will be a wedding in Lichfield a week before the Feast of St. Martin. There are terrible rumors, which I fear are true, that this wedding will be contested by Lord Tutbury. They say he is angry because he was betrothed to Anne of Boston, but the betrothal was revoked after a wealthy wool merchant, Geoffrey Wool, countered with a much better marriage proposal. Lord Tutbury, they say, has vowed to wreck the wedding at all costs. I also hear he has the tacit support of his overlord, the Earl of Stafford, meaning Lord Tutbury can do as he pleases with little fear of punishment. Something bad will happen on that day, Gregory. Perhaps it would be good if you were there so you can record it in your chronicle, and if need be, hold Lord Tutbury accountable.

The little town of Lichfield felt big. It seemed all of Staffordshire was on hand for the wedding. The inn was full, as were the local priories. Peasants and gentry alike boarded travelers in their homes and barns, and a tent city sprouted up in the flatland north of Lichfield's timber rampart. Gregory arrived early and took a room in the inn's dusty attic. He had a bed, a bench, a chest, a table, and a chamber pot. He spent his days writing and his nights drinking ale and talking with the growing number of people in town for the wedding.

"The nuptials will be like no other in the history of Lichfield," the taverner said to Gregory. "This wedding will make the town famous."

"I don't know if fame is in the offing," Gregory replied, "but with as much ale as you are selling, it will surely make you rich. I am not convinced this wedding will be as eventful as predicted, but I must admit I am curious."

"You won't be curious for long," the taverner said. "Lord Tutbury is furious, and even when he is in a good mood, he's as mean as a starving bull."

Gregory learned many more details after arriving in Lichfield. Tutbury was thirty years older than the sixteen-year-old bride. Though he came from an old family that traced its pedigree back to Normandy, the family had fallen on hard times. Tutbury, with a few bastards but no legitimate heir, needed a bride to sire a proper brood. He also wanted to restore his fortunes by taking control of Anne's business. When her father died, she'd inherited his shipping interests in the busy channel port of Boston, the proceeds from which would substantially increase Tutbury's coffers.

Gregory learned opinion was divided. "Tutbury should accept his fate and look for a lamb in another pasture," one merchant said. Still another commented, "Tutbury is a lord, and it is God's work that his will be served."

Merchants married for business and money, the townsfolk said, and that was the case with Geoffrey and Anne. A wool merchant and a ship owner. Together they might build an empire. But it was also believed the two had fallen in love at first sight and that many of their letters had gone back and forth between Lichfield and Boston since. Those who supported Geoffrey urged him to move the wedding to Boston where Tutbury had no influence. In Boston, they said, the wedding could go as planned. Geoffrey refused.

Talk at the inn and in the tavern was that Geoffrey's family came to prominence as wool traders in Lichfield. If Geoffrey married upward into a family more wealthy than his own, the townsmen said, he needed to do it in his hometown so all could witness his ascension.

"Geoffrey needs to have his wedding here so he can show Tutbury and the rest of us his time has come," a shoemaker said.

A spicer, on the other hand, derided the decision. "Geoffrey's pride has made him a fool, I fear, and his foot will be caught in Tutbury's trap."

The purported beauty of the bride intensified the matter. As told by the townspeople, Anne of Boston was more delicate than a red summer rose, more melodic than a wren, as graceful as a gentle bend in the river, and more inspiring of hope than the light of dawn. The purest of virgins with eyes as green as the fields, hair as gold as treasure, and a spirit as strong and steady as the ocean's tide, Anne of Boston, they said, was the most comely woman in the realm. And while opinions varied as to who should have her hand and where the wedding should take place, all seemed to understand why Tutbury was acid with envy and why Geoffrey was full of pride.

Gregory returned to the inn and climbed the steep stairs to his attic room. He sat at the table, lit a candle and a piece of frankincense, dipped a quill into the inkhorn, and started writing again. Two hours later, as he lit a new candle, the cathedral bells rang. Gregory stood from his desk, went to the window, and opened the shutter. From his vantage point in the attic, he had a clear line of sight down Tamworth Street. Several mounted men-at-arms in glinting mail, and bearing black and white pennons, rushed across the muddy bridge and through the gatehouse. Two horses pulling a wagon, and a chaotic gaggle of courtiers and household servants on foot followed them. Lichfield, subdued all day by the cold, windy drizzle, came alive with bells, trumpets, blessings, and laughter. As the procession made its way down Tamworth Street, and as it passed the inn where Gregory lodged, an elegant, bejeweled hand pulled back the wagon's thick blue curtain. A teenage girl leaned out and waved to all the townspeople who stood in the rain to greet her. Sparkling in the dreary twilight, Anne of Boston had arrived.

he Bishop of Chester, overlord of Lichfield, decreed that the gates should be locked the day of the wedding. But from what Gregory heard, it would do no good. The scuttlebutt was that some of Tutbury's men were already in town, lying low until wedding day. If true, their presence did nothing to hamper preparations. Rakers cleared Tamworth Street of dung and refuse. Porters erected a pavilion outside the cathedral where the banquet would be. The shops and stalls of the market bustled with nobility and commoners buying new clothes and accouterments. Drovers arrived with their pigs and cattle. A wagon loaded with casks of wine creaked into the market. As the town readied itself, minstrels rendered songs of love, loss, war, and honor. A troupe of jesters on tall stilts entertained with juggling and jokes. Up and down Tamworth Street, homes had sprigs of greenery hung over the door signifying bride's ale for sale and consumption. Watching the people of Lichfield embrace this wedding, Gregory realized they thought they could muscle Tutbury aside and hold the event as planned. Foolish or not, Gregory respected the tenacity of Lichfield and its favorite son, Geoffrey Wool.

Gregory tossed and turned the night before the wedding. He awoke the next morning, both groggy and excited, to the bells of Prime. He broke his fast with a hunk of cheese, a crust of bread, and a glass of mulled wine. He said his prayers, washed his hands and face, and cinched the cloak with a silver and emerald brooch. With his beaver skin hat snuggly on his head, he stepped into the blustery autumn day and walked to Lichfield Cathedral. His cloak whipped and snapped behind him as a series of powerful gusts swirled down Tamworth Street, and he held his hat steadfast to keep the wind from carrying it away. The scents of festival—roasting pork and beef, baking bread, and mutton stew—wafted on the wind from the kitchens of the cathedral close. By the time he arrived, Gregory felt tardy. Hundreds of people abuzz with talk and speculation were already there. Gregory sought out a new acquaintance, Roger of the grocer's guild, and joined the morning's conversation.

"Good to see you, Roger," he said.

"And you, Master Gregory," he replied. "So what do you think will happen today? Does Lord Tutbury ruin the wedding or does he lose his nerve?"

"Surely he will think better of it," Gregory said. "He really has nothing to gain. Think about it. Even if he succeeds and Geoffrey and Anne do not wed this day, she would never consent to take his hand in the future. If I were Lord Tutbury, I'd find something better to do."

"But you are from London, Master Gregory, where things change each year," Roger said. "Out here on the manor things tend to stay the same, and Tutbury's family has been in power since before the cathedral was built. If he did nothing, it would be seen as a sign he does not believe in his own lordship. If that happens, peasants begin demanding higher wages, merchants start driving harder bargains, tax revenue goes down, and the king starts looking for a new Lord of Tutbury. Lords rule by the sword, Gregory, and Tutbury will use his today."

"That's a shame," Gregory said. "When will lords start using their brains?"

"Brains?" Roger laughed. "There are plenty of people in Lichfield who are jealous of Geoffrey because of his success, but deep down they love him because he and his family have brought prosperity to this town. And marrying Anne of Boston? It is a good thing for all of us."

He and Roger milled through the crowd, greeting merchants, gentry, and nobles, all of them in their finest. Recurring gusts of wind rustled hoods, tunics, and mantles. At times, it grew so loud people had to speak up in order to be heard. A friar said it must be due to the wings of a thousand angels descending on Lichfield to bless the wedding. Several people agreed, but Gregory wasn't so sure. What this wedding needed was protection. And indeed, a dozen armed men gathered near the pavilion and scanned the crowd for trouble.

When the bells of Terce rang, all eyes turned toward Vicar's House, an old hall at the entry of the cathedral close, where the bridal procession began. Flanked by an armed retinue, bridesmaids, and minstrels, Anne made her way down the cobbled lane leading to the steps of the cathedral where the deacon and Geoffrey awaited. Clutching a bouquet of garlic and herbs, she wore sweeping sheaths of green silk trimmed with velvet and ermine and a blue mantle to show her purity. Woven into her garments was a glittering universe of jasper, sapphires, and emeralds. Her golden hair was parted in the middle with braids coiled over each ear, and on her head was a wreath of ivy. She moved with dignity and poise and her face showed solemn joy. As she made her way through the divide in the crowd, her perfume of musk and rose oil filled the air. She took her place on the cathedral steps next to Geof-frey, who with a blush and a smile, seemed swollen with elation. When the couple held hands and presented themselves, hundreds clapped and cheered.

The deacon cleared his throat and led them in their vows, but he stopped at the sound of a shrill hue and cry. With a collective gasp, the entire gather-ing turned toward the commotion. A child ran up the cobbled path scream-ing, "The market is on fire! The market is on fire!"

Like everyone else, Gregory craned his neck for a view back toward town. He smelled burning thatch and timber and saw an ugly ribbon of black smoke curling in the air. All at once, the serenity of the wedding collapsed into the mad confusion of a disaster.

People ran, screaming and cursing, back to town. Men-at-arms drew their swords. Visiting noblemen exchanged frozen looks of shock while a friar proclaimed the fire was God's punishment for an unholy union.

Gregory kept his eye on the bride and groom. They shared a long em-brace, kissed on the lips, and then whispered to each other. The deacon whisked Anne into the safety of the cathedral while Geoffrey tore off his foppish shoes and ran barefoot down Dam Street back to town. For a long moment, Gregory, seized by indecision, just stood there. The sound of his name broke the spell.

"Gregory, come help us!" Roger pleaded. "You are one of us now, so come and help us save our blessed town!"

Gregory joined a long line stretching from the fish pond to the market. Over and over he passed a full bucket to his right then an empty bucket to his left. He knew it wasn't enough. The strong winds from the morning had not subsided. With each successive gust, the flames licked higher and higher.

Tufts of burning thatch leapt from one roof to the next, setting the town ablaze. People ducked into homes and workshops to save what they could by piling their possessions in the street. Others, who saw their lives in ruins, just sat and wept. As Gregory scanned the wreckage all around him, he saw a new calamity—a gang of men opening the oaken doors at Tamworth Gate.

"Look!" Gregory yelled, pointing his finger. "The gate is open!"

A group of armed riders galloped through. Shimmering in the haze of the heat, they appeared as phantoms in their black capes and armor. A knot of men-at-arms and townsmen bristling with swords, axes, pitchforks, and staves sounded their battle cry—For Lady Anne!—and rushed forth to meet the intruders. A struggle ensued in which the townsmen, formed behind a defiant wall of shields, halted Tutbury's charge. More people from the town quit their lost attempt to douse the fire and took up arms with whatever they found. The people of Lichfield soon outnumbered Tutbury, and he and his men fell back as rocks, arrows, and firebrands rained down upon them. Geoffrey, bare-chested and dark with soot and ash, stepped out in front of the line and clumsily brandished his blade. Shoulders heaving and sword hand shaking with fear, he leveled a gaze at his rival.

"Lord Tutbury, you have destroyed my workhouse and my wool," he said. "You have burned the town and wrecked many lives. The damage you have done this day will take years to repair. But still you have lost. I will take Anne's hand in marriage and Lichfield will rebuild. Return to your backwater manor and leave us be."

"The day is not yet done, Geoffrey," Tutbury said.

He pushed the helm's visor down over his face and dug his spurs deep into the flanks of his white charger. The horse whinnied and lurched forward. Tutbury cocked his sword high above his head, stood in his stirrups and brought the sword down with all his lordly might. Geoffrey held his sword above his head with both hands and parried, but in so doing, was knocked to the ground. Tutbury swung his horse around and positioned himself for the kill. As he did, a teenager stepped forward and caught Tutbury at the shoulder plate with a billhook and pulled him from his horse.

The teenager dropped the hook, pulled a knife, and got on top of Tutbury. He pushed up the visor and laid the knife at Tutbury's eye. The teen looked up at Geoffrey and said, "Let me finish him!"

"No, boy," Geoffrey said. "He has finished himself."

The teenager got up and so did Tutbury, who spat at the ground and remounted. "You can have your whore."

He motioned to his men and they galloped back through the gate. A long silence ensued, the only thing audible the crack and spit of the embers that used to be the town. Then came a tender voice of concern.

"Geoffrey? Geoffrey?"

Everyone turned in the direction of the voice to see Lady Anne. The crowd parted to reveal Geoffrey, sword in hand, standing heroically at the head of the makeshift Lichfield army.

"Oh, Geoffrey," she said, and raced to him. He dropped his sword and pulled her into his arms.

regory lost everything in the fire. Oxford and Simon le Clerk. All of it gone. He would have to start his chronicle over, and just the thought of it made him tired. But he knew a good place to begin.

They said the wedding would make Lichfield famous, and indeed, they were right. Two smoldering hearts grew into an inferno, and as an army stood as witness, the flames of their love curled so high they singed even the silk trim of Heaven's embroidery. But there beat a third heart, old and empty and blackened well before it burnt in the blaze.

A WINTER
WAITING
FOR LETTERS

regory climbed into the saddle and Moonbeam clopped out of the stable, one of the only structures spared by the fire. She ambled down Tamworth Street and through the stinking wreckage as glum townspeople dug through the smoldering embers of their lives. Out through the gate Gregory rode, breaking free from the soot and ash of Lichfield and galloping over the verdant country plain. Hunkered down in the saddle, swathed in his leather and wool, and with his belly sated with cheese, almonds, and a slice of pork gelatin, Gregory was comfortable and confident as he headed east. But as he topped a rolling hill, he wheeled Moonbeam around and took a long last look at the charred town.

He shook his head and made the sign of the cross. Lichfield would pay the price for its defiance. Winter beckoned. The grain stores ruined. People had no place to stay. Gregory sighed. Having seen the town before its destruction, he appreciated the despair and understood the hardships to come. He took a deep breath and exhaled through his nose. He worked his spurs and Moonbeam trotted back down the hill, across the plain and back through the gate. Curious townspeople watched as he made his way to the blackened remains of the market, where people gathered to greet him.

"Master Gregory, you are back," Roger said, as a cautious smile crept across his face. "I thought you'd left us."

"Not yet, Roger," he said and dismounted. "I cannot leave with a good conscience with so much work to be done."

"May God bless us all." Roger wrapped his arm around Gregory's shoulder. "And what work is it you intend on doing?"

"What I do best—write, drive hard bargains, and make arguments in my best interests. And in the foreseeable future, my interests are Lichfield's."

He managed to secure a room, which he shared with Roger and three other merchants, in the solar at Vicar's House in the cathedral close. The cathedral and its associated buildings sat apart from the town so none of them burned. Many townspeople crammed into the complex, living in attics, cellars, or the nave, and in lean-tos against the cathedral's walls. Others stayed with friends and family in the villages outside Lichfield. The poorest of the poor found shelter in the various priories and monasteries out in the county. The burned out hulk of the town stood vacant, save during the day, when townsmen cleared debris and piled it outside the city's palisade. Both Martinmas and Christmas came and went with enthusiastic prayer and subdued celebration. Stomachs growled, people shivered, and infants and the elderly died at night. Numerous quarrels broke out between people living too close to one another without their usual comforts. A knife fight, a fist fight, a husband and wife screaming at dawn. This happened daily, and as the winds blew colder and colder, the collective mood of the town grew foul.

Yet Gregory found reason for optimism. A de facto command center formed in the cathedral's chapter house, and Gregory thrived at its center. Equipped with a desk, ink, quills and a stack of parchment, he wrote what he hoped was a provocative letter. With solemn conviction and the authority of a London lawyer, he told a detailed account of Tutbury's raid. He pointed out that Tutbury had the tacit support of Earl Stafford and recommended the earl be held accountable for the actions of his vassal. Since the wedding took place at the cathedral under the authority of the deacon, the raid on it, argued Gregory, constituted an act against God. He gave the body count, three dead by fire and four dead in battle, and recounted the hardships of a people who lost nearly all their possessions, housing, and food stores. He ended the letter with an impassioned call for justice and an unabashed request for assistance.

It is not your sin for which to atone, but it is a disaster deserving of your mercy. It is your Christian obligation to bear the burden of charity, so please, reach into your godly heart and take hold of your compassion.

Benedictine monks from Canwell Priory took his letter and copied it so that within a few days, two dozen editions existed. Riders took the letters to all corners of the realm, from Exeter to York and from Shrewsbury to Dover.

"Most will not care, but at least everyone will know," Gregory said to the cadre of monks.

"You must have more faith in the Christian heart, Master Gregory," a monk replied. "Your letter will find its way into the bosom of benevolence."

Gregory knew Lichfield needed more than that. The rebuilding of the town would revolve around the lure of high yields for goods and services rather than alms and philanthropy. He wrote a second, personalized letter to his friends in London. He explained the situation in Lichfield and said a great opportunity existed to both make money and serve the betterment of mankind. He requested that the guild give audience to Geoffrey Wool, a merchant who had recently taken control of a significant shipping interest in Boston. Gregory also wrote letters on behalf of the Lichfield merchants, who sent those letters to their business associates in other towns.

Each morning after Prime, he went to the chapter house and sat at his desk. He grew to love the morning light as it filtered through the stained glass, bathing the vaulted room with soft hues of blue and gold. He became comfortable with the oftentimes idle chatter of the monks and especially liked the distant echo of their Gregorian chants at Terce, Sext, and None.

Accustomed to fresh fish, meat, and white bread, he hated what had become of his diet, stale rye and dreary bean pottage, but said nothing of it. Instead he ate what was served and stayed at his desk and continued writing—and not just letters, but the chronicle itself.

As weeks passed and as the frigid days came one after the next, and as candle after candle melted into the tray, he noticed a depth and clarity in his words that had not been there before Lichfield. The suffering of the people, their stubborn belief they'd survive, the burst of joy at the arrival of a cart-load of grain and salted fish, three thieves strung from the gallows, and the cathedral bells marking yet another day of resilience. His chronicle started to breathe. Even with an empty stomach, cold feet, a runny nose, and a painful cough, Gregory felt a warm jubilance churning from deep within.

Gregory knew his inner joy meant nothing to Lichfield. Like everyone else, he started to wonder if anyone would respond to the town's call for help. The letters went out well before Christmas. Now it was early February, and with the exception of a few small donations from the local nobility, such as the grain and fish, nothing had arrived. People complained of being punished for their sins. More alarmingly, people asked if this was not the fault of Geoffrey Wool, who, consumed with vanity, demanded the wedding take place in Lichfield rather than doing the sensible thing and moving it to Boston. People said it was Geoffrey's fault, not God's or Lord Tutbury's, the city lay in ruins. Gregory, the Canwell monks, and the cathedral's deacons discussed the matter one morning while gathered in the chapter house. They agreed if things didn't change, the same people who rushed to Geoffrey's defense might be the same ones who would drag him to the gallows.

"I propose that Geoffrey be publicly and officially asked to leave town," a deacon said, to murmurs of support.

"But if he leaves, his departure would only confirm the worst claptrap being said of him," another deacon replied, to nods of approval.

"Geoffrey must be punished," the deacon said. "His presence here is an insult to all those who are paying the price for his arrogance. Be rid of him, and be rid of him now!"

"Oh, but how you enjoyed his tithe all these years," the other deacon said. "Patience and friendship are easy in the good times, but now that things have changed, it is time to dump the pot?"

"Do you accuse me of treachery?"

"Yes. I do. We have known him since he was a child. He was baptized in this very church."

The argument devolved into a shouting match, with both deacons pointing fingers and then shoving each other. Gregory and the Canwell monks wedged between them and tried to calm them down, but the deacons pushed their way through and came nose-to-nose. They were about to start throwing punches when a signal bell sounded. Someone of importance had arrived.

Gregory, the monks, and the deacons dashed out of the chapter house, through the choir, down the central nave, and through the front doors to the cathedral steps. The shivering, bedraggled townspeople had formed a semicircle around a rider wearing a bearskin cloak, encrusted with snow, over his armor.

"Gregory of Bordeaux," he bellowed. *"I have messages for Gregory of Bordeaux."*

All eyes turned toward him.

Gregory stepped forward. "I am he."

The rider dug into a large saddlebag and pulled out a thick pipe roll of parchments wrapped in waxed leather. "These are for you."

Gregory took the roll and tucked it underneath his arm.

Gregory wiped a snowflake from his eyebrow. "Who are these from?"

"You must be important." A knowing smile crossed the rider's face, "for these are from important people. And for all of you—" he raised his voice for all to hear, "—there are victuals enough for a month on the way from Leicester."

As the townsmen issued a collective sigh of relief, one of the deacons walked down the cathedral steps and over to the rider. "Will you stay with us for a while? Though our means are modest, our hospitality is keen."

"My good deacon, I do not have time for timid fires, thin wine, and gruel." He smiled the grim, broken-toothed smile of a knight. "An arrest warrant has been issued for Lord Tutbury, and I ride with the Sheriff of Staffordshire."

The rider wheeled his horse, slapped the reins, and nearly trampled a few townspeople slow to part and get out of his way. The deacon and Gregory turned and looked at one another, but neither figured out what to say. Finally, the deacon pointed at the pipe roll under Gregory's arm and said, "I believe we have something to read."

Once inside, Gregory peeled back the waxed leather binding to find several scrolls rolled one inside the other. He thumbed through them. From the difference in handwriting from one to the next, Gregory counted five letters. He looked up at the deacons and monks crowded around his desk. "We planted the crop, and now we shall see the yield."

The first letter was from Alan Spicer, the dean of the Guild of Merchants in London. The guild would be honored to meet with Geoffrey Wool, Alan wrote, and his presence in London was expected forthwith. The second letter came from the London Guild of Goldsmiths. In eternal gratitude for Gregory's prior and future legal support, the goldsmiths donated enough silver to build a dozen two-story row houses. The third letter was from Jean du Mont, Gregory's cousin who ran the winery. He had found an unclaimed shipment on the wharf of sixty tuns of cheap Spanish wine and had bought it for a third of its value. He traded the wine for domestic goods such as candles, pots, rough finished wool, leather, salt and pepper, cheeses, and dried fruit. The merchandise had already been loaded onto a ship bound for the port at Chester. The fourth letter was from John, Gregory's friend and business associate in Oxford. An old merchant's hall was being rebuilt in stone. All the usable timber salvaged from the remodel would be donated to Lichfield. The timber, precious and exorbitantly expensive oak imported from the Baltic, would have to be claimed forthwith. Otherwise, it would be sold at auction.

Gregory giddied as he stretched the fifth letter across his desk. This one was on the highest quality vellum Gregory had seen in years, and written in a fine hand. Before even reading it, he knew this letter carried with it an official heft and importance. It was from the Earl of Southampton. Gregory plunged into the document, and as promised, read it aloud to the monks and deacons gathered about the table and over his shoulder.

Master Gregory,

   The court received your letter with much astonishment. The account of Lord Tutbury's raid on Lichfield is still the talk of London. You are truly a gifted storyteller, and if your letter is any indication, your chronicle will be one for the ages.

   You are to be commended for your courage in telling the truth, that Tutbury planned and led the attack which ended with the burning of the town and the deaths of seven people. But what is still not known is the extent of Earl Stafford's involvement in the incident. It is a matter of record he is Tutbury's overlord, but beyond that, it is next to impossible to prove his involvement. The problem, Master Gregory, is your letter openly stated Earl Stafford tacitly supported the raid, a claim you should not have made. With the exception of the ones written to your close associates, I know your letters were supposed to be anonymous. But someone in Lichfield identified you as the author and your name was mentioned more than a few times at Westminster. Earl Stafford asked the king to charge you with slander, a crime for which you could be hanged, but I convinced him to wait until more is known.

   The king agreed to fine Tutbury £500 to pay for the rebuilding of Lichfield. He refused to honor the fine, so a warrant was issued for his arrest. He is to be brought before the king for questioning. For your sake, you should hope he implicates Earl Stafford in the raid. If not, the king's men will come looking for you. Earl Stafford is not a popular man, as you know, and he is not as powerful as his grandfather was. But he is still a dangerous man with a large affinity and enough money to ensure his justice will be done. You did the right thing by telling us about Lichfield, but in the future, be careful not to make accusations you cannot prove. I thought you, as a lawyer, would have known better.

You have put me in a bad position. You are my chronicler, so I cannot sit idly by as people mention your name and slander and the gallows in the same sentence. And in truth, I sought you out, not the other way around, so I owe you my support because ultimately I am the one who put you in the position you are in. But please remember you work for me. As it stands, I am currently working for you. You should know that if not for me, the man who delivered my letter would instead have arrested you. This cost me as I had to use a favor I had wanted to keep. Since I became earl, I have been able to stay out of Stafford's sad circle of plots and schemes. Now he eyes me with suspicion. If you put me in a position like that again, I will drop you from my employ forthwith. If this sounds harsh, that is my intention. You have made a powerful enemy, Master Gregory, and if you continue to make powerful enemies, then my reputation will begin to suffer. I'm sure you understand.

Please know you still have my full backing and confidence. Your account of the attack on Lichfield was wonderfully done, and I cannot wait to see what else you encounter during your travels throughout the realm. Another rider will soon arrive with your pay, and it should be enough to keep you in good stead through the spring. What I want you to do with some of the money is hire someone to ride with you. Someone you trust, someone who is strong and knows how to use a weapon. You will continue to go into dangerous places, and if you continue to travel alone, then you will not travel for long.

Godspeed, Master Gregory.

Richard Beaufort, Earl of Southampton

Gregory was no longer giddy. In his life, he had never once thought himself destined for the gallows. All that changed with this dreadful letter. He had a sick knot in his stomach at the thought of his name being linked with slander. And it embarrassed him that he had caused Southampton so much trouble. He looked up at the monks and deacons, who matched his dour expression with baleful looks of their own.

"It seems in my haste to impugn Tutbury, I have impugned myself."

"Don't be too hard on yourself, Master Gregory," one of the deacons said. "I once farted in front of the Archbishop of Canterbury—during Mass."

Gregory and the others split with laughter, and during the humorous respite, Gregory reminded himself help was on the way, Tutbury would see justice, and Southampton stood by his side. Perhaps he had enemies, but he still had blessings to count.

God finally pried the spring from the cold grip of winter. Almost at once the chill lifted and the trees and fields grew sweet again. Peasants planted crops. Hired hands sawed, lifted, hammered and framed the town back into shape. Each day wagon trains, heaped with goods and pulled by teams of draught horses, rolled through the town's gates. Food and household items were expensive and strictly rationed, a daily reminder Lichfield remained in danger. But the collective mood of the town was one of relief. The sun had replaced the clouds, and instead of howling wind, the breeze blew with the green aroma of life.

Gregory had many reasons to feel optimistic. All around him were signs his letter-writing campaign had worked. Several merchants told him the town could have rebuilt without him, but his work had speeded up the process tenfold. Geoffrey Wool, with the help of the London merchants, had made a small fortune on finished textiles from Flanders. He manned the center of the rebuild. Financing much of the work from his own purse and overseeing it with a firm diligence, Geoffrey emerged as the undisputed leader of this community as it struggled through its most trying time. He wanted to strengthen the town gates, reconfigure the market, and erect a guild house of stone. All buildings would be roofed with slate, not thatch.

New drains needed to be dug out. Taxes on incoming trade goods needed to be raised, while the town's tax owed to the Bishop of Chester would be lowered. The opportunity inspired Geoffrey, and as the weeks passed and as Geoffrey grew stronger and wiser, Gregory felt a deep sense of gratification—his introduction to the London merchants proved crucial to Geoffrey's upsurge, and thus, to the rebirth of the town.

One night, while Gregory wrote into the wee hours, the experience of Lichfield overcame him, and in an emotional burst, he worked his quill across the parchment.

> *While it only takes a few hands to destroy a city, it takes many to put it back together. None of us want hardship, but it is in the bleakest hour where we find our courage, not to gloat and to preen, but to remain and endure. No sword can slay a generous heart, and no fire can destroy a willing soul.*

Gregory became part of the Lichfield community, and it would have been easy to stay. People waved at him when he walked down the street, bought him ale at the tavern, and invited him into their newly built homes for supper. The merchants promised him a prime spot at the market, and said they would elect him as dean of the guild. In Lichfield, Gregory could grow fat and happy. But he knew it was time to leave. The chronicle whispered, and Moonbeam, grown restless in the stable, needed to run. As he prepared for his departure, the words of Southampton haunted him. "If you continue to travel alone, then you will not travel for long."

 regory pulled his horse to a stop at the top of a high ridge. From there he saw cranes in the meandering river down in the valley, a stand of budding alder, and a swath of heather and bellflowers. The warm morning sunlight shimmered on the river's green waters. A gold eagle banked through the sky as a gentle breeze kissed the upland. Gregory

took a deep breath. He smelled the dense sedge from the river bank and detected the faint fragrance of honeysuckle and rose. Songbirds, flittering in the shrubs and bushes, serenaded with their sweet refrain of spring.

As he savored the wonders of nature, Gregory knew he had been right to leave Lichfield. The grueling churn of business in a town not his own had nearly gotten him down. He had lived with the stink of fire and the weight of expectations for four months. The constant tap of hammers, the rhythmic grinding of the saws, and the incessant chatter of a small town had exhausted his patience. Enough was enough. Firm in his decision and prim in his farewells, he doffed his hat and rode out through the Tamworth Gate.

But he hadn't left alone. During the upheaval of Lichfield, Gregory had gotten a good look at the essence of the townspeople. While many had distinguished themselves for a variety of reasons, none had proved more heroic than Warren, the teenager who had unhorsed Lord Tutbury. A broad-shouldered farm boy with a warm, gap-toothed smile and an impeccable set of manners, Warren had enhanced his reputation through the struggle with Lord Tutbury. But he had been held in high esteem long before the raid.

The townspeople knew of his qualities and weren't surprised he'd shown courage in battle. In the aftermath of the raid, Warren helped enliven the mood of the commoners. Clever and sincere, he found ease in jest and in consolation. As the town rebuilt, he never went without a tool in his hand or a load on his back. He arrived at dawn, stayed until dusk, and toiled at the center of the busiest work gangs. He dug foundations, laid roofs, and sawed timber. After winter broke, he plowed and planted fields.

When Gregory found out Warren knew how to ride, he realized the boy was the one he needed as he continued his journey. He also knew prying him from Lichfield would not be easy. When he first broached the topic, Warren's blue eyes glittered with intrigue, but then they showed caution.

"I must first ask my parents."

Warren lived on the outskirts of Lichfield in a thatched one-room house of wattle and daub. A poor man's house, a ploughman's house, a house of toil and song. At the end of a worn path, near a proud oak, at the edge of a wheat field, an honest hearth of the soil. Gregory stood outside the front door as Warren conferred with his parents, and though he could not discern the words being said, he knew from the rise and fall of conversation that the talk was heated.

Warren emerged a while later looking glum. "My parents do not want me to leave. But I do not agree."

"Let me talk to them. Perhaps we can reach an understanding."

He gladly accepted the cup of ale offered to him, and looked across the table at the man and wife staring back at him. Stout and stubborn folks, Warren's parents, with the old Saxon looks of the countryside. Born and bred on the plough, raised in the row, and schooled on reap and sow, these were the weathered warriors of the harvest, the humble hub of the great English wheel.

Gregory removed his hat, set it on the table, and took a sip of ale. "I need your son to accompany me on my journey. True quality is hard to find, but indeed, you have bequeathed it to your son."

His father propped his forearms on the table and leaned in. "His quality is needed at home," he said, and turned up his face in a show of concern.

"I do not doubt you," Gregory said. "But he is more valuable with me, out there, than he is with you, in here."

"Do not speak riddles, stranger, for I do not like them," his father said, and clinched his meaty right hand into a fist. "Tell me what it is you want, and I will answer yes or no, but try and trick me, and you will leave with less than you came with."

"I am Gregory of Bordeaux. I am a chronicler, and I work for the Earl of Southampton. Perhaps you have heard of him?" From the thoughts that seemed to turn in the father's eyes, Gregory could see he had gained his attention. "The earl gave me money and told me to hire a man," he continued. "If I hire your son, Warren, then he not only works for me, but also for the earl."

As his parents exchanged looks of wonderment, Gregory pulled the coin pouch from his belt and plopped it on the table. Warren's parents looked at the pouch, then at Gregory, then back at the pouch, and then at Warren, whose face spread into a backroads grin. Gregory knew they had heard how loud and heavy the pouch had landed on the table, and he knew there was more in that pouch than they had ever seen in a lifetime. Gregory drained his cup of ale, and put his beaver skin hat back on.

"This is no riddle," he said. "I have already made arrangements to pay for your son's manumission, so he will have no duty with the Bishop of Chester. And for your household, a full mark. But your son must swear an oath of loyalty to me and ride out on the morrow. Do we have a deal?"

Warren's parents stood from the table, and Gregory gave them that clever look he used down on the gritty London waterfront. The father held out his calloused hand. "Deal."

"And God bless you," Warren's mother said.

"Your son is now free." Gregory shook the father's hand. "When you next see him, he will be a man of the world."

THE
GATEHOUSE AT
NEWARK CASTLE

hey spent the night in a village outside Nottingham. Gregory treated Warren to a venison feast and a pot of ale. The only travelers lodged in the inn that evening, they had free run of the place, eating with their elbows out, slurping the ale in big gulps, and speaking as they pleased. They imbibed excitement because the next day they would make the final leg to Newark Castle. Guy de Coutances, a French knight captured five years earlier, had been held in the dungeon there, but was about to be transferred to the remote Hinton Priory for a life of silence and prayer. A sad fate for sure, but a fate Gregory thought worthy of his chronicle. He learned of the knight through a letter from the Bishop of Lincoln. Ransom is the devil's work, but if you write about it, perhaps you can expose its folly.

Gregory pulled off a crust of bread, sopped it in the spicy broth and took a bite. He washed it down with a chug of ale. When his cup went empty, Warren refilled it. And so the evening went, as the master and the page inaugurated their fellowship.

"At the time of his capture in Normandy, it was believed Guy de Coutances would fetch a high price," Gregory said. "But after years of failed negoti-ations with his captor, the nobleman's family decided to promote a younger brother and not pay the ransom. This Guy de Coutances once had an income of one hundred livres a year, but now he is worthless."

"So what will we do when we arrive at Newark?"

"What do you mean? We will eat, drink wine, and rest our bones in front of the fire."

"That's not what I meant." The boy frowned. "I mean, how will you ap-proach this old knight who is surely in no mood to talk about his failed life?"

"Oh, but he will want to talk," Gregory said. "I represent the last chance for his story to be told. I perhaps cannot save him from the monastery, but if he makes it into my chronicle he becomes immortal. And immortality, Warren, is what we all seek in one way or the other."

"I understand it was your letters that brought so much help to my home-town. And from what I was told, the arrest warrant issued for Lord Tutbury was based on your testimony. How does it feel to wield such power when you do not wield a sword?"

"My parents knew the importance of words, and that is why they made arrangements for me to go to school," he said. "What I have begun to learn is the written word must serve the law. It must serve the interests of mankind. Words are at their best when they are true."

"What is it like? To write words?"

"There is a great burden. You must do a lot of work for other people. You must write what they say, not what you think they say, and not what you want them to say."

"I should like to learn my letters one day."

"If you stay with me for long enough, then you surely will."

"Do you think this knight, Guy de Coutances, knows how to write?"

"I don't know, but my guess is he can't even sign his name," Gregory said. "He is a knight, so he was born and raised to kill. That leaves little time for grammar."

"Do you think a man who could write and wield a sword could be powerful?"

"So powerful, in fact, he might just attract the ire of a jealous king," Gregory said. "Why? Would you like to be such a man?"

"Now that I think about it, yes."

Gregory gave him a sharp look of warning. "You can share your dreams with me, and I will encourage them," he said. "But in mixed company you should watch what you say and to whom you say it. The wheels of this world turn slowly, Warren. And if you get in front of those wheels, you can be run over by them. Understand?"

"Yes, Master Gregory."

Gregory and Warren trotted their horses into Newark at the end of a hot and dusty day. The bells of St. Mary Magdalene signaled Vespers as a golden sunset peeled across the sky. Merchants and workmen packed up their goods and tools. A gang of boys and their dogs scampered through the market. Laughter and singing sounded from the tavern. Gregory nodded courteously to a local who looked at him with wary eyes.

Near the bridge across the River Trent loomed Newark Castle, its red sandstone glowing in the twilight. Somewhere down in the belly of the stronghold sat de Coutances, and Gregory was eager to speak with him. However, a severe lord, Miles le Gaunter, held the castle in the Bishop of Lincoln's stead. Gregory knew le Gaunter would have pointed questions, and he was equally sure he would deliver pointed answers. Indeed, the bishop had told him any hospitality offered at Newark would be forced and perfunctory, and Gregory would do best to come and go as quickly as possible.

He turned to Warren. "Say nothing to no one. You are no longer in Lichfield where everyone knows your name. You are a stranger here and Lord le Gaunter is dangerous. Keep quiet and do as I say."

The boy nodded in silence and coaxed his horse forward in the direction of the castle. As they approached, Gregory saw armed men peering down at them from the gatehouse windows.

A man stuck his head out and sneered. "Bordeaux, is that you?"

He looked up and pulled Moonbeam to a stop. "It is I."

Gregory assumed he waited while one of the guards went to notify Lord le Gaunter. Remaining straight and unflinching, he kept his eyes on the gatehouse, knowing anything—an arrow, a crossbow bolt, or a stone—could come racing his and Warren's way at any moment. At last a new face appeared in the gatehouse window, a round, sickly face with one sad eye and a liver spot on the cheek. Framed by a shiny mail coif and creased with a terrifying frown, this was the face of power in this part of Nottinghamshire.

The face of Lord Miles le Gaunter.

"The Bishop of Lincoln, my overlord, says I must let you in so you can talk with that shitpile of a man, Guy de Coutances," le Gaunter said. "But for some reason I cannot understand why anyone would want to record the story of a worthless bucket of piss such as he."

Gregory removed his beaver skin hat, ran a hand through his tuft of brown hair, and cleared his throat. "My lord, I find it interesting you speak so poorly of him now, seeing that for years you thought he was worth a fortune."

"Lower the drawbridge!" Le Gaunter's face disappeared from the gatehouse window. As soon as the drawbridge was down, le Gaunter, on foot and pointing his finger, stormed across it with his men.

The lord confronting him was hardened by axe and sword, and though Gregory was unsettled by the sight of this enormous trunk of a man with his toothy underbite and slouched shoulders, he couldn't hold back a smirk as le Gaunter, red with rage, stopped at the edge of the drawbridge.

"From the smile on your face, I can see you don't know why I'm so angry."

"Oh, but I do." Gregory put his hat back on and tugged it down low over his brow.

"And why is that?"

"Because if I tell the story of Guy de Coutances, then I tell the story of you and your failure to collect your ransom. You feel this story will reflect poorly on you and your abilities—especially if Guy slips from your hands and into those of the monks at Hinton."

"You chroniclers think you're smarter than you really are," growled le Gaunter, his hand on the hilt of his sword. "You can stay and do your work, but it is salt fish and stale bread and the fires will not be lit for you, Bordeaux."

Gregory and Warren spent two tense, hungry days and nights at Newark Castle. Gregory asked that Guy de Coutances be brought up from the dungeon and into the gatehouse. While Warren stood guard, Gregory and Guy sat at a small table in a dank little room with a candle flickering between them. As they shared stale crusts of bread, molded cheese, and watered down wine with an edge of vinegar, Guy told his story. Le Gaunter's men stood at the foot of the gatehouse singing bawdy songs, telling filthy jokes, and issuing threats to disrupt their sessions. Gregory and Guy managed to shrug off their crudities and over the course of two days he had five sheaths of parchment for his chronicle.

No physical hint remained of the man Guy used to be. Gaunt with a straggly yellowish beard, bloodshot eyes, and deep valleys around his chapped and crusted lips, he was the detritus that remains after the flood has receded. Gregory felt a bit of sadness for Guy, whose noble life had changed as the result of a simple skirmish near his hometown in Normandy. But Gregory's sympathy recoiled as their talks continued. Guy spoke not of his fondness for family and friends, nor of his duty to God. Yet his eyes glimmered as he boasted of horses and whores, of gaming and war, and how he missed the silk and steel of lordship. Guy was angrier with himself for having been captured than he was with his family for having promoted his younger brother to the position of heir. In Guy's world, only one person counted—Guy. Five years in the Newark dungeon had done nothing to squelch the pride he'd felt on his last day of freedom, when he'd donned his splendid armor and dashed out to the skirmish in a flurry of plumes and pennons.

"If ever I have the chance," he said, "I'll reclaim the lordship of Coutances, even if it's over the dead bodies of my father and brother."

"But your fate says otherwise," Gregory replied. "Soon you will be taken to Hinton Priory in Somerset. If you have not been told, that is a Carthusian house. You will live as a hermit in a cell, and the rest of your life will be spent in silence and prayer. While many houses flout their duty to God, the same can-not be said of the Carthusians. They follow the rule with the utmost severity."

"The Carthusians?" His lip quivered. "But I thought I was going to Grey-friars in London."

"Where you would eat fresh meat and fish and dabble in the sins of the flesh? No, I'm afraid you have been lied to. Lord Miles le Gaunter wanted you for your money, but now that he doesn't have it, he will punish you for the rest of your days."

Gregory didn't think the sorrow on Coutances face could grow deeper, but indeed it did. His brow furrowed into sharp ruts of despair, a tear ran down his ashen cheek, and his blackened teeth clinched into a grimace of old, incurable pain. A foul odor wafted his way as Guy's soul seemed to escape him on the wings of a long, lonely sigh.

Hands trembling, Guy tried to take a sip of wine, but it ran down the cor-ners of his mouth and into his beard. He dropped the cup, put his hand to his forehead, and heaved with weeping. As he cried, he mumbled of the darker side of lordship—rape and pillage, burning and looting, the cruel imposition of taxes and flagrant corruption. Innocent men falsely accused, virgins de-flowered, and families, both noble and common, destroyed. "These things are what an heir needed to do to inherit an estate and its revenue. I only did what others before me had done. I always knew it was wrong, but I did it anyway—for my avarice and greed."

Gregory, in cold silence, deftly worked his quill against the parchment to preserve each word Guy uttered. From the corner of his eye he glanced up at Warren, who listened and leaned motionless against the archway. Gregory was not surprised Guy had opened up about his life. Now that grim Hinton Priory was the known destination, this was the day of reck-oning. The nobility donated money to churches and sponsored the found-ing of abbeys and priories. They paid people to mourn at their funerals. In their wills, they left money to pay people to pray in perpetuity for their souls. Gregory knew these things and accepted them as the way of the world. But what he also knew was those with money always got a return on their investment. Holding a stake in an abbey meant having a powerful abbot as an ally. And to pay the indigent to mourn and to pray was to earn an accolade for Christian charity. Yet how many nobles, or anyone for that matter, would admit their sins when they, like Guy de Coutances, had nothing to gain? This is the question Gregory pondered as he dipped his quill into the ink well.

> *When a man is born in a trap, he knows the truth only when he is caught. If he escapes, he will learn to lie again. If not, he will realize acceptance resides with us, and forgiveness resides with God. Perhaps it is best not to sidestep the snare.*

The wagon train arrived the next afternoon. The Carthusians, soaked with the day's somber rain, trudged through the mud with dour purpose. They went there not for pleasantries but to seize a man. Clad in black habits and hoods and walking with the assistance of great staves, these were the hardened men of Christ whose sole mission was to build a bulwark against the apocalypse. To claim a nobleman like Guy and to harness his prayers was a big grab for the Carthusians, who no doubt would pound him into the man they needed him to be. From a window in the gatehouse, Gregory and Warren watched them approach the castle. The clink of chains grew loud as the drawbridge lowered. Miles le Gaunter, dressed in a fine green tunic and a feathered cap, walked across the drawbridge leading a donkey. Riding the donkey, backwards, was Guy, his hands in irons behind his back. Despite the indignity, Guy held his head high. He looked up at Gregory and gave a wry smile. A Carthusian monk handed le Gaunter a small leather sack, took hold of the reins and led Guy and the donkey to the wagon train. With the rain coming harder and thunder rolling in the sky, the Carthusians pulled out of town.

Gregory heard the urgent steps of many men running up the spiral staircase to the second floor of the gatehouse. Le Gaunter burst through the door. He and his men poured into the room and surrounded Gregory and Warren.

As a drop of spittle ran down his underbite, le Gaunter flashed a facetious smile of hospitality and mockingly bowed down. "Master Gregory of Bordeaux, I pray you have seen and heard great things to write about. We at Newark Castle are so pleased to have assisted you in your endeavor to write Southampton's chronicle. Unfortunately, we no longer have the means to support you. Our stores of food and drink are low and we need to make room for other guests who are already on their way."

"Am I correct to assume your hospitality ends immediately?"

"Ah, Bordeaux, you are ever so smart," le Gaunter said. "And if you are not on the road by Vespers, I will be forced to accommodate you and your page in the comfortable quarters recently vacated by Guy de Coutances."

"That will not be necessary, my lord."

"And one more thing...." le Gaunter's sad eye flashed malicious and bright. "It seems your horses escaped from the stables yesterday and my men had to track them down and bring them back. A time consuming task. I'd like to think a man of your standing would be more than willing to compensate my men for all the work they did for you. Am I right?"

"You most certainly are." He looked up at the tall, stooping knight. "What do you think is fair recompense? Perhaps a shilling?"

"I was thinking more like a pound."

Gregory had a pound, but he did not want to give even a farthing to le Gaunter. He cursed himself for having been so arrogant upon his arrival. Had he been meek when he and le Gaunter had first met, perhaps he would not be in this situation. But he had let his vanity reign, and in a flash of hindsight he knew he had cajoled le Gaunter in an attempt to impress Warren. He had let his tongue wag, a mistake. But he guessed he was bigger than this cheap local lord, and believed the odds stood in his favor if he chose to go bold.

"My lord, I agree with you. One pound is a sufficient fee for the toil and trouble of your men. But you must keep in mind those are not my horses. They belong to the Earl of Southampton, and he keeps an estate in Leicestershire, not too far from here. Perhaps you should keep the horses and seek the pound from him. I would be more than glad to walk merrily on my way."

Le Gaunter breathed through his nose and glared at Gregory, who returned his gaze without blinking. Dripping hatred enveloped the men as
the bells of Vespers gonged. Le Gaunter pushed back his cloak to reveal the
pummel of his sword. Gregory held out his open hands to show he wielded
no weapon. The ringing ended, the hiss of a burning wall-mounted torch
the only sound after the bells stilled.

"Bordeaux, I can kill you."

"Yes, my lord, you can," Gregory replied.

"But I don't need blood on my sword, not today at least." Without taking
his eyes off of Gregory, he motioned to his men. "Ready their horses!"

Soon thereafter, Gregory and Warren galloped out through the gatehouse and into the churning storm. Their steeds, Moonbeam and Tamworth, raced long and hard through woods and fields, down drover's roads,
over hills and dales, and across swollen streams and marshes. They found
shelter in an abandoned barn on the outskirts of an abandoned village in a
forgotten nook of a forgotten valley. Warren built a fire, roasted a few pieces
of salted fish, and sprinkled them with black pepper. In his pack he found a
crust of bread, a handful of nuts, some dried fruit, and a hunk of hard goat
cheese. They ate in silence.

As they settled down for sleep, Warren leaned up on his elbow and
looked across the whispering fire. "Master Gregory, who owns our horses?"

"We do."

"And not the Earl of Southampton?"

"No, Warren, those are our horses."

"And you didn't pay le Gaunter the pound."

"No. I paid him no pound, and nor shall I ever."

The Jury at Corby Speaks

hielding his eyes from the morning sun, he knew which way was east. Other than that, Gregory hadn't a clue. Far from Newark, he hoped, with food and comfort on the near horizon. Following a byway little more than a rabbit trail, he and Warren made their way through the fragrant, blooming wilderness and by noon reached one of the old Roman roads that crisscrossed the realm. Parched and hungry, they headed north.

Gregory felt ragged. Damp clothes from last night's rain. Chafed skin. Bones aching from the grueling ride out of Newark. He had hit his head on a low hanging branch the night before, and his head still ached. Briars had torn at his knee. A blister bulged from his left big toe, and back at Newark Castle, in his haste to leave, he had slipped on the gatehouse stairs and twisted his ankle. Things could be better, he knew. He could be in London, sitting at his shop counting his coins and writing contracts for the guild, sipping on Clairac at the Purple Pot Tavern amidst gossip and humor, and eating spiced beef and buttery white bread as minstrels regaled him with song. Yes, things could be better.

Still, he was in good spirits. He had gotten more than expected from his meetings with Guy de Coutances, and in addition to Guy's story was the unexpected behavior of Lord Miles le Gaunter. Indeed, Newark had been a bonanza. But something nagged at Gregory. He had made a mistake, something he did not often do. He had chided a powerful lord, and it had nearly cost him his life. Warren's as well.

He looked over at his young country page, whistling a tune and gazing into the sky as his horse walked slowly down the road. "Warren, I think I need to apologize to you."

The boy stopped whistling and turned to him. "Apologize? For what?"

"My conduct at Newark Castle. I was reckless with Lord le Gaunter and in so doing, I put you in unnecessary danger."

"You should not apologize," Warren said. "I agreed to face danger when I chose to ride with you. I made an oath and pledged my loyalty, so whatever comes our way I must accept."

"That is one way of looking at it. But with your oath comes a responsibility on my behalf. If you are to be loyal, then I must be worthy of your loyalty. You are not a servant, Warren, but an important part of what I'm trying to do. I have taken you from your home, your family, and your friends. You deserve my best, and that is not what you received at Newark."

"I could disagree, but I will accept your apology. But I do want to ask you a question. Guy de Coutances. You two spoke French so I did not understand what was said. But I know he told you many things. In the end he broke down. I have never seen a man shed such tears. What did he tell you?"

"Oh, he confessed his sins," Gregory said. "He parted with his anguish and surrendered to his fate. Even battle-hardened men like Guy will cry when they reach the end of one life and the beginning of another."

"What will happen to a man like Guy de Coutances?"

"He will pray for the souls of all mankind, and then he will die a saved man."

"And what about Miles le Gaunter? What will you write of him?"

"He spoke English, so you know all I know," Gregory said. "If you wrote the chronicle, what would you say?"

Warren leaned back in his saddle, tilted his head up, and laughed. "I would say he has great hospitality, serves wonderful food and drink, and is gifted with horses."

Gregory looked over and laughed. "Yes, dear Warren, Lord le Gaunter will be remembered in history as the greatest of hosts."

They could have gone on like that all day, riding casually and laughing as they conversed. Gregory and Warren had a natural rapport. The young page had much to learn and Gregory much to teach, and talk bounced earnest and easy between the two. But levity was not the way of the road, and sensing danger, Gregory pulled his horse to a halt and motioned for Warren to do likewise. Searching the landscape in front of him, he noticed movement in a stand of oak down the road to his right. With a squinting of his eyes he narrowed his focus on the largest tree, and to his dread, spied a man peering out at him. Warren pulled the mail coif up over his head, donned his conical helm and slid the great billhook from its saddle strap. The man stepped out from behind the tree and into the middle of the road. He quickly wound up his sling, and from an overhead position, launched a stone. It sped past Gregory's face and slammed into Warren's helm with such force the brim bit back into his forehead and drew blood. Gregory looked over his shoulder and saw two more men, armed with heavy knives, creeping towards them.

"There is no need for weapons, lads," Gregory called. "I have coins I will gladly give."

As he awaited a response, the sling man launched another shot. It caught Gregory flush behind the right ear in a sickening crack of bone and stone. He felt his teeth crunch and tasted blood. His vision flickered and his ears grew loud with ringing. Yelping in pain, he put his hand to the back of his head. Moonbeam reared and Gregory, blind and flailing for the reins, was thrown. He extended his right leg to brace his fall, but it snapped on impact. Gregory slumped in a heap, broken, bleeding, and helpless. As his vision dimmed, he prayed that God might help him, and if it was too late for help, that God might have pity on his soul.

All at once, the men charged. Warren slid off Tamworth and as the assailants closed, stood guard over Gregory. Once in striking distance, Warren roared and stepped forward with his billhook gripped in both hands. He caught one of the men by the thigh, and with a quick turn and pull, put him on the ground. As he recoiled and readied for another strike, a second man stabbed down at him. The knife glanced off Warren's helm and raked against the coat of mail. Warren slid to his right, swiped the billhook in a terrific arc, and spilled the man's guts. He collected himself, and with all of his ploughman's power, thrust out the butt end of his weapon and caught the arriving sling man square in the mouth. The two attackers who remained alive were now down, one holding his shattered face and the other staunching the ragged wound at his thigh.

From behind the nose guard of his helm, Warren flashed a bloody smile of battle. He put the billhook to the throat of one man and then to the throat of the next, to show them their lives were his if he wanted. They collected themselves and slunk back into the bush from whence they had come. The dead man, his warm entrails oozing out onto the dusty road, attracted flies as hungry crows cawed from the trees. Warren flung off his helmet and crouched on both knees at Gregory's side.

"Master Gregory, are you alive?" He cradled Gregory's head in his hands.

"I am alive, dear boy. But I fear I shan't be for long."

Gregory awoke with a groan. He writhed with a spasm of pain, but the pain meant he was of the earth, so he was glad to have it. He leaned up on his elbow and looked around the room. A soothing fire crackled in the hearth over which hung a pot of what smelled like simmering beef stew. He saw a large and comfortable room, tidy and organized yet thick with the odds and ends of a meaningful life. Pots and pans and jars and half barrels, a colorfully embroidered wall hanging, plates and bowls and cups stacked neatly on a shelf. All manner of utensils, cured meats and encased cheeses, bundled herbs, and full sacks of burlap dangled from the rafters. A small, spotted dog jumped up onto the bed and licked Gregory's hand. He patted the dog's head as he peered deeper into the room. Two people sat at a long table on the other side of the hearth. Despite the shifting shadows cast upon him by the fire, Gregory discerned Warren, who appeared to be talking in-depth with a woman in a veil. Gregory tried to rise, but the stiffness in his bones told him to do otherwise. Instead he cleared his throat, and to his cheer, Warren bolted up from his chair and raced across the room.

"Master Gregory." He flashed his gap-toothed smile. "You have been at rest for two days. It is through God's mercy you are awake!"

"Yes," Gregory said with a cough. "I am awake. But beyond that, I cannot say too much."

Warren pumped his fist and laughed. "You are awake and you are alive and you will get better. The worst of it has come and gone. Look, your leg is in a splint."

Warren pulled back the blanket. Gregory looked down at his right calf, held in a wooden frame wrapped with leather. The sight of his leg reminded him of the fall but nothing else.

"You were made to sleep by a potion of cabbage juice, henbane, hemlock, opium, vinegar, and the gall of a castrated boar." Warren turned up his mouth in an expression of disgust. "A poultice of rosemary and onion was stuffed up into your armpits to suck out the poisons from your head wound. Master Gregory, you were a sight to see."

"How long did I sleep?"

"Two days," Warren said. "And you snored so loud, I could barely hear myself think."

"Dear heavens. In my frailty, it seems I am a nuisance."

"A nuisance?" Warren said. "Someone tried to kill you, yet you live. My esteem for you has grown because now I know you have the will to survive."

"I appreciate your support," Gregory said. "And with God's grace I will soon be out of this sick bed and back in the saddle."

"In time, Master Gregory, I am sure of it."

Gregory glanced up at the woman standing next to Warren. "So who do I have the honor of meeting this day?"

She sat down at a stool next to the bed. "I am Margery Alesworth. And as long as you are in my care, you will heal."

"I thank you for what you've done," he said, gesturing at his splinted leg. "I don't want to be a cripple for the rest of my days."

"The bone set well," Margery said. "You will walk again and with all the strength you once had. But you should also thank Warren. He kneeled at the foot of your bed each day and prayed."

Gregory looked over at his page, who, bashful in the face of praise, awkwardly looked away.

"Where am I?" Gregory said, returning his attention to Margery.

"You are in the village of Corby, in Lincolnshire," she said, and dabbed a damp cloth at his forehead.

Her voice soothed him. The direct voice of a confident and experienced person, and in it he found solace. The doubts nagging at him just moments ago shooed away like squawking fowl. Even though she wore a veil, Gregory saw her red hair greyed at the peak and temples. Crow's feet spread from the corners of her green river eyes, and lines of laughter and sorrow graced her handsome cheeks. In the frame of her veil, he saw a country lass who had grown into a wise woman, a sharp wit yet to be ground on the millstone of compromise. Gregory didn't know exactly how he'd come to be in Corby. But he knew why. For the first time in years, his heart bloomed like a field of foxgloves.

"I have beef stew, Master Gregory," she said.

"Beef?" he said, and his mouth watered.

Propped up by Warren on one side and Margery on the other, Gregory hobbled to the trestle table and managed to sit down with his splint leg propped on a stool. He tried his best not to be ravenous, but soon abandoned his attempt at civility. He spooned the stew into his mouth with wolfish gulps, over and over again until he emptied the bowl, save for the broth, which he sopped up with a crust of bread. He ate another bowl and gulped down a cup of ale. When Margery asked if he'd like a strawberry pie, he nod-ded his head and dug into it without saying a word. Soon sated, he returned to the bed and fell fast asleep with the spotted dog curled up beside him.

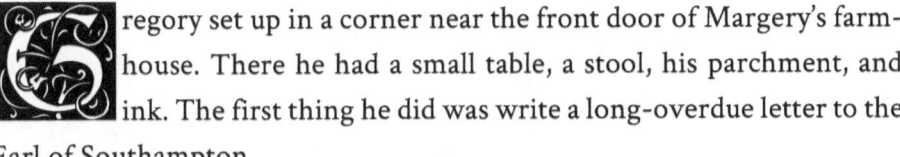 regory set up in a corner near the front door of Margery's farm-house. There he had a small table, a stool, his parchment, and ink. The first thing he did was write a long-overdue letter to the Earl of Southampton.

> *It appears I have made another enemy. Lord Miles le Gaunter of Newark, he of the slouched shoulders and the dreadful underbite, refused me hos-pitality when I visited his castle. He is a vassal of the Bishop of Lincoln, a friend of mine who I will visit soon. I have resolved not to speak ill of le Gaunter while in the presence of the bishop, as I cannot afford to tarnish what little affinity I have outside of London. But you should know this lord tried to extort a pound from me, under threat of taking my horse, Moon-beam, before I left his fortress. If you should see him at court, you might consider telling him you are aware of how he treated me.*

He also wrote a letter to his cousin, Jean du Mont, and asked him to share it with his friends and associates.

> *I fell from my horse and broke my leg while being attacked by highway-men. But my leg has been set and is healing, and I am safe and happy in the quaint village of Corby in Lincolnshire. I am staying with a villager named Margery Alesworth, and if she lived in London, I think I would have wed her by now. I have also taken on a page. His name is Warren and he is from Lichfield. He is a simple sort with an unblemished heart and the strength of a bear. He is smart, too, and if I have my way, he will learn his letters in good time.*

He soon found himself in a comfortable routine. Wake at dawn, write until midday, eat dinner, sit outside for an hour or so and watch the peasants work the fields, return to his chronicle and write until supper. Warren, meanwhile, found work replacing the roof at the parish church of St. John the Evangelist, and in little time had coins in his pocket and friends who called his name.

In the evening they converged with Margery at the hearth table to eat and drink and talk and laugh. Friends and relatives stopped by for visits and Gregory and Warren found themselves in a warm community of people centered on Margery. Gregory had yet to ask of her his probing kinds of questions, but he guessed she was a person of standing. Her farmhouse, after all, was made of stone, not of timber, and the roof of slate, not of thatch. She could afford beef, lamb, pork, fresh trout, white bread, sugar, saffron, and wine. She had a chest full of neatly stacked robes and mantles of all colors. Embroidery depicting the birth of Christ adorned the wall. Her table was set with linen, a silver-plated ewer, and spoons. Even the guest bed Gregory and Warren slept in had a padded feather mattress.

She had a large barn behind her farmhouse where she housed a team of oxen, a horse, pigs, cows, and goats. Her material possessions impressed him, but they didn't come close to comparing with the woman herself. When people visited, they didn't just come for company, but for empathy and advice. Jovial in one moment and serious in the next, she had the depth to embrace the layered needs of her community. Coins changed hands, promises sworn, and truths told to the young and old. From the window near his table, Gregory watched as she conducted business in the street or spoke with ploughman out near the fields of wheat and barley. Ever busy, she never walked alone but with a friend, family member, or associate. Gregory had never met a woman with as much practical authority, and indeed, in her uniqueness is where he found her beauty. He also knew she must have been tough to have obtained her position, and that's why each time she walked through the door he felt a heartbeat of joy. In her arresting presence had become, of late, his favorite place to be.

"How is your leg, Gregory?" she asked as she entered the room. "And how is your chronicle?"

"Both are doing fine." He took a sip of wine. "I'm going back through my short stay at Newark Castle. There is much that needs to be written about what happened there."

"Gregory, can you join me at the table?"

By the tone in her voice and the concern in her eye, he knew she wanted to talk about something more pressing than his broken leg and his writing.

"Of course." He rose, braced by a pair of crutches. As he made his way to the table, she stoked the embers and added more fuel to the fire.

She poured two cups of wine and took a seat. With a sharp glance and a gesture of her hand, the servant girl left the room. Gregory laid the crutches against the table and sat down. Looking into her eyes, which showed a steeliness he had never seen, Gregory was nervous. "How long have you been here?"

"We arrived two weeks ago tomorrow," he said.

"And I have enjoyed every day of it. It is good to have men in the house."

"Even if one is yet a cripple?"

"Yes." She reached out and touched him on the hand. "Gregory, people are starting to talk. I'm sure that does not surprise you."

"In a village like Corby, no, it does not. But what do they speak of?"

"I haven't wanted to pull you into this," she said, "but now it seems I must. A month ago, during court, Lord Corby brought a lawsuit against me. He wants to take my land. People are asking me if you will take my case. Will you?"

"Margery, you saved my life! Of course I will take your case, and I will also waive the fee! Tell me what it is Lord Corby wants, and I shall make him regret he ever wanted it."

Margery poured more wine and told her story. "The old Lord Corby was a nasty man. He had a greasy beard, a hideous goiter around his neck, and his clothes stank of urine. He drank too much, would break wind in the middle of a conversation, and was ever quick with a demeaning word, let me tell you. Meticulous in his collection of taxes, too, and when it was time to hang a man, he always sat front and center. But he was fair. He honored his word, and he was just in court. His bailiff and his priest were honest, and they worked with the villagers to make sure the manor functioned as it should. We had a nice Saturday market, and each year, the old Lord Corby threw a wonderful Christmas feast at his hall. Those were the good old days."

"And what happened?" Gregory asked.

"He choked on a fish bone and died. During Lent three years ago."

"Before we go any further, I am curious," he said. "How did you amass such an estate?"

"I inherited a freehold from my father, and I am twice a widow with twice the dower. But I assembled much of it on my own. I control seventy five acres and four rent houses."

He took a sip of wine. "Margery, you're richer than me."

She went on to tell him that with cash rents and no debt, she dabbled in all manner of trade—wool, timber, spices, textiles, metal works, victuals, and livestock. She also kept bees for honey and wax, and by her own account, brewed the best ale in all of Lincolnshire—thus her surname, Alesworth. "After the old Lord Corby died, he was replaced by his son, who we call the new Lord Corby. He is a goat's ass of a man, and soon after he was sworn in, things changed."

"Let me guess," said Gregory. "An insecure son wants to prove he is superior to his father?"

A sad smile came to her lovely face. "I'm afraid so. The bailiff and the priest, the ones who witnessed all the records, they disappeared not long after the new Lord Corby came to power. There is no longer justice at court, either. He raised the tax on the annual fair and on all the goods going in and out of town. He called in all the debts of the poor and seized the holdings of those who could not pay. He raised the tax on the miller, so the price of bread went up. And if that wasn't enough, he cancelled the Christmas feast last year."

"And now he's coming for you."

"And I don't know how to stop him. He claims my original freehold, the one I inherited from my father, is forfeit because my father gained title to it through an illegal transaction—with the old Lordy Corby! Since I pledged that freehold as dowry in both my marriages, it voids the property left to me by contract by my late husbands—"

"—Or so the New Lord Corby claims."

"Yes, and the only way I can maintain title is if I pay a fine equal to the revenue the land has generated over the last twenty years."

"And what is his estimate?"

Margery sighed. "One hundred-and-fifty marks." She took a worrisome sip of wine. "I do not have that much silver."

He kept a straight face, but inside, sickened at the thought of such an exorbitant fee. An amount of that magnitude could bankrupt even the mightiest of London merchants, and would surely destroy Margery. He would have to examine her deeds most carefully. "You will not need the silver if you have the deeds. You do have them, right?"

"Yes."

"If your deeds are good then the new Lord Corby has no case. My guess is he's hoping you do not have them."

"I can get them tomorrow, I promise," she said. "But please, for the rest of the night, let's forget about the lawsuit. I want to hear about Gregory. You are a lawyer, a London wine merchant, and a brave chronicler riding through the realm. Surely you have a story to make me forget my troubles."

"If you pour me another cup of wine," he said with a smile, "I'm sure I'll have no problem telling you a tale."

She obliged.

They raised their cups, tilted them toward each other, and then took a drink. Gregory gazed into her eyes, which sparkled in the light of the hearth fire. He wanted to lean in and kiss her, and guessed she would be amenable. But instead, he stymied the temptation with another taste of wine. He put the cup down, rested his elbow on the table, and leaned his head on his hand. "I have lived in London for many, many years, but I spent my childhood in Bordeaux, where I was born. ..."

ne night after Margery and Warren went to sleep, Gregory lit a candle and a piece of frankincense. He spread the deeds out over the table, pulled the chair up tight, and poured over the documents. Dating back to the first year of the reign of King Edward, they told the story of peasants who found their freedom in the soil. Piece by piece and year by year, a fertile estate emerged on the northern outskirts of Corby. In the deeds lived the works of John, the prudence of Ian, and the patience of Roger. Margery appeared in there, too. Her leases and rents and trades and purchases—the dealings of a talented landlord in command of her world. Each deed precisely written, witnessed and signed by the bailiff, Clifford Townes, and John of Gainsborough, the parish priest. The new Lord Corby might want to take control of the land, but legally, Gregory knew he had no case.

Rats will gnaw at anything if you let them. He shook his head, rolled up the deeds, and tied them off with a leather strap.

He then wrote a few letters to Lincolnshire nobles he did not even know. But he wanted to meet them, so he invited them to the Saturday market at Corby. He implored them to bring coins, for there would be much to buy, and to bring their associates, for there would be entertainment they would not want to miss.

Gregory looked up from the letters and saw dawn creeping through the cracks in the shutters. He snuffed out the candles and slid into bed.

o further appreciate the land under Margery's control, Gregory walked every inch of it, from the dead oak tree to the apple orchard, from the bend in the road to the beehives, and from the creek bank to the cow pasture. As he hobbled along on his crutches, Warren at his side, Gregory spoke with the tenants who worked the land. In Margery's estate lay the innards of Corby, the blood, bone, and marrow of a vibrant community. Gregory estimated up to half the population was somehow tied to the tract, which meant whoever controlled the deeds

controlled the town. During Gregory's tour of the estate, he heard plenty of gripes and grievances.

"Growing up, Margery was a good girl," said one of Margery's cousins, a ploughman. "But year by year, she grows fonder of silver than she does of her own kin."

"Back when Margery was married to Roger, things were as they should be," said another ploughman. "Roger took care of the fields and she took care of the home. Now that she is in charge of all of it, she has forgotten her place is in the hearth."

But she also had her share of supporters.

A milkmaid who lived in one of Margery's rent houses said, "She patched the roof and had a well dug, and when my daughter died, she paid for the funeral. If all landlords were like Margery, we would all be happy."

Walking the land and talking to the people were brazen acts sure to attract the attention of the new Lord Corby, and that's what Gregory wanted—a curious lord who might show his hand before the next session of court. To Gregory's pleasure, he appeared unannounced at the Saturday market. Gregory, Warren, and Margery visited at a stall and looked at ells of blue velvet when the market went silent. Gregory turned, and there he was, on his horse, in the middle of the street and at the front of his armed retinue. Their eyes locked and Gregory knew—here before him sat the enemy. He wore a green wool cap with an ostrich plume, a matching green woolen tunic, and black boots with spurs and silver buckles. His thin brown moustache was waxed at the ends, and his goatee ended with a waxed point. On his left arm he wore a heavy leather glove up to his elbow, and on that glove perched a peregrine falcon. Rather than ride a horse that fit him, the bantam Corby sat on a giant bay charger. His legs didn't hug the horse's flanks but instead flared out in a buffoonish show of conceit. In silence, he waited as curious onlookers gathered. Once the market was crowded and appropriate for theater, the new Lord Corby coughed up a ball of phlegm and spit it at Gregory's feet.

"Lick it up, boy, or I will have you whipped and thrown in the stocks." He held his head with the casual aloofness of authority.

"It's good to know the great Lord Corby has learned his manners. I have been many places, but never have I been greeted with such courtesy. But alas, I cannot oblige your request. You see, I am a free man of London, and I do not lick the snot of bumpkins."

Loud with gasps and murmurs, the townsfolk, craning their necks and standing shoulder to shoulder on their tip toes for a view, closed in so Gregory and the new Lord Corby faced each other inside a large circle. This encounter, anticipated for weeks, would at last unfold with half the county bearing witness. This was as Gregory had hoped and as he had planned, so he grew confident knowing he had chosen the time and place of conflict, and that the right people watched.

During his tour of Margery's estate, Gregory learned the obvious—the new Lord Corby was reviled. But he also learned a few unexpected things. Corby, the third of three sons, had never been groomed to be the lord of the manor. His lot was to freelance and earn a place in a household higher up on the manorial chain. From what Gregory had learned, the old Lord Corby had hoped his youngest son would leave and never return. But both of the older sons had died, and the title went to the youngest by default. In addition to the petty fines and fees he had levied against his own tenants, the new Lord Corby had also reopened old boundary claims against vassals and rival rulers of other manors in Lincolnshire. The short of it was the new Lord Corby was never meant for this role and had made a fine mess of things. In the marketplace with his gleaming warhorse and his falcon, his boots and his spurs and his armed retainers, the new Lord Corby projected unassailable power.

But Gregory knew otherwise.

Village spies no doubt told the new Lord Corby a lawyer from London was in town, he worked for the Earl of Southampton, and he planned to represent Margery Alesworth in court. A stranger in black, Gregory was sure they had told their lord, and a cunning fellow, too. Deep in the belly of his hall, there was no telling what the young lordling had heard. But his presence here in the market was proof he'd heard something, and that he was with his full retinue was proof he had expectations.

Not wanting to disappoint his host, Gregory stepped further into the confrontation. He pushed up the brim of his beaver skin hat, and his lip curled into a daring smile. The new Lord Corby, shooing away a fly, responded with a dangerous grin.

"So I understand you will oppose me in court next week. Why?"

Gregory shrugged. "Because Margery's deeds are good and your claim is dubious. I have argued cases at King's Bench and Common Pleas for years, Lord Corby. Believe me, you cannot win this complaint. And if we do not get satisfaction here, then I will appeal it to circuit court in Lincoln. There you will have to answer to a royal judge."

"But my scribe," Corby gestured toward a tonsured priest in his retinue, "has poured over the manor records. He assured me that John, Margery's father, did not have the right to enter into a freehold contract with my father, because he did not have the right to sell. John's deed is the mother deed, and if that one is forfeit, then it stands to reason all the others are forfeit as well. You might know the law in London, but we know it in Corby, too."

"The deed shows the requisite fee was paid and the contracts were sworn and witnessed by the bailiff, and then signed by your father," said Gregory. "The metes and bounds are good, too. Freeholds are legal and this one is legal, and I'm sure the jury will agree."

The mere mention of the word jury made the new Lord Corby flinch. With a collection of twelve free men to learn the facts and arbitrate, the schemes of an unpopular lord could easily be thwarted by an honorable jury. Corby must have realized a few of the jurors stood in the Saturday market crowd, and perhaps they had come there to watch him abuse his authority, because Gregory saw a look of chagrin dawn sharp and bleak in his face.

Rather than let Lord Corby regroup, Gregory pressed the advantage. "Lord Corby, you have inherited your father's land and title, but it seems you did not inherit his common sense," Gregory said, leaning on his crutches with his arms crossed over his chest. "Your father helped build this village, and it is a nice one. I should know, for in my travels I have seen some real pigsties. But now you say your father erred, and for that you want to punish

Margery with a fine of one hundred and fifty marks? Perhaps it would be wise to continue counting your coins and forget about Margery Alesworth. If you push this thing too far, you could wind up being the loser."

The new Lord Corby glanced at a group of his peers—fashionable country squires who glared back at him with unfriendly eyes. He looked down at Gregory and then back at the squires. A deep furrow of confusion appeared in Lord Corby's brow. These men, all of them Lincolnshire landholders with rights of their own, and all of them jurors at various points in the past, never appeared in person at Corby's Saturday market. Their householders came instead, so to see them here this day was a surprise for everyone, including Lord Corby.

He held out his hands in a show of bewilderment and said, "What are you doing here?"

"We were invited, Lord Corby," one of them said.

"By who?"

"That, we do not know," the nobleman said. "The letters were anonymous."

Lord Corby turned to Gregory. "Lawyer, did you do this?"

A big smile spread across Gregory's face, but he said nothing.

"Seize him!" commanded Lord Corby. "Seize him, I say, and throw him in the stocks!"

When his men came forward, Warren and then Margery stood in their way. Many people in the crowd, including the squires, joined them. When they did not budge, and when it was clear the only way to apprehend Gregory was to hack through the crowd, Lord Corby, flustered and muttering, called off his men. As he and his retinue pulled out of the market, Gregory put one arm over Margery's shoulder and the other over Warren's.

"The jury has spoken," he said.

That night, Gregory, Warren, Margery, and her closest associates gathered around the hearth at Margery's farmhouse. They drank ale and rehashed the events from earlier in the day. The look on Corby's face. The unexpected presence of the squires. The tables turned at last. Gregory, with ink and parchment at hand, wrote as the party crept into the wee hours.

Though a man cares only for the opinions of his equals and betters, what others think of him still counts. The baker of bread and the keeper of bees may not have hawks and hounds, but they remember the times and know the difference between good and bad. A local lord can afford to be unpopular, if such is his way, but not to be loathed by all.

Looking out over a misty morning field stretching north from Corby, Gregory felt the first autumn chill. His writing done, his leg healed, and Moonbeam hungry for travel, the time to head to Lincoln had come. He knelt down, plucked a long blade of grass, and tucked it in the corner of his mouth so the seed head dangled and danced in the breeze. He watched a red and mustard sunrise break over a stand of distant beech, and heard the geese honking as they flew overhead. The little spotted cur that always followed him milled about and sniffed as dogs do. Gregory made the sign of the cross and recited a joyful psalm. In that final moment before the world was awake in full, he peered into the well of his soul. Reflected in the still water was the face of a happy man. He looked over his shoulder, back toward town. Warren, with both horses fully rigged in tack and saddle, waited in front of Margery's farmhouse.

"Master Gregory, you have seen the sunrise many times," he called, with his hands cupped around his mouth. "I thought you said we would leave today."

With a smile and a cordial shaking of his head, Gregory made his way back to the farmhouse, where Margery also waited. Standing on the flagstone at the front door sill, she wore a yellow veil, a blue wildflower behind her ear, and a flowing green robe of worsted wool. Barefoot, too, and hands on her hips. The fading features of youth glowed bright and beautiful in her face, and as Gregory climbed up on his steed, he knew he would not soon see the equal of this aging country lass.

He dug into a saddlebag and fetched his fur-lined under-bonnet, which Margery had made for him, and put it on. Over that he pulled his beaver skin hat and then slid his hands into his gloves. He hoped to appear gallant and dashing, mounted on noble Moonbeam and preparing for the road. He arrived in town broken and bleeding, so it was important to him that he rode out sitting tall and strong in the saddle.

"Does this please you?" He made a grand gesture of coaxing Moonbeam around in a prancing circle before waiving out his right hand.

"Oh, Gregory, it pleases me so." She clutched her hands tight to her chest.

"I will return," he said. "And I will bring you a gift so splendid it will be unlike anything you have ever seen."

"I hope as you say," she replied, her voice almost a whisper.

Gregory didn't gallop out of town. He took it nice and slow and savored the pain of leaving her behind. Each time he glanced back, she kissed her fingertips and waved, until at last she and Corby disappeared from view. A sad longing came over him as he looked out at the road ahead. With each step of his horse, he moved further away from what he wanted. The jasmine in her hair, the sweet sparkle in her eyes, and the arousing comforts of her womanhood—Margery already haunted him with her assortment of delights. He thought about the last two months and how he had healed and how he had won. Always the stubborn merchant, always the crafty lawyer, so much of his life had been consumed with the quest for status and riches. But what he had done in Corby had come from the gut. Luring a corrupt manorial lord into an ambush in his own market was one of his finest moments. And he had done it to prove his mettle for Margery, whose high opinion he had come to crave.

He couldn't help but reflect on his most treasured memory of his time in Corby, and a small smile played on his lips.

One Saturday evening the villagers gathered at Margery's house to celebrate over the new Lord Corby's decision to withdraw his lawsuit. Once the party was loud with laughter and the songs of ale, Gregory and Margery had snuck away to a little loft up in the barn where they coupled with sincere and thorough ardor.

"I know you will not stay, and I know I cannot go with you," she had said, and kissed him on the neck. "But remember this night and what we have shared. When it is cold and you are lonely, and when you are tired and frightened and surrounded by strangers, know that I think of you."

He didn't need the cold or loneliness, the exhaustion or the fright. He thought of nothing but her as he rode toward Lincoln.

regory and Warren made camp in a glade deep in a forest of willows. Warren watered and fed the horses, pitched the tent and built the fire. He rummaged through a saddlebag and pulled out the victuals Margery prepared for them—pickled herring, smoked pig's feet, yeasty bread with honey and strawberries, and a skin of her famous "big" ale. They ate and drank and talked until the moon was high and shining in the sky. Warren wanted to know all about London, and Gregory was eager to oblige his curiosity. The conversation meandered through the dark and squalid streets of the capital, and Gregory found himself laughing as he told of the petty indignities of London life. While the city was sophisticated, he said, it was also provincial and potbellied with self-importance.

"And what about someone like Margery?" Warren said. "Could she make her way in London?"

"Margery is too decent for London," Gregory said. "Besides, she is rooted in the soil of Lincolnshire, and if she were not there, she would surely wilt like a rose plucked from the bush."

Warren took another swig of ale. He wiped his mouth with the back of his hand. "Do you love Margery?"

"Margery? Love?" Gregory pressed his hands close to the fire. "My heart is too jaded for love."

"Master Gregory, I do not believe that, and neither do you."

APPLES
BAKED IN
CINNAMON

hey wheeled their horses to a stop and marveled at the view. Out on the horizon atop a distant hill climbed the tallest man-made peak in all of Christendom—the spire of Lincoln Cathedral. Against the backdrop of a grey sky, the cathedral seemed an enormous, shining ingot of hope, laid to Earth by the hand of God himself. Across from the cathedral rose the stout walls and towers of the old castle. Clustered in between were the thatched roofs and steeples of the city.

Gregory took a long look and smiled, then glanced over at Warren. "Well, lad, what do you think?"

"I think I have never seen such a thing," the boy said with awe. "The cathedral—it is taller than anything I could have ever imagined!"

"Which is one of the reasons you are on this journey with me," Gregory said. "I told your parents you would return to Lichfield a man of the world. And God willing, you shall."

"I have never been to a real city," Warren said. "Only Lichfield and the villages nearby."

"You will enjoy Lincoln," he said. "We will eat and drink, and I will buy you something nice in the market for all you have done for me. Lincoln is known for its fine cloth, and before you leave, you will have some of it tucked in your bag."

Both of them coaxed their horses into a mild gallop, and they shared enthusiasm as their mounts went faster and faster. Soon they ran at full speed, their legs outstretched and trampling the road beneath them. Moonbeam snorted and flexed, and Gregory pulled away until he led Warren by a furlong. When he reached the city gate, he pulled Moonbeam to a stop, turned and feigned boredom as Warren rumbled up the road, the sheen of embarrassment on his brow. When he and Tamworth arrived, Gregory laughed and clapped Warren on the shoulder.

They rode across the crowded bridge at High Street and then up the steep hill to the market at Bailgate. Gregory laughed as Warren shook his head in wonderment, looking up and down and then left and then right. He smiled as Warren caught the eye of a prostitute, flicked a farthing to a cripple, and gawked at the impressive collection of tools and weapons on display at the blacksmith's shop. A woman yelled from the window of a three-story home leaning out over the street. A woman in a similar house yelled back at her. Gamblers gathered round a cock fight. Franciscans with tonsured hair and grey habits begged and preached while buyers haggled with merchants. Brawny boys toted barrels and crates and large earthenware jugs. They sang as they toiled in the muck and mud of High Street. Posing and primping with their hooded hawks were the noblemen, their shoulders draped with flashes of scarlet and green. The bells of Sext rang. Then came a gust of wind dancing down the hill, and on that wind rode an odor so rank and nasty both Gregory and Warren contorted their faces into frowns of disgust.

"Master Gregory, what is that terrible smell?"

"Ah, my boy, that's the smell of the city, the stink of freedom."

leanor of Brittany was dead. She returned to Dinan to see her parents, ate infected oysters during a feast, and died three days later. Her family buried her heart at the Basilica of St. Sauveur in Dinan, but her corpse was packed in salt, wrapped in a waxed cowhide, and shipped across the channel and up the river to Lincoln. From there, the corpse would travel overland to Lancaster, where her grieving husband, the Lord of Lancaster, awaited. Fearful his beloved Eleanor would be tormented during her stay in purgatory, he had sent out a summons to all the holy houses in Lincolnshire requesting prayers. Since the funeral cortege would take a week to reach Lancaster, he also wanted people to travel with the body and read psalms along the way. In return, he offered food and coin to anyone who made the journey.

Gregory drank a sip of wine and gave a sour smile as a servant set a new flagon on the table. With a piece of bread, he sopped up a lick of goose gravy and took a bite. A minstrel in a far corner of the hall strummed on his lute, and the new log on the fire spit and crackled with comfort. He had left Warren at the inn and had come alone to dine with an old family friend, the Bishop of Lincoln, at his palace just south of the cathedral.

"Why doesn't Lord Lancaster come and retrieve his wife himself?" Gregory asked. "If he loves Eleanor as much as he says, he should be more than glad to do the praying."

"Who knows the ways of lords?" the bishop said. "But from what I hear, he is bad with the gout."

Once back in Lancaster, Eleanor would be buried in the yard at the Priory Church of St. Mary, a fitting end for a woman who had born her husband three sons and a daughter as beautiful as a rolling river pearl.

"But I suspect he is anxious to get her in the ground for other reasons," the bishop said in the secretive voice of gossip.

"Do tell, Lord Bishop," Gregory said.

"Oh, I really shouldn't," he said. "It is only hearsay."

Gregory turned his face and looked at the bishop with a taunting pout. "You should not begin a story you are not prepared to finish. Tell me, Lord Bishop, or I should think you are holding out on me."

Gregory and the bishop had known each other for nearly two decades. When just a young apprentice cellarer at St. Paul's, the bishop would stop by the wine shop and purchase a pipe or two when the cathedral expected guests. Gregory, himself an apprentice under his father's instruction, grew to know and admire the bishop during his many visits. As Gregory came of age, and as the bishop rose up through the ranks at St. Paul's, the relationship strengthened. After Gregory and his cousin took control of the family business, the bishop transferred to Lincoln to be groomed for further advancement. But he stopped by the wine shop at Royal Street each time he came to London for business. Though more professional than personal, and though neither was in the inner circle of the other, Gregory and the bishop considered themselves good friends. And now they met in Lincoln, just the two of them, across a long table attended by servants.

"I have heard from more than a few people Eleanor poisoned her oldest brother-in-law so when he died, her husband, the second son, would become heir to the fiefdom of Lancaster," the bishop said. "Those same people told me she had the first son of her youngest brother-in-law drowned, and the second thrown from the battlements of Lancaster Castle. This way, there were no males in the family line to challenge her offspring."

"I know people will kill for power, but infanticide is the Devil's work," Gregory said. "Do you believe what you have heard, for if you do not, Lord Bishop, you have shared a vile rumor."

"I believe," the bishop said. "I would not repeat it to you if I did not know it to be true."

A flagon of crisp Rhenish wine and a platter of baked apples glazed with honey and cinnamon arrived for dessert. Having already eaten cheese and bread, peppered cabbage and onions, goose meat pie, and venison and frumenty, Gregory was sated and half-drunk after finishing this welcomed feast. He leaned back in his chair and licked the succulent honey and cinnamon from his fingers, and in a bowl of water washed his hands. As he dried them with a linen, he looked over at his host and knew he hadn't dined with the Bishop of Lincoln simply for the sake of sharing a fine meal. The bishop wanted something from him, and it was only a matter of time before the bishop made his intentions known. Rather than wait, Gregory decided to do what he always did. He forced the issue.

"Lord Bishop, you have stuffed my belly and gotten me soused, and now I am ready for you to ask of me what you want."

Holding out his hands for emphasis, the bishop gave what Gregory thought was a false smile of innocence and said, "I do not ask anything of you. You are an old friend and you are here to enjoy my hospitality. Judging by the look on your face, I have succeeded in making you happy."

"Yes, Lord Bishop, this is the best meal I've had since leaving London a year ago," he said. "But I also know a bishop never gives without receiving."

The bishop laughed. "You know us too well, Master Gregory. And you are right." He cleared his throat and gave Gregory a serious look. "I want you to travel to Lancaster with Eleanor of Brittany's funeral cortege."

"Come again?"

"I want you to travel with the funeral cortege."

"Why would I do that?" he said. "The cortege is a false show of piety for a person who is not worth my prayers, and who is not worth God's grace."

"I don't expect you to pray," the bishop said. "But there is a young Benedictine monk, Marcus from Burwell Priory, who arrived in Lincoln yesterday. He is making the journey and I would like you to keep your eye on him."

"Why is this Marcus so important?"

"They say he is a rare man, very eloquent and even exquisite in his speech," the bishop said. "He is peasant born but has learned his letters. Outside of that I don't know much about him. But a man in my position is always on the lookout for new talent."

Gregory wasn't convinced. There had to be more to the story. With both elbows he leaned over the table and stared deep into the bishop's old brown eyes, where a ripple raced across calm waters. The bishop must have known what Gregory had seen because a meek sadness replaced the pomp that had shown in his eyes earlier when the honeyed apples had been served. Gregory no longer looked at the mighty Bishop of Lincoln, who could raise an army and damn a man to hell, but an old man with a wounded heart. In reading the bishop's face, Gregory figured out who Marcus was and why the bishop was curious about him. What he didn't understand is why the bishop had chosen to bring him into the situation.

"Lord Bishop, you have revealed your secret, but why have you revealed it to me?"

A tired smile of relief came to his face and a glint showed in his eye. "You are Gregory of Bordeaux, and I know you will do the right thing."

They tilted their cups toward each other, exchanged looks of agreement, and then took deep quaffs of the crisp white Rhenish wine.

They gathered in the morning at the steps of the great cathedral. The mourners, in their rough wool and tattered cloaks, stood near the covered wagon that carried Eleanor of Brittany's salted corpse. Eleanor's household servants, not hiding their disdain for the rabble that had arrived for the cortege, clustered around the wagon and murmured to themselves. At the center of this crowd was a monk, a full head taller than the vagrants surrounding him, who pulled people to his chest, one at a time, for a dramatic hug and a dour kiss on each cheek. The cold drizzle captured the pink morning light and pulled from it a hue of sadness. Despite the sound and movement, all seemed silent and still. Gregory and Warren, mounted on their fidgeting and impatient horses, stood on the outskirts of this somber scene. Perhaps a group of angels, plucking at stringed instruments and with blessings at their lips, peered down from the heights of the cathedral's bell towers. But when Gregory looked up, he saw no smiling, haloed faces looking back at him.

The driver of the wagon whipped the rumps of the horses, and the wheels creaked and churned through the mud. The mourners fell in behind the wagon and followed, and thus began the funeral cortege for Eleanor of Brittany. Though the procession moved slowly down the sunken, potholed road, the Lincoln skyline, punctuated by the cathedral's astonishing central tower, eventually faded from sight.

Gregory and Warren followed from a distance and kept their conversation to themselves.

"Master Gregory, I have seen the indigent, and I myself have always been poor. But I have not seen such poverty until today."

Gregory had seen this a thousand fold in London. People who lived and died in the streets, always with a hand out, always with an empty stomach, and always the first to shiver and freeze in winter. They limped with clubbed feet, cupped their hands over harelips, and skulked as the unwanted spawn of crooks and castaways. Some insane and some just stubborn, both easy to shun. Alas, the world was cruel, and there wasn't enough to go around.

"What you see are those who have been tossed onto the dung heap of our imperfect world," Gregory said. "They are the dregs of the realm, many of them by no fault of their own, but still they are God's children and deserve His grace."

"But Master Gregory, we are part of this procession, so what does that say about us?"

Gregory chuckled at Warren's sharp reply. "I don't know, because I don't know exactly why we are here. But we have food and coin of our own, so we need nothing from Lord Lancaster and will say no prayers for his dead queen."

Gregory didn't want to tell Warren what the bishop had told him. Not then, anyway. The cortege would take a week, and Gregory didn't know if his page could keep a secret that long. A murderous queen. A grieving lord. An illegitimate monk. A toxic brew spilling out of Warren's mouth in front of a throng of starving mourners. Gregory could do without the risk. Tell him all, he would, but only at the end of the procession, not the beginning.

The cortege paused for a brief repast of unleavened biscuits and watery ale. Eleanor's household, ladies-in-waiting from the lower nobility, did not mingle with the mourners, who hacked and coughed and picked at their scabs as they ate and drank. But the monk, who Gregory knew to be Marcus of Burwell Priory, stood among them, sipping a cup of ale and nibbling at his bread. The black hood and tunic did not hide his long, striding bones, nor the broad yoke of his shoulders. He pushed back his cowl and scratched the back of his neck. The ring of hair around his freshly shaved tonsure was thick and dark, and in his features showed the strain of youth giving way to maturity. Gregory did not want to stare, but he was curious to see if Marcus had the Bishop of Lincoln's likeness. And when the monk gestured to a mourner and turned his head just so, Gregory indeed saw the long, crotchety face of his old friend in the young countenance of this man.

The cortege resumed its westward trek. Marcus, behind the wagon but in front of the mourners, turned to them and walked backwards as he read in English from his Book of Hours. His voice came as a clarion call, a divine blast from atop a mountain, a deep and unflinching tenor of absolute passion.

"I waited, waited for the Lord, and He stooped down to me. He heard my cry, He drew me from the deadly pit, from the miry clay. He set my feet upon rock, and made my footsteps firm. He put a new song into my mouth, praise of our God. Happy the man who has placed his trust in the Lord and has not gone over to the rebels who follow false gods. How many, O Lord, my God, are the wonders and designs that You have worked for us. You have no equal. Should I proclaim and speak of them, they are more than I can tell! You do not ask for sacrifice and offerings, but an open ear. You do not ask for holocaust and victim. Instead, here am I. In the scroll of the book it stands written that I should do Your will. My God, I delight in Your law in the depth of my heart. Glory to the Father. From the earth You formed me, with flesh You clothed me. Lord, my Redeemer, raise me up again on the last day."

Gregory and Warren looked at one another with raised eyebrows. The mourners responded with a resounding, "Amen!" Even Eleanor's household, their faces touched with the shine of appreciation, turned and looked Marcus's way. It had been a long and soggy day with fits of rain and drizzle, but now it was as if the sun shone on a field of shimmering wheat. Marcus, his head held high and his green eyes flashing, managed to prance even as he walked backward. He licked his fingertip, flipped a page, and read another psalm.

"Your justice I have proclaimed in the great assembly. My lips I have not sealed. You know it, O Lord. I have not hidden Your justice in my heart but declared Your faithful help. I have not hidden Your love and Your truth from the great assembly. O Lord, You will not withhold Your compassion from me. Your merciful love and Your truth will always guard me. For I am beset with evils too many to be counted. My sins have fallen upon me and my sight fails me. They are more than the hairs of my head and my heart sinks. O Lord, come to my rescue. Lord, come to my aid. O let there be rejoicing and gladness for all who seek You. Let them ever say, 'The Lord is great,' who love Your saving help. As for me, wretched and poor, the Lord thinks of me. You are my rescuer, my help, O God, do not delay!"

Again the mourners responded with a heartened, "Amen!" The forgotten, the maligned, the crippled, the crazed—they crowded around Marcus, their savior. He reached out and pulled an old lady into his embrace, and then kissed the forehead of a baby riding the hip of his bedraggled mother. A wretched man with one eye wept, and a teen with deep pock marks raised his hand and shouted, "Amen, Marcus. Amen!"

That night, on the outskirts of the village of Bradford, the mourners built a bonfire. Gregory and Warren had their own fire and did not attend. But from where they sat, they saw the silhouettes of the mourners, suspended in a spell of feverish excitement cast by Marcus. Moving in and out of the shadows thrown by the fire, he gestured with his shoulders and his arms and his hips, and made of himself a grand spectacle. So full was his voice, Gregory and Warren heard him as he spoke not of God and His grace and the salvation of Eleanor's soul, but of coveted pleasures.

"Beef, pork, cod and bread, fruit pies and ale, and a handful of pennies—a world of exultation awaits us in Lancaster," he said.

Warren got up and paced through the firelight of their small camp. He stopped and put his hands on his hips. A worried expression came to his face. "Will Lord Lancaster make good on the promises Marcus is making?"

"That is the question, isn't it," Gregory said. "Lancaster was a fool to have offered food and money in the first place. He has lived in the comfortable confines of his castle for too long and has forgotten how gullible the down-trodden can be. I assure you these people will arrive at the gates of Lancaster, and when they do, they will demand satisfaction."

Gregory was shocked the next morning when the group of mourners appeared to have tripled in size during the night. A good hundred people now walked in the funeral train, and Eleanor's household servants, who at first had shunned the mourners, had joined the crowd. Gregory and Warren exchanged knowing glances, for they had arrived at the same conclusion—Marcus had passed a point of no return. For good or ill, these people belonged to him.

Observing the crowd, Gregory noticed most of the people in the cortege at Bradford were downcast or lame. But among them moved men who appeared to be hardened criminals who bore the marks of punishment—missing hands and ears, carved off noses, brands on their foreheads, and missing tongues. They wore heavy knives at their belts and stood as sentries at Marcus's side. As the cortege ground westward, Marcus read the psalms with ever more fervor, and his followers responded in kind. And when night came, in a field outside Kildwick, they lit another bonfire. The people gathered around the flames as Marcus, his voice a grandiloquent treble, stoked their desires with stylish tales of Lancaster.

"When we arrive, the gates of the golden city will open to us, and Lord Lancaster, a just and benevolent man, will reward us for keeping his beloved Eleanor safe in the bosom of our savior, Jesus Christ. If you are hungry, fear not. At Lancaster, the fires of the lord's kitchen will be lit. Loaves will be pulled from the oven, meat will roast on the spit, and a thick broth will roil in the pot. A chicken for everyone, I say, and frumenty and fried fish and wheels of cheese. A cask of ale and a pipe of wine, and servants to keep our cups ever full. Roasted pears and strawberry pie, honey-glazed almonds and apples baked with cinnamon. We will eat until we can eat no more, and once we have emptied our bowels, we will eat again. If you find your purse has no pennies, be certain Lancaster will open his vault and lavish you with coins. We will strut to the market and buy dyed velvet and worsted wool and have their tailors make us fine tunics and mantles. The people of the city will marvel at how handsome we look, and we will say to them, 'We have done God's work and we are worthy.' The walls of Lancaster are not made of stone, my friends, but of silver and pearl."

Among the crowd, Gregory and Warren stood up front and only a few feet from Marcus. With his arms folded across his chest, Gregory affected a stance of nonchalance, even though the fire and Marcus's orations were intense. He so badly wanted to say something, to denounce Marcus as a fool and to implore the rabble to return to their hovels. But he knew his words would be used against him, and with the mob becoming more delusional by the day, he refused to make that mistake. Instead, he studied Marcus. He noticed the crooked vein in his neck that bulged when he hit his high notes, and the preening glare in his green eyes as he inspired the disenchanted. Not yet young and not yet old, Marcus enjoyed the sweetness of his years, when boyish good looks and the silver of wisdom appear together.

As his oratory continued, Gregory noticed how he veered from innocence to degeneracy, and how his optimism would always drip away into a bucket of despair. A sin had been growing inside of him for a long time, and with the support of a starving mob and a core of criminals, that sin might just soon see the light of day.

Gregory and Warren made to leave and head back to their camp, but before they slunk away, Marcus held up his hand and motioned for them to stop.

"Do not leave just yet," he said in a forced tone of hospitality. "You have traveled with us for three days but you still have yet to introduce yourself. Who are you, man in black, and why do you travel with us but do not pray?"

Marcus tilted his head back and to the right and served a look so laced with lunacy, Gregory went cold with fear. He responded with a measured look of reason as he made eye contact, first with Marcus, and then with the felons and dregs gathered around him. Here in the glow of the firelight sniffed a hungry pack of wolves, and Gregory knew if he said the wrong thing, they would smell his mistake and tear him apart.

"I am a humble chronicler from the south," he said, "and I travel with you because I wanted company and protection on the long trek to Lancaster. My name is Gregory of Bordeaux, and I applaud what you are doing in the service of Eleanor of Brittany. When she is in Heaven, she will look down on you and smile."

"A chronicler," he said with unexpected exuberance. "And what, may I ask, do you write?"

"At this very moment, I observe a man on the verge of greatness, a man who in just a few days will forever earn the gratitude of Lord Lancaster," he said. "And, I believe, you will be feasting on roasted pears, strawberry pie, honey-glazed almonds, and apples baked with cinnamon."

"So you will write of me?" A maniacal smile spread across his face.

"Oh, yes. Marcus the monk from Burwell Priory who made the dangerous journey from Lincoln to Lancaster in the twenty-fifth year of the reign of the great King Edward—one of my best stories yet."

"Well, then," he said, in a voice of pride and danger. "I will give you something to write about."

Gregory and Warren returned to their camp.

"I think we should leave," Warren said. "I think we should get on our horses and forget all about this damned funeral cortege. I do not like what I see, and I fear we are in danger."

"Your fears are not misguided," Gregory said. "But we must stay, and do you know why?"

"Please, tell me, for as I sit right now, I do not know."

"Because justice will come of all this, but only if we stay. We must see the truth so we can speak it. Marcus's tongue might tell lies, but the same should not be said of ours."

"Well, if we stay, I will make sure to sharpen my billhook," he said.

"No, it is already sharp enough," Gregory snapped. "To do so now would be to provoke them. Please, go to sleep, but do so with one eye open."

Gregory lay down, locked his hands behind his head, and used his pack as a pillow. He looked into the night sky, at the crescent moon, a dagger of clouds, and a vast swirl of stars. Serene, bright and happy in Heaven. The stars shared the night with the moon, which shared the sky with the sun, which shared its warmth with the earth, which fed mankind. Surely God's work. But what did mankind do? They toiled and sang, ate and drank, solved problems and built cities, made laws and raised children, and died with the Lord's grace. They also lied and cheated and made war. They did their best to destroy what they'd worked so hard to build. Even as it perplexed him, Gregory still believed in mankind. But he knew there was still much to learn from the sun, moon, and stars.

The next morning, the funeral cortege, with Marcus leading, entered its fourth day famished. The pale drifters, nourished with nothing more than a thin broth made from boiled leather and wheat husks, found strength in Marcus's incessant plaudits and woeful cheer.

"God made this gorgeous day for us," he bellowed. "And since this is God's work, there is no man who can keep us from what is ours. If they say no, we will say yes. If they lock the door, we will open it. God says the meek shall inherit the earth, and since we are meek and since we are on earth, we will inherit our rewards today!"

In his zealous reading of the psalms, Marcus had his followers in a righteous, belligerent mood by the time they reached Skipton. Strung out on the Word of God, thirst, and hunger, the crowd, which over the days had swelled into a foul horde, rejoiced at the sight of the town. Tucked into a bend in the River Aire, Skipton resembled many other towns, a jumble of thatched homes and halls, a wharf, a rutted high street, and a proud parish church. What made Skipton different, at least on that day, was that it sat empty. The townspeople had grabbed what they could and had taken refuge behind the stout walls of the adjoining castle. They watched from its battlements as Marcus and his wretches spilled toward the town.

"Be on your way, rabble, or we shall unleash the garrison," came a voice from the castle's gatehouse.

Marcus, standing with his felons near the city gates, looked toward the castle and yelled, "Feed our empty stomachs with pork and beef, and wet our parched lips with ale. Once you have done that, we shall be off to sleep and will leave tomorrow when the rooster calls at dawn."

"All we have for you, vagabond, are swords and spears. We will feed you with steel and flame and will quench your thirst with your own blood!"

"Then open your gates and come out with your garrison," Marcus said.

He walked to within bowshot of the castle walls, took the big cross from around his neck, and held it high above his head. His challenge provoked a hail of bolts and arrows, but none of them struck him. The townspeople, peering down from the wall, heckled him with insults and expletives, and more arrows whistled past his head, but Marcus did not budge. The castle gates did not open, and no soldiers sallied out. The horde erupted with a filthy cheer of defiance. Marcus, his face alight with savage confidence, turned to his followers.

"God," he said, "has granted us the town."

As the horrified townsmen watched from the castle walls, Marcus and his men breached the city gates. The looting of Skipton commenced. They kicked in doors, torched homes, and picked cellars clean of food and belongings. They tapped casks of ale and wine, slaughtered cows, and cooked on an open fire on the green at Holy Trinity Church. As the horde stuffed its gut and slaked its thirst on the bounty of Skipton, the sacking progressed with hysterical joy. Amid the boisterous singing and bouts of laughter came shrieks of rape and grunts of murder. A man and wife pulled from their attic and strung from the gallows. An ancient oak hacked and felled. A boy's throat slit, his body dumped into the well. So it went, deep into the night, until Skipton was a burnt and bleeding corpse. Gregory and Warren watched the atrocity from the top of a nearby hill.

Taut with anger, Warren looked at Gregory. "Is there anything we can do?"

"Most certainly." Gregory spit for emphasis. "We will go to Lancaster and prepare for Marcus's arrival. When we see him again, I will have his death warrant in my hand."

They mounted their horses and fled west to Lancaster. Gregory thought about the Bishop of Lincoln, and his opinion of him changed. The entire time Gregory had known him, the bishop—the pious, fastidious, and dili-gent bishop—had an unknown, unwanted son tucked away at Burwell. In and of itself, that was no great crime. Bastards from all walks of life littered the realm. But if the bishop's son pillaged Skipton, then what crimes was the bishop capable of? Sons, after all, tended to turn out like their fathers.

As Gregory rode on through the night, his thoughts turned to the chron-icle and what he would write next. Marcus of Burwell Priory, he guessed, would be his new topic.

A fabulist with a golden tongue is ever eager for the day of plenty, but when it arrives, more often than not he chokes on his own inventions.

No Pride in Death Warrants

regory stood at the entrance to Lord Lancaster's hall and watched his servant flood his filigreed goblet with wine. Fat, draped in fur and silk, seated in a huge oaken chair and with brindle hounds at his feet, this was a lord's lord. With an almost imperceptible nod of his bearded chin, he admitted Gregory into his hall, but only after he had taken a deep drink from his cup and wiped his face on his sleeve. He stared at Gregory with a mix of contempt and curiosity, and the scrutiny unnerved Gregory, who did his best to maintain a show of confidence as he entered the hall.

Laden with booty from the crusades, the room glittered with gems and glowed with the motley hue of Oriental rugs and exotic wall hangings. At his feast table, set with silver plate, Gascon wine, and juicy sides of game, congregated the keepers of the old guard, those who ruled the world and who never wanted it to change. Hunkered in his sanctum among his retainers, his fawning servants, and his balladeers who sang of love and war, Lord Lancaster entrenched himself in familiar comforts. So intimate was the setting, Gregory felt like an intruder. Knowing it was dangerous to present bad news to a ranking lord, and guessing Lancaster was already deep into his hogshead of Sauternes, he made a careful measure of risk and reward.

In a sincere show of deference and respect, Gregory doffed his hat and bowed low. Even though he saw the lout in Lord Lancaster, even though he noticed the rosacea on his nose, and even though he knew his title rested on the dark deeds of his deceased wife, Gregory kept a polite face and unassuming posture. The music went silent along with the talk and laughter. The lords looked up from their trenchers of meat. The hounds cocked their ears and heads.

"My Lord Lancaster," Gregory said, "I have heard tell of your splendid court, but nothing prepared me for the magnificence in front of my very eyes."

"Spare me your dribble, scribe," grunted Lancaster. "You came here with news, so tell it."

"Your queen, Eleanor, has been abducted by the very people entrusted with the keeping of her soul, my lord, and they will not relinquish her until you have emptied your coffers and depleted your larder," Gregory said. "They are headed this way, and there are many of them. If you do not bend to their demands, they threaten to damn Eleanor to the eternal furnace of hell."

Lancaster sat up in his great chair and gripped its carved arms with his thick, bejeweled hands. His right eyebrow curved into a steep arch, and the left side of his mouth bent into a scowl. "And how is it you know this story? Are you their messenger?"

"No, my lord." Gregory held out his hands in an emphatic gesture of subservience. "I am the accuser."

"What do you mean?"

"I rode with them from Lincoln. They started with the psalms, but as the days passed, the crowd grew violent. Their leader is a young, peasant-born monk—Marcus of Burwell Priory. I rushed here to tell you he has sacked Skipton, and I fear he has done the same, or will do the same, with Gargrave, Clapham, and Ingleton. Your city, my lord, is also on his list."

"But he is a monk!" said Lancaster. "I am a lord! He cannot possess anything I cannot take, including my wife's dead body. And if it is food he wants, then he can starve. If it is coin he fancies, then he shall never have two far-things to shove up his ass!"

"He is a man who grew up nurturing a dream, a dream of being a man of consequence," Gregory replied. "That dream was a pup that became a wolf, and now it has escaped its cage. My lord, if he were to get inside the city, then he will surely loot it. Perhaps it would be wise, my lord, to ride out and meet him. The gates are strong, but they are built for battering rams. This Marcus, I assure you, strikes with a much mightier weapon."

Lancaster leaned back in his cushioned chair, stroked his greying beard, and studied Gregory. The two of them locked gazes in the haze of the hall, and as they did, Gregory tilted his chin and pursed his lips to show he had no fear. He saw the old lord thinking, as Gregory had hoped, about everything he said. He knew Lancaster pondered the embarrassment he would suffer if a peasant horde somehow slipped into town and plundered it. More impor-tantly, he guessed Lancaster feared the chance that Marcus, the impover-ished monk who had prayed for the salvation of his wife's soul, might arrive as a sympathetic figure. Plenty of people in Lancaster needed a meal and a penny. Perhaps some of them would open the door and invite Marcus in.

Lancaster rose to his feet. "Men of this court, prepare to ride at dawn. We will hunt tomorrow, and this wretch, Marcus of Burwell Priory, is our prey."

The massive gate of oak and iron creaked open. Lancaster and his knights hoofed out into the mist across the frosty field. Their helms shone with the salmon blush of dawn, their breath foggy with autumn chill. Gregory and Warren struggled to keep pace with the lords but equaled the squires and pages. With the blue silhouettes of the Pennines rising in the distance on either side, they hastened through the sleeping valley.

They rode hard until the morning shroud gave way to a dry, bleached noon. They stopped, rested their horses, ate cheese and jerky, and drank small ale. They mounted again and rode with the urgency of knowing with each passing moment they closed in on their quarry. Gregory and Warren exchanged glances of excitement. They rode with the posse comitatus and felt the thrill of the hunt and its promise of adventure. Their knowing glances betrayed a collective elation because the longer they rode, the stronger Moonbeam and Tamworth became. No longer at the rear with the squires and pages, Gregory and Warren remained right there with Lancaster and his ablest men-at-arms.

Barreling into the afternoon, something finally appeared on the horizon they had expected to see—a large curl of black smoke rising into the air. At Lancaster's command, the war train wheeled to a halt. Horses whinnied with impatience and knights fidgeted with their armor as Lancaster and a few of his most trusted men huddled in a circle. Two scout riders went on ahead.

Lancaster watched them leave, and without taking his eyes off them, roared, "Scribe!"

Gregory made his way through the bustle of knights, and when he reached Lancaster, gave a look of deference and said, "Yes, my lord?"

"Do you have what you prepared last night?"

"Indeed." He reached into the chest pocket of his cloak and pulled out a rolled parchment tied off with a piece of leather. He tried to hand it over, but Lancaster waved him off.

"You wrote it, and you will deliver it. And when you do, I want you to give him my demands."

"Which are?"

"He is to deliver my queen, Eleanor, and his person into my custody forthwith. Or else." He narrowed his eyes.

The scouts soon returned with news. Marcus and his horde. Bentham in ruins. Lancaster and his retinue surged forth, crested a hill, and there before them in a crook on the River Aire was Marcus and his followers, rejoicing as the shattered village burned.

As Lancaster's retinue sped toward Bentham, Marcus rallied his people. They formed a knot, lifted their fists, and sounded a defiant cheer. By the urgency of his pointing and gesturing, it was evident Marcus gave orders. His followers soon retreated down to the waterfront, protected by the river in back and by Bentham's burning timbers in front, and formed a defensive position. The glint of hooks and blades proved their arms, and they voiced resistance in their shouts and jeers.

Lancaster pulled up short of town, stopped and waited. The two sides sized each other up in silence as the fires died down. Lancaster, with three dozen swords and lances, found himself outnumbered twenty to one. Marcus made an ugly face and spit, and then stepped over to the wagon carrying the salted body of Eleanor of Brittany. With a heave, he pulled it out from the back of the wagon and handed it off to two of his felons. They hoisted it up over their heads, grabbed firebrands, and marched to the back of the multitude. Marcus snapped his fingers. People gathered stray pieces of wood and burning embers and followed the felons. In short work, a large bonfire burned on the banks of the waterfront.

"If you are the great Lord of Lancaster, then I will tell you the obvious," Marcus called in his round and ringing voice. "I have built a funeral pyre for your queen. If you do not give us what is rightfully ours, and what was promised to us by you and by God, so help me I will burn her as if she was a pagan."

Gregory glanced sideways at Lancaster's reaction. The old lord seemed perplexed. Wrinkles gathered at his eyes, his brows bunched together, and he breathed a long, thoughtful exhale through his nose. A swirl of ash raced out from the charred town, a gasp of wind whipped at his beard, and the flames of the pyre, the ones that would consume his beloved and send her to hell, taunted with the voices of a hundred demons. Lancaster sat transfixed, old and obese in his ornate saddle. His knights, confused by their lord's indecision, mumbled amongst themselves. Gregory and Warren exchanged looks of surprise, for neither of them had expected this. After what seemed to be an eternity of silence, Lancaster spoke.

"Scribe," he said. All eyes turned to Gregory. "You know him, right?"

"I don't know him, but I know more about him than you and your men."

"The terms," Lancaster grunted. "Give him my terms. Show him his death warrant and give him my terms. He does not fear my sword, but perhaps he will fear your words."

Gregory looked over at the rabble and shuddered. He rode out in front of Lancaster's line, turned in his saddle, and said to Warren, "Come, come, lad, it is time for the dirty work."

Warren unloosed the billhook from its rigging and trotted out to join Gregory. As he did, Gregory grew frightened and proud. Seasoned by the day's ride and sitting tall in his saddle, Warren showed his peasant's pride in the bristling plume of crow feathers adorning his conical helm. With wind-burned cheeks and wary eyes peering out from behind the nose guard, Warren looked ready to serve a death warrant on Marcus. A dangerous game, Gregory knew, and he did not want to lose his page. But he believed it was Warren's time to shine. So they trotted their horses into the smoldering hulk of Bentham. They pulled up at the edge of the gutted market, a short stone's throw from the mob.

Gregory held the death warrant above his head to signal he had come with a message. Marcus and his felons—wiry men with cropped blond hair and pale blue eyes—came out to meet him. When it looked like they would come too close, Gregory warned them by shaking his head.

"Stay your distance, Marcus," he said. "My man sharpened his billhook just this morning."

Marcus heeded the admonishment and stopped his advance. "Gregory of Bordeaux, is it?"

"Yes, and I have come with an important message from Lord Lancaster."

"You left in the night," Marcus said. "I was troubled by your departure. But I never imagined you'd be so foolish as to return with a cohort too small to stop mine."

Being so close to him, Gregory saw in sickening detail how Marcus had descended deep into lunacy. He had traded in his Book of Hours for a hand axe. He still wore the big cross around his neck, but now had a second cross drawn in blood on his forehead. He had shaved off the rest of his hair so he no longer had a tonsure, and instead of wearing a monk's habit and sandals, wore boots, breeches, and a blacksmith's thick leather apron. Gregory turned his nose in disgust when he noticed Marcus's bloody hands bore the stigmata. A hodgepodge of dementia, a man overcome by the conceit of his rotten soul. He felt a stab of sadness and sympathy for him. Still, he managed to clear his throat and speak with stridence and venom.

"You are charged with arson, rape, and murder, and you are to hang. You said you wanted to give me something to write about, and indeed, you have. You see, I pulled out my quill and authored your death warrant." He tossed the document at Marcus's feet.

Marcus yanked it off the ground and unrolled it with an expression of sour disregard. His lips moved as he read to himself. Finished, he looked up from the parchment with a vehement shaking of his head. "Your accusations are false, for I have done none of these things."

"Oh, but you have," Gregory replied. "I watched you consent to the sack of Skipton. And you have now done the same at Bentham. As the leader of this squalid army of simpletons, the blood is on your hands. Indeed, if it pleases God, you will hang, and you will hang soon. Lord Lancaster offers these terms—hand over his queen and turn yourself in and your followers are free to go."

"And if I don't?"

"Then he will wait you out, starve you out, and slaughter your people, bit by bit and piece by piece, until you are alone and helpless."

Marcus breathed through his nose and his face grew pale with an old and angry pain. The eyes that once twinkled with confidence now burned with the fury of a man insulted and crazed. Ever ready with a lustrous strand of words and a trove of provocations, the monk seemed miffed that on this day, Gregory proved to have a superior tongue. His teeth chattered and his whole body rippled and shook. A vein bulged in his neck and blood pulsed from the stigmata. He slid the axe from his belt and hefted it at his side. "Gregory, I think you are wrong about who is going to die."

He cocked the axe over his shoulder and lunged.

Gregory, sitting motionless in his saddle, watched the attack unfold—

Marcus's mouth wide and gaping, his eyes bright and yellow as a waning moon, a bead of sweat falling from his chin, and a glinting axe blade arcing toward the kill.

"God have mercy on my soul," Gregory whispered. He made the sign of the cross and prepared for the worst.

Before the axe hit home, Warren made a play with his billhook. He wedged it up under Marcus's apron, clutched the bill with both hands, and coaxing Tamworth backward, tugged with such force he yanked Marcus from his feet. Warren spurred Tamworth forward, dragging Marcus behind him and back toward Lord Lancaster and his knights.

Marcus's felons raised their knives and closed in on Gregory. With a great whinny and a flash of hooves, Moonbeam reared, turned, and in a spray of turf, dashed to safety.

arcus received a fair trial, but no one stood in his favor. Gregory and the leading burgesses from Skipton, Ingleton, and Bentham appeared in court and pointed accusing fingers at him. He remained vociferous in his denial of any wrongdoing. He somehow freed himself from the shackles and lurched across the room with his hands outstretched in an attempt to strangle Gregory. It took five men to hold him down, and as he panted and seethed, the trial continued and ended in an hour. Marcus was dragged off, held in the gaol overnight, and hanged outside the castle wall the next day at Sext.

In the hours leading up to his execution, children of the streets scurried from house to house and from storefront to storefront, spreading the news that Marcus of Burwell Priory, once head of a heathen army bent on destroying Lancaster, was to die at Hanging Corner. What seemed like the entire city came out for the spectacle. They pelted him with refuse and abused him with taunts as men-at-arms led him to the gallows. A priest read him his last rites, and soon thereafter, he dangled from the end of a rope. Gregory and Warren attended the execution but did not join the crowd. High above the throng, they watched from the battlements. They remained there long after everyone else had dispersed, looking down at the lonely corpse draped in pauper's wool.

"Before we left Lincoln, you said the bishop wanted you to keep an eye on Marcus," Warren said. "Why?"

"Oh, that." Gregory leaned back on the battlement and crossed his arms. "If you promise not to tell anyone, I will tell you why."

"All your secrets are safe with me."

"Marcus was the bishop's bastard son. And the bishop wanted me to accompany him to find out what kind of person he was. If Marcus proved to be smart and useful, I was to recommend he be hired into the bishop's staff, or someone else's staff, where he could be legitimized. But as you know, that was not the case."

"His bastard?"

"That is not so rare, is it?"

"No, but the bishop is a powerful man. Do you think if Lancaster had known about Marcus, somehow his life would have been spared?"

"Perhaps," Gregory said. "But for all the wrong reasons. You see, Lancaster and the bishop are peers, but they are not necessarily friends. Had Lancaster known Marcus was his bastard, he would have used it to threaten the bishop's reputation, and in the end, to extract some kind of concession from him. Marcus would have been a pawn in Lancaster's game of power."

"But you could have told Lancaster, right? And you could have profited by so doing?"

"Yes," Gregory said with a thoughtful nod. "But I have known the bishop for many years, and my loyalties lie with him."

"I know you will write of Marcus in your chronicle, but will you let it be known the bishop sired him?"

Gregory looked off into the sky and gave a troubled laugh.

"Yes," he said. "But by then it will be of no use to Lancaster."

"But it will blacken the bishop's name."

"Perhaps, but a story is not good if it is not true."

"Will the bishop retaliate? After all, it was our witness that sent his son to the gallows."

"We will know in good time." He gave Warren a sharp glance. "That man down there in the noose tried to kill me, but you did not let it happen. You are only seventeen, but you are already a grown man."

"When he came at you, the world slowed down," Warren said. "I saw everything in great detail, and I knew what I had to do. It was only later that I felt the fear. Master Gregory, I don't care what you know or what you don't know or what you will or will not tell. Marcus deserved to die. He committed crimes against man and God, and he deserved to die."

"I feel as if I did the right thing, but believe me when I tell you, there is no pride in writing death warrants."

"That is not the first, right?"

"Nor will it be the last."

"In your time at the London courts, how many have you written?"

"Too many, dear Warren. Too, too many."

They did not dally in Lancaster. The morning after Marcus's execution, Gregory and Warren headed north to Warton, where they rested their horses and replenished their supplies. Talk as they did of many things, their conversation always turned back to the funeral cortege. One night, as the candles guttered in the trays, and as Warren stood near and looked over his shoulder, Gregory put ink to parchment.

It is a shame when there is no place in the world for a man who finally becomes what he is meant to be. He arrives late and at the wrong place while in servitude to his long neglected ambition. Marcus of Burwell was better off in the priory, reading and writing and tending the fields. But the dead queen inflamed his poisoned heart, and mercifully led him to his doom.

THE BATTLE OF OSBERT'S FIELD

They guided their horses up a path of steep and narrow switchbacks to the summit. From atop the high peak, they saw the green, lichen-clad mountains rippling out into the horizon in all directions. A stand of spruce sprawled over a ledge, and a birch woodland burst with autumn orange and gold. A bright blue lake, twinkling with sun and wind, curled through the valley like a silk ribbon. An osprey skimmed the lake and banked upward with a wiggling fish tight in its talons. A herd of sheep grazed in the fells while a wall of dark clouds rolling in from the Irish Sea promised rain and gales. Vast and beautiful, yet empty and bleak. Gregory and Warren enjoyed the panorama until, mindful of the coming storm, they descended the mountain and rode hard out over the moorland heath, where the red grouses flittered about, and on into the village of Keswick.

They headed north through the county of Cumbria to the fort city of Carlisle, where knights amassed for a raid into Scotland. For years, the borderland was the scene of strife between English lords pushing north and Scottish chieftains pushing south. Mercenaries, horse thieves, cattle rustlers and common outlaws, all of them flourishing in the lawless hin-terlands for the betterment of their own accounts, fought for their version of honor and duty. King Edward, who had already crushed Wales, now focused on Scotland. Royal favor, a few pounds of silver, and perhaps an estate for anyone brave enough to ride into the charred wilds and return with a chieftain's bearded head.

The risk had no shortage of takers. Looking to make their name in battle, impoverished knights and unknown squires from across the realm flocked to the borders for a chance to write their name in King Edward's good book. They all knew the army would come one day, and when it did, the king's bar-ons would be at his side and the glory would be theirs. But before that day, the raids offered a chance for the landless, indebted, and otherwise disgraced to stake their claim. Those hopeful men, clinging to their swords and their dreams, descended upon Carlisle in droves. And so it was this city, encircled by a grimy wall and anchored by a mean tower, into which Gregory and Warren arrived on a dismal day of wind and rain.

As their horses trotted under the arch at Botchergate, Gregory looked at Warren, and in a low voice of warning, said, "Let me do the talking. These men slit Scottish throats, and they will slit ours, too."

A room became available at the Red Horse Inn when Gregory agreed to pay double the going rate. He and Warren napped, woke to a meal of bread and cheese, and then went downstairs to the tavern. Gregory had never con-sidered going out on a raid in Scotland, but from Lancashire, the border was so close he decided he would. Now in Carlisle, he had no second thoughts, but he guessed this would be the most dangerous leg of his journey. He looked around the tavern, surprised at how quiet it was. Out in the streets chaos jostled as young lords, drunk on ale and delusional with the promise of opportunity, paraded about on their steeds. But inside the Red Horse, somber men huddled over their candlelit tables and talked in hushed tones. No wonder. These people knew the truth about the raids—few returned and fewer still found the fame and fortune they craved. Gregory wasn't sure why he was prepared to take such a chance. The question of Scotland nagged at him. But the results would come sooner or later, and only then would he know if he had been right or wrong to head north.

A wench approached the table. Gregory ordered a flagon of Rhenish wine and a bowl of roasted chestnuts. As he and Warren ate and drank, they talked about all they had seen and done. They agreed while it had been an adventure, the adventure had just begun. Gregory promised he would take Warren to London and show him the great market at Cheapside when their travels ended. They would shop for horses at Smithfield, take a barge down the River Thames, and one night visit the stews in Southwark.

"Your promises, they do not seem out of reach," Warren said. "At the end of this journey, London."

"I will not ply you with fantastical notions, only with sound ideas," Gregory said.

Thoughts of the easy leisure of London had them both feeling warm and happy in this cold, angry town. But as their conversation rolled into a crescendo, Gregory saw something that made him catch his breath. The man who just walked in. He took off his drenched cloak, handed it to a servant, and found a seat in the corner. Gregory watched as he ordered food and drink and spoke softly to the page who accompanied him. For the longest time, Gregory could not figure out his identity, but the face was somehow familiar—the square, stubble-lined jaw, the blue eyes, and the trace of rugged nobility across his brow. Warren gave Gregory a quizzical look as he cocked his ear in the direction of the newcomer. From what little Gregory heard of his accent, he knew the man hailed from the north. And that's when he realized who it was—Walter of Helmsley, the young Yorkshire knight who had so fabulously failed at Oxford when he'd jousted Eustace of Dover for the Lordship of Laugharne.

Gregory slapped the table and laughed. "Warren, my boy, I think this chronicle just got a whole lot better."

Still appearing confused at his benefactor's behavior, Warren gave him a curious look. "What makes you say that?"

"Oh, you will know soon enough." He took another quaff of Rhenish wine and smiled in delight.

He waited until Helmsley finished eating. When the serving wench brought a new flagon to his table, Gregory knew it was the right time to approach. He nodded to Warren, who followed him across the crowded room. At the table, Gregory gave a perfunctory bow. In mid-drink, Helmsley looked up over the brim of his cup and frowned. He set it down hard on the table and wiped his mouth on the hem of his green jupon.

"Yes?" He propped his elbows on the table.

"Are you by chance Walter of Helmsley?" Gregory said.

"Yes," he replied, blue eyes flashing. "And who is it who disturbs me while I enjoy ale with my page?"

"My apologies." A sly smile crept over his face. "I am Gregory of Bordeaux. I was at Oxford when you jousted with Eustace of Dover. May I sit and have a drink?"

"Only if you are buying," he said. "Since Oxford, things have not gone well for me."

"Oh, I have a few farthings to spare." Gregory took a seat. "So tell me, what became of you after the tournament?"

Helmsley took a deep drink. For a long while he looked into the flickering candlelight but said nothing. Gregory figured the past tumbled around in his mind. He clenched his teeth, tightened the grip around his cup, and continued to stare balefully at the flame. He filled his cup, took another drink, and in that last swallow seemed to find the courage to speak of his undoing.

"I returned home in shame," he said. "Soon after, a messenger from King Edward arrived and told me my claim to Helmsley was forfeit, that I had to leave by the end of the year or I would be forced to leave. I have been landless and without a title ever since. I hired out my sword in Durham and in Northumberland, but was not invited to join a household."

"That is too bad." Gregory sighed and shook his head. "What happened to you at Oxford? I was there, and I saw it with my own eyes. You, much more than Dover, caused your downfall."

"Must you remind me?" he said. "This time a year ago I sat in my hall with my wife and my men, drinking and laughing by the fireplace while venison roasted in the kitchen. I was a lord, and on most days, I was content. But how could I say no to King Edward? They said Dover was no match for me. But when I arrived in Oxford, the moment was too big. The city. The court. The crowds. I had never seen anything quite like it. I drowned myself in a pot of ale and embarrassed the king, and now I am here, in this shit-pile of a town, hoping someone will give me a few pennies to ride north and kill Scots."

"Where is your wife?"

"In York," he spat. "She has not spoken to me in a year. I hear she has taken a lover—a deacon at Holy Trinity church—and is with child."

Gregory reached across the small table, put his hand on Helmsley's shoulder, and looked into his eyes.

"Your fortunes will soon improve," he said, his tone soothing, consoling. "You were a lord before and you will be a lord again."

Despite his show of confidence, Gregory felt great pity for Helmsley. He had ridden into Oxford with such martial pride and had appeared invincible prancing down High Street on his white charger. On the verge of becoming a lord in Wales, he held the golden chalice in his hand but drank from it too soon. A simple lapse in judgment, a youthful act of bravado, an instant when he thought he'd won the prize before he'd played the game. In that moment he'd lost it all, and in front of the smirking students and masters of Oxford. Now a landless cuckold with only an unshaven page as company, he relived his ruin in a town where no one was supposed to know his name.

"How do you propose I reclaim my status?" Helmsley said.

"That question requires many answers," Gregory said. "But it starts here in Carlisle. I will find you a suitable host for your venture north, and God willing, you will begin to right the wrong of Oxford."

 regory and Warren walked through the market, loud with the ringing hammers of the forge, down Butcher's Row, up Baker's Lane, and across the green to the townhome where Lord Osbert

of Kent held court with his retinue. They waited hours for Lord Osbert to finish his meal. Once bloated with bread, beef, and ale, he consented to Gregory's request for an audience. He and Warren entered the hall, a dreary room of bare wood and stone, and gave an obligatory bow. Osbert nonchalantly plucked a piece of gristle from his teeth, flicked it to the table, and smacked his lips. He pulled a mantle of luxurious grey mink over his shoulders, in part to ward off the chill, but more importantly, Gregory surmised, to draw attention to the fact he possessed such an opulent and beautiful piece of fur.

Osbert gave a smug smile and made a benevolent gesture with the sweep of his hand. "Gregory of Bordeaux, my steward tells me. Why is it you honor me with your presence?"

"I assure you, Lord Osbert, the pleasure is all mine," Gregory replied. "I have traveled far and wide, my lord, yet but once have I seen a fur as precious as yours, and when I did, it lay draped over the shoulders of our dear king."

"A gift," he said, and tugged at it again. "You see, a man as humble as I cannot afford to buy such things."

Gregory usually laughed with scorn and chided such false expressions of modesty, but standing in front of a dozen mercenaries at Osbert's court, having heard of Osbert's penchant for unexpected fits of belligerence and having heard he had participated in the massacre at Berwick just a year earlier, he thought better of it. Instead, he shed the troublesome pleasantries and went straight to the point.

"I understand you ride north."

"You have heard no lies," Osbert said.

"I want to ride with you."

Osbert and his men laughed. "I'm looking for warriors, Bordeaux, something you are not."

"True, but I'm a chronicler, and I want to write about you and your triumphs against the enemies of our king. We will all die someday, Lord Osbert, but if your sword swings true in Scotland, and if I write about it, then you will live forever."

Osbert exchanged looks with his men, and after a long moment of silence, they seemed to find Gregory's proposal acceptable.

"I will bring you north with us. Are you bringing the peasant boy with you?" He nodded toward Warren.

"Yes, my lord, he rides with me. But I also have a second man, Walter of Helmsley, and his sword is at your command."

Three days and no Scots. Hilltop after hilltop, cupping their hands over their eyes while searching the horizon, and nothing. Vacant valleys and shimmering lochs, emerald steeps and mossy outcrops. A land of barrenness and beauty, where the heart of man rocked in a cradle of stone and the blood ran cold as the rivers. This is where the corncrakes cried, the plovers sang, and the red foxes roamed—a land of heath and moor and pewter skies. Gregory had never seen a Scot. He had heard people tell of them, and the telling was never good—bearded, blond-headed devils on tireless ponies, armed with blades that never went dull, filled with an unquenchable thirst for merriment and battle. Birthed from the mountains, suckled on the wind, and thick with the nourishment of rain, the Scots were the stubble of the land. To try and uproot them was folly, but here Gregory traveled, with a nervous hand on the reins and a troubled look over his shoulder.

Osbert of Kent didn't wear his mantle of mink. Arrayed in his black kit of steel, wool, and leather, he looked like a prowling angel of death, ready to vomit fire and blood on the land of his enemies, to drown them in a river of urine, or to bury them in a landslide of excrement. Restless and aching to send souls to Heaven and Hell, he drove his band of mercenaries deeper and deeper into the borderlands. Snow fell and still he went forth on the rutted road to Edinburg. Jesting, shouting, and singing, he and his men grew boisterous in their venom, calling, "Come out, come out, you dirty Scots, and meet your maker."

On the fourth day, the Scots answered Osbert's challenge. On top of a hill appeared a dense line of footmen bristling with spears, bagpipes droning. A blue banner whipped in the wind while a man beat methodically on a drum. Their stink filled the air and hungry crows circled above them. Gregory trembled as Osbert and his men readied their lances. Among the Scots only one, their chieftain, was mounted. He rode out on his pony and brandished his sword.

"Who is first?" he called, and the black pony reared and whinnied.

Before anyone else responded, Helmsley trotted his horse a few feet out from the line.

He looked back at Gregory, and with a grim smile, said, "This isn't Oxford, lad."

He pushed down his visor, took his lance from his page, and settled into his saddle. He spurred his steed and drove over the field. His lance tilted.

The chieftain waited for the moment of reckoning. In the blink before the lance impaled him, he turned and lowered his shoulder.

Helmsley missed.

As he made his pass, the chieftain hefted his sword and gave a stroke so powerful and true, it cut through Helmsley's helmet and split his skull down to the bottom of his neck.

Helmsley's life spewed out from the wound. His limp body slid from the saddle to the ground in a gruesome heap.

A stab of guilt plunged into Gregory's heart at the sight of Helmsley lying dead in the field. Young Helmsley, abandoned by his wife and his king, cast out from his castle and made a drifter because his poise did not equal his pretensions. Gregory had found him at the height of his vulnerability, and instead of telling him to go south, where it was safe and where the money was easy, he had told him to go north, where he was no match for the men he would encounter.

"Dear God, have mercy on his soul," Gregory said, "and give me the wisdom to grant better counsel."

The chieftain high-stepped his pony down the line of footmen. The bagpipes droned as the Scottish battle cry grew earsplitting and dreadful. With lowered spears and shrieks and shrills, they swarmed across the field. Osbert and his knights bunched together, lurched forward on their mounts, and with the earth shaking beneath them, lowered their lances.

Watching from atop the hill, Gregory winced with sorrow and sickened when the two lines collided. A clap of groaning agony, the splitting of wood and the ringing of steel—both sides gave battle in the dank pit of the human heart, where hatred, not reason, resides. Osbert and his men hacked with their broadswords. They bashed through the enemy shields and poised themselves to break the stubborn Scottish line. And at that very moment, when it appeared Osbert would have his day, the truth of the matter emerged.

Gregory's eyes widened and his mouth fell open. A fresh detachment of Scottish riders crested a hill. They swept down toward the battle. Pulling their swords all at once, it looked like a bolt of lightning flashed on the hillside. Heartened by the arrival of allies, the footmen pressed forward. One by one, and sometimes in twos and threes, Osbert's men fell. But there was not an ounce of cowardice among the remaining. Those who could wheeled their horses around. With shouts of "For the King!" they barreled toward the oncoming cavalry.

As the Scots trapped and killed Osbert's remaining men, he fought hand-to-hand with the red-plumed chieftain. Their swords rang out, they cursed, and their steeds stepped and jostled for the advantage. A death match between equals, Osbert and the chieftain, heaving with exhaustion, traded strike and counter strike. Neither could crack the other.

The fight wore on. The chieftain's mount grew quicker. He guided it around so he was suddenly on Osbert's blind side. Osbert turned to confront the danger. The chieftain stood in his stirrups, howled to whatever god would listen to him, and with his enormous sword gripped in both hands, swung it into Osbert's neck. His head tumbled across the turf and his corpse fell from the horse.

Gregory felt no sadness as Osbert's yolk leaked out. Indeed, he welcomed the man's ugly death. A day earlier, the warlord had told Gregory that his men had murdered three hundred women and children and looted the parish church at the sack of Berwick. Even in war—and even if Scots—by Gregory's count it was three hundred too many. Though he would never admit it to anyone but perhaps Warren, he had found himself rooting for the Scotsman, and when he triumphed, he felt a sense of satisfaction for which he was almost ashamed.

Another howl sounded from the Scots, and their chieftain pranced before them on his rugged pony, coaxing it into high steps and hoof-shuffling circles. The bagpipes blared and the drum rumbled as the clansmen celebrated their win. Over the din of victory hung the anguish of the injured, the cries of the dying, and the putrid gas from the bowels of the slain. Then one of them separated himself from the rest, pointed up to the top of the hill, to Gregory and Warren, and many Scottish eyes turned to the pair of strangers who'd arrived with the enemy.

"What do we do?" Warren asked.

Gregory held back his own surge of panic. "This is not our fight."

"Master Gregory, what do we do?"

Gregory considered flight. But even with fast horses, they did not know this inhospitable land. Damn, we could win the race, but we wouldn't survive the journey. His composure wilted into trembling as the chieftain peered up and caught his gaze. When he and his cavalry galloped up the hill, Gregory realized what he needed to do.

"Get off your horse, get on your knees, and put your hands behind your head," he said and dismounted.

Warren looked at Gregory and then looked back at the chieftain and his retinue. To Gregory's holy dread, it looked as if Warren waffled between pride and fear. He did not immediately dismount, and for a moment, a moment in which he squared his jaw and clutched the shaft of his billhook, it appeared to Gregory as if Warren would fight the chieftain.

"Warren, if you value your life, get off your horse. Now!"

Gregory closed his eyes and sighed with relief when Warren finally dismounted. Gregory didn't know if submission would work, but once in the position of surrender, they could only wait and pray.

"God, shine on us a light of peace," Gregory said, "for too many have perished this day."

The chieftain and his riders reached the plateau and circled their captives. Nimble on his panting pony, the chieftain rode up to within a few feet of Gregory, pulled his steed to a halt, and quite casually crossed his hands over the saddle's pommel.

Gregory slowly lifted his head. So close was he that he smelled the pony's fetid breath, saw the fog of battle in the chieftain's trinket eyes. A nasty little scrap of a man with a chapped face and a missing front tooth, he wore black boots, a fine coat of mail, a short crimson cape, and glittered with silver and gold. The red plume danced in the breeze, as did the blond curling locks flowing out from beneath his helm. The blade at his hip seemed too big for this diminutive man, but Gregory had seen him wield it with such skill, he knew that not to be true. Smoldering like hot coal, plumb with certitude, and as taut as the ropes of a coiled siege engine, here was the Scot of hushed English tales.

"Your king will never take this land," the chieftain said. "What you saw today will happen again and again."

"But my king is not known for prudence in war, so he will come," Gregory said. "You proved yourself today, but you will have to prove yourself again."

"There'll be proof enough when I piss down his throat," he said. "But please, let us not waste our breath speaking of King Edward. I have a question for you. How many men have I killed today?"

"By my count, two," Gregory said.

"And why should I not kill two more?" He looked at Warren, then back at Gregory.

"Because your victims were landless mercenaries not worth a shilling in York. My man and I, on the other hand, are worth many pounds back in London."

"And what makes you so valuable?"

"I am a chronicler, and I will bring everlasting glory to those who employ me. Just as they have read of Julius Caesar and Charlemagne, so too will they read of our time—and perhaps even of you," Gregory said. "If you do not believe me, I have ample proof."

"Priest," said the chieftain, and a tonsured elder dressed in black emerged from the group of spearman that had made its way to the top of the hill.

Cautiously, Gregory reached deep into the breast pocket of his tunic where he kept his letters of recommendation. On folded pieces of parchment inside a waxed leather wallet were the letters, each of them bearing a seal. He pulled out the wallet and handed it to the priest, who opened it and thumbed through the parchments.

Gregory knew the names he'd see—Jean du Mont, Alan Spicer of the London Guild of Merchants, the London Guild of Goldsmiths, Anne of Boston, Geoffrey Wool, Joan the Widow, the Bishop of Lincoln, the Lord of Lancaster, and most importantly, Richard Beaufort, the Earl of Southampton. Gregory despaired of playing all his cards at once, but he also knew the more he was worth, the longer he and Warren would live. So play them he did, hoping his letters trumped the chieftain's sword.

The priest took his time reading the letters, his lips moving in silence, and from time to time, a bushy eyebrow arching in welcome surprise. He looked up from the letters and gave Gregory a subtle wink.

"God has smiled on you today—Gregory of Bordeaux." He turned to the chieftain and held up the letters. "He speaks the truth, my lord. He knows powerful people in the south. If there is a ransom to be paid, his people can pay it."

The chieftain nodded. A frightening smile crept over his face as his red plume bent and fluttered.

"Welcome to Scotland," he said. "You will stay at my castle for a year, and at the end of that year, if the ransom hasn't come… well, you are a chronicler. You know how that story ends."

Under close guard, Gregory and Warren galloped off with this hardened, bloody band of Scots. Gregory looked over his shoulder for one last glimpse of the battlefield. Footmen had already gathered up the horses and had stripped Helmsley, Osbert, and the others of their belongings and armor. Crows and rooks pecked at the scattering of naked corpses.

Dear God. Helmsley had been correct. This wasn't Oxford.

Hours later, Gregory, Warren, and the Scottish war train arrived at the gates of a gloomy castle perched in the corner of a cliff overlooking the sea. He had seen it on the horizon, and as he rode through the gate, it seemed to glare down at him. The tower keep, tall, damp, and dark. As Gregory looked up at the tiny window at the top, his stomach went queasy and he frowned. Throughout the day, many thoughts had run through his mind. Now that the tower loomed over him, and now that he felt the breathing of its stone, all his brooding came together in a passage he knew he would one day include in his chronicle.

In this world there are good men, bad men, and those who are neither. While one finds his endeavor in the works of charity, his brother might crave pillage and spoils. Still there are those who have no druthers, and are at the whim of circumstance. They must take what is given and hope for the best, but as we must know, hope without choice brings rarely a happy end.

The gate closed behind them. At the gruff command of one of the riders, Gregory dismounted. A footman apprehended him. He wrenched Gregory's arm behind his back, put him in a headlock, and dragged him off to the tower.

"Scribe, enjoy your stay," he heard the chieftain say. "And don't worry about your page. He will ride with us."

A BARBARIAN IN SWINTON'S TOWER

Twenty pounds of silver, the price for his life. Gregory didn't know if he was worth it or if his people would pay it, but he didn't share those doubts with his captor. He wrote letters describing his plight, that he was held by Swinton the Red, a fierce Scottish chieftain, and that his life was forfeit in a year if the ransom wasn't paid.

> *Bring your silver, for prayers are not enough to save me. I was a fool to have come to Scotland, and now I ask you to pay the price of my asininity. I promise you, should I make it home alive, you will be the beneficiary of the wisdom I now learn.*

Swinton housed him on the top floor of the tower, where he had a splendid but monotonous view of the North Sea. He soon wearied of the calling gulls, the crashing waves, the howling wind, and the big black rat that crept into his room each night to lick from his empty bowl of gruel. In the first week, he went stir crazy and descended into a tirade.

"You Scots are not born of the womb but are hatched from eggs," he yelled from the window.

The boys of the village responded by launching rocks from their slings. One of them caught Gregory above the left eye, cutting him badly and knocking him to the floor as he clutched at the wound. Gregory yelled from the window no more. Swinton's priest, Malcolm, was kind enough to have a desk and chair, iron gall ink, quills, and parchment delivered from Kelso Abbey so Gregory could write. And write he did, pushing back against the grinding solitude of captivity with the people and places of the chronicle.

The joy of Lichfield before the marriage between Geoffrey and Anne will always live in my heart. Spices and incense burned at the town's four corners, and boughs of greenery hung from the walls. Colorful braids of all manner of cloth hung from the banquet canopy near the town hall. Whole hogs roasted overnight, and tremendous sides of beef turned on the spits. In every oven loaves baked, and in every pot ale brewed. All along Tamworth Street, one heard the strings of lutes and the whistle of pipes, and the peasant girls kicked out their feet and made of themselves coquettes. No one paid mind to the curfew, and the night watch saw fit not to enforce it. Everyone was invited to the wedding, and on its eve, commoner and noble alike gathered at the tavern. Parish priests and cathedral deacons even came that night, trying to be discreet as they emptied their cups and motioned for more. A hearty cheer sounded in the tavern when word came that two pipes of precious Saint Sulpice had arrived from Chester. Someone leapt onto a table, hoisted a tankard, and bellowed, "To Lady Anne!" and the dozens in attendance lifted their drink and repeated after him. The next day, their refrain became their battle cry. And so, too, was it on my lips as I picked up a stone and rushed to the fray.

He sat at the desk when the sun rose in the east, and sat at it still when the sun set in the west—day after day, week after week, and month after month. Writing until his fingers hurt, his ass ached, and his back stiffened. Malcolm struggled to keep him supplied with enough candles and rush lights, especially when the days grew short and the nights shimmered black with the darkness of the sea.

Gregory realized anything he had written prior to his imprisonment was little better than scratch. Now working with the fever of a man uncertain of his future, Gregory cracked into the very heart of mankind and wrote what he thought would stand the test of time. He didn't stop at what he'd seen since he'd left London long ago. He wrote his own history, and how he'd grown up on the wharves of Bordeaux, how he still remembered the ringing of the bells at St. André, and how he sailed across the sea to London with his parents when he was eight.

I am Gregory du Mont, but I am known, and proud to be known, as Gregory of Bordeaux. My father, Henri, was a wine merchant in London, and my mother, Herleve, kept his accounts. I grew up in the family business, and before I had hair on my privates, I could turn a farthing into a penny and a penny into a pound. Before I could read and write, I knew the difference between a Sainte Croix and a Sauternes, and between a Moissac and a Bergerac. I am known to be a critic of the men of the holy orders, and to chide them when they fall short of their sacred duties. But if there is one thing I can say of both the episcopal and the monastic, it is that they never cheat on their wine. When a ship laden with their tuns arrives in the London pool, you know it will be a good day. The bidding is always keen and the price never falls short. I do not kneel and pray with bishops and abbots, and nor do I seek their social graces. But by my merchant's blood, I must respect what they do, for my family and I grew wealthy off the fruits of their labor.

I had two sisters before me, and both of them died while I was a child. I barely remember them, but I know my parents loved them dearly. Sabine and Hélène were their names. Each year during the Feast of St. Agnes, we said a special prayer for them. When I was sixteen, my parents died in a shipwreck while sailing back to Bordeaux. The boat capsized during a storm. The fishermen who rowed out to the wreckage found only one survivor, a deckhand, who came to me months later to tell me my parents would never return. I am now twenty-nine, but that wound has yet to heal. My father left a will, so I inherited the wine shop on Royal Street and the silver he'd saved for my education. It took me many years, and indeed, I suffered the sting of the rod many times, but I earned my degree in law and was admitted to the courts. With the help of my cousin, Jean du Mont, I surpassed what my father had achieved. You see, to my family I owe my sadness and my joy, my pain, and my plenty.

If he still lived by the time the ransom arrived, Gregory was worth two years' income for Swinton the Red. It was no surprise, then, that he was kept far from starving. Still, Gregory grew sick of the dreary pottage of cabbage and beans, and turned up his nose at the flat ale brought to him in great quantity. On Christmas day, a guard served him a boiled egg, a roasted chicken leg, a pear fritter, and a half gallon of Spanish wine. He gnawed that bone until the cartilage was gone, and then he broke it open and sucked out the marrow. He saved the wine until last and drank it in big gulps until he was happy and sad and drunk and looking out the window across the frigid, moon-kissed tumult of the North Sea.

The tower stood at the far end of a walled courtyard, accessible only by a drawbridge across a steep ravine. Inside the squalid bailey stood a timber hall, a chapel and barracks, a kitchen, workshops, and stables. Outside the wall on the other side of the drawbridge was a jumble of huts and thatched houses. Though Gregory wrote with purpose, he still took breaks. And when he did, he opened the shutter, leaned into the window, propped up on his elbows, and looked out onto Swinton the Red's little salt-swept chiefdom by the sea. He grew to recognize the people of this settlement and knew their routines—a scullery maid who walked to the kitchen each morning with a babe on her hip, the spinster with the limp who always arrived at church a bit late, the red-headed apprentice working the bellows at the forge, and the parish priest, God bless him, who kept unseemly hours. Whenever he was at the window, someone always looked up at him, pointed a finger, murmured to a friend, and on occasion, made an obscene gesture. He guessed word had spread that a London scribe was captive in the tower, and Swinton would have his head if the silver did not come. He understood their curiosity but was uneasy with being on display.

He scratched into his beard and pulled out a louse. He cursed it and crushed it between the nails of his thumb and index finger. Gregory had never worn a beard until now. He kept his face, the back of his neck, and the area behind and above his ears razor-shaven. In London, he went to the barber once a week, and on the road, Warren did the honors. A close shave followed by a hot, wet cloth wrapped about the neck—now that was comfort. If ever he had the chance to shave, he would, and never again would he have a beard.

He missed his beaver skin hat, Cordovan boots, and garments of Flemish wool. It irked him not having his silver brooch and black cloak, his kid gloves and brass spurs. Upon his arrival at Swinton's stronghold, Gregory was shorn of all his possessions, including his clothes, and in exchange was given rags. Wearing, as he was, a pair of peasant's clogs, a gown of rough, undyed wool, a reeking wolf-skin coat, and a kettle cap of matted deer fur, he felt like a barbarian. Gregory knew it was vanity that teased him. His life was at stake. He knew he was blessed he had not rotted out on the moor with Osbert and Helmsley. Still, he'd been born into money, and there was never a time when he could not afford the trappings his status allowed. Vanity be damned. He missed his finery.

The tower was always cold, even in the spring and summer. The wind never stopped howling. The shutters never stopped creaking open and shut. Even when the sun was high and bright in the sky, a biting draft circled in the room. He had no fire until the autumn came, when he had just enough fuel to keep from freezing. In the dead of winter, his teeth chattered day and night. He could barely keep his quill straight due to the shivering of his bones. He awoke to find snow drifts in the corner of his cell and icicles at the window. Crouching in front of the brazier with his hands held to the fire, his breath came out in great bursts of fog.

If the cold wasn't enough, there was the stench. Built into the wall was a garderobe—a wooden seat over a chute that emptied into a dung heap at the bottom of the tower. But Gregory was not allowed to use the garderobe. He was forced to use a chamber pot, which he was not allowed to empty. Instead, a crone came to his room only once a fortnight to empty the bucket out the window. The pot was not big enough to contain two weeks of waste, and by the end of each fortnight, the bucket overflowed with what Gregory called the devil's juice.

"You are a prisoner of Lord Swinton," the steward had told him, "so you shall live with the stink of your own shit. If ever you are caught using the garderobe, we will pull out a tooth. If you use it a second time, we will put out an eye. And if there is a third time, then you will not have a hand with which to write your chronicle."

Warted hags came to his room, dumped the bucket, set it back in its place, and left with a crafty smile. Except for one of them. She picked up the pot, and instead of heading to the window, moved toward the garderobe. She turned to Gregory and said, "Scribe, I could dump this in the wrong place, and so could the others, and in no time, you'd be so deformed even your own mother wouldn't pay a farthing for you."

Gregory bolted up from the desk, and in a hot panic, lunged toward the garderobe. He positioned himself between it and the hag, and guarded over it like it was a hoard of gold. The hag leaned back and cackled with laughter. She went over to the window, dumped the waste, turned to Gregory, and held up the pot for emphasis.

"I don't want to see you lose a tooth or an eye, dear boy," she said, her voice thick with sarcasm. "I just wanted to remind you that you are no better than a bucket of shit. From now until the day you die, remember that and perhaps you will live a long life."

From then on, he crouched in front of the garderobe whenever one of the hags came to dump his pot. Captivity will make a man do strange things. He wished he did not know that to be true.

From his tower perch, he saw Swinton was an active warlord. He and his men frequently marshaled in the courtyard before rumbling over the drawbridge on their ponies and into the borderland. Returning days or even weeks later, battered and bruised and laden with loot, they feasted in the hall, the hours loud with singing, peals of laughter, and the droning of pipes. Gregory longed to be a part of these celebrations, to guzzle wine and ale, to sink his teeth into a side of beef and to meet Swinton and his fellow clansmen. He wanted to know their story and include it in his chronicle. But most of all, he wanted to see and speak with Warren.

The only glimpses of him were when he left or arrived with Swinton and his men. Had he not known Warren well, he would never have guessed him to be an Englishman from Lichfield. Among Swinton's grim warriors, he held his own. His face dark with stubble, geared in mail and swift on his horse, he looked like a blood member of the clan. Gregory shook his head with resignation when, upon returning from a raid, one of the village girls rushed out to greet Warren as he dismounted. Alas, he was one of them. Yet even if Warren thrived with the Scots, Gregory still worried. What if he died on one of these raids, far from family and home? Gregory had faith Warren would always make it back, but what was he becoming? If Warren developed a taste for death and became no better than a browbeater with a blade, then Gregory knew he would have failed. He hoped the Warren he knew from Lichfield, the earnest kid with the kind demeanor and the helping hand, was so deeply ingrained nothing could take it out of him.

That's how Gregory spent his time—cold, hungry, and alone with his life, unkempt and foul and wishing for the comforts of yesteryear. He took solace knowing if he survived the isolation and indignities of captivity, he could survive anything.

"God, let me out of this stinking hell and I will please You with good works."

Though restless, aching, and sick with worry, Gregory managed a smile. A substantial stack of parchments in Latin sat on the desk. Everything he had seen since the Earl of Southampton hired him was now on the record. He had taken it a few steps further and included his memoir, a lively portrait of London, and a scathing rebuke of the assumed power and privileges of the nobility. He goaded the church, too, and like a few chroniclers before him, mocked its greed and its relentless meddling in secular affairs. He predicted in time the force of commerce and trade would topple the old order and cities, not churches and castles, would rule the world. Gregory knew he could be made to pay for such thoughts, but up in Swinton's tower, he stood upon one thing, the truth as he knew it.

Speak it now, or be forever a fraud.

If the best thing you have ever done in your life is to simply be born, then you have not done much. Men with impressive titles oftentimes come to London, where they do little more than eat and drink and gamble on sport. It is their right, they say, to take much more than they give. Perhaps they are correct, but it is foppery to believe things will never change. With nothing but a strong back and callused hands, a ploughman from the shire will steal away from his family and friends for a chance to flourish in London. So many of them fail. They regret the risk they took because they never receive the reward. Huddled up and miserable in their hovels, they long for the verdant fields of their youth. But they know down deep inside, despite their disappointments, it was best that at least they tried. And even though they are polluted with envy over those who succeeded where they did not, they know those men are just like themselves, though blessed with more luck and guile. Motivated by dreams and burdened with sorrow, they trade in their bondage for the dire uncertainty of life in an unforgiving city. They bring with them their outdated habits and ancient superstitions, but also ideas and ingenuity. A new day has dawned in London, as many well know, yet there are those who refuse to awaken, and who hide from the rising sun.

rom the window in the tower he had seen the castle's comings and goings for nearly a year—warriors, villagers, merchants and peddlers, priests and emissaries from other clans. They

all seemed to blend into a moving tapestry that wasn't black or brown or green but a drab mixture of the three, a swatch of poverty hanging about the heads and shoulders of the people who called this place home. And that's why, looking out beyond the village to the rolling field, Gregory's heart raced with hope. The three men approaching on horseback weren't from around there. Isolation in the tower had done many things to Gregory, but it had not diminished his keen eyesight. He saw a knight in a blue and gold surcoat, his page attired in the same livery, and a hook-nosed priest in black.

Sitting on nervous horses twitching and snorting in the frigid morn, they waited as Swinton and his riders trotted out to greet them. Gregory was too far away to understand what was said, but the priest gestured as he spoke and Swinton gestured in due turn. The conversation must have gone well because the priest made a graceful sweep of his hand, and Swinton, speaking to his men, flashed a smile and put on what appeared to be a gold ring. As the discussion continued, the knight pulled a bulging money sack from his saddlebag and handed it to one of Swinton's men.

Dear God, let that be twenty pounds of silver.

The two sides continued to talk for a long while, and to Gregory's surprise, the priest handed Swinton a scroll. He did not read it, but nodded his head and tucked it away. The priest pointed up to the tower, at Gregory, and Swinton and his men laughed. Soon thereafter they turned their ponies and headed back to the castle. The knight, the page, and the priest stayed put.

As Swinton clacked across the drawbridge, he looked up to the tower. "Gregory, you turd heap of a man, you whore boy of London, you are free! You were worth your price in silver, but believe me, had it been a farthing less, I would have gladly had your head!"

Ignoring the taunt, Gregory neatened the stack of his writings and gathered them up under his left arm. He walked over to the leaking chamber pot and picked it up with his right hand. Just as he did, a guard unlocked the door and walked in.

Gregory stepped over to the garderbobe, looked at the guard and said,

"The fee has been paid, and now I am free. I am Gregory of Bordeaux, you mutt, and from hence forward, I will shit at a time and place of my choosing."

He took the pot and dumped it down the chute and then threw it against the wall. He stormed out of the filthy room and down the spiral staircase to the courtyard where Swinton awaited. The chieftain, still on his pony, held up his hand to show the gold, ruby-encrusted ring on his right pinky.

"Your friends in London do good work," he said. "If you are ever back this way, perhaps we will agree to a similar arrangement."

"Perhaps, Lord Swinton," Gregory said, wisely backing off the tantrum he'd thrown just moments ago. "Despite nearly dying of frost, I did manage to make good use of the year."

"Yes, I see," he said, glancing at the parchments under Gregory's arm. "My crones tell me you worked on it every day, and my steward tells me I spent a fortune on candles so you could write into the night. But I don't mind. It was me, after all, who had the desk and parchments brought over from Kelso Abbey. You do know that, don't you?"

"No, I did not," he said, deflated. "I thought it was Malcolm the priest who supported me."

"Malcolm," he said, and laughed. "Malcolm does not do anything unless I say so. Right, Malcolm?"

"Yes, my lord," he said, from within the crowd of onlookers.

"You were smart to think your friends would pay the ransom, for they have and you are free," Swinton said. "But you are not as smart as you think. The whole time you were in the tower, you didn't write the chronicle for you or for the Earl of Southampton. You wrote the chronicle for me!"

"Whatever do you mean?" Gregory said, becoming ill with the realization he had been duped.

"I fed you, I bought the candles and the ink and the parchments, and you wrote it in my castle," he said. "That is *my* chronicle. If you didn't want me to have it, you shouldn't have written it."

"You will take this from me?" Gregory said, holding out the parchments. "This which took me a year to write and which means nothing to you?"

"Am I in it?"

"Yes," Gregory conceded, after a long pause.

"And maybe the bishop in Edinburg wants it for his own collection, and would pay a pretty fee for its delivery?"

"Maybe."

"So you see, it is much more meaningful to me than you thought," he said, and nodded to a few of his men.

They closed in on him. One pried his left arm out and grabbed at the parchments, and another punched Gregory so hard in the face he saw stars and fell groaning to the ground.

"Now get up, you lice-ridden whelp, and leave my castle or you will hang before nightfall."

On his hands and knees, Gregory spit a gob of blood and gathered himself. He made it to his feet, and with blurred vision, stumbled out over the drawbridge and through the village. He ran to the knight, page, and priest, calling, "Please don't leave me!"

He tried to run faster, but one of his clogs fell off and he stumbled to the ground. As he struggled to regain his feet, panting and distraught, he heard the dreadful sound of hooves coming from behind. Too fearful of what he'd see if he looked over his shoulder, he peered into the eyes of the priest, who seemed puzzled by what approached. Gregory could bear it no longer. He rose to his feet and turned, expecting to see Swinton bearing down on him with his enormous sword. Instead he saw something that filled his heart with a swift and cresting wave of joy. Warren, stalwart and handsome in the saddle, and silvery Moonbeam, cantered across the field.

"Dear Warren, my boy." Gregory's voice cracking with emotion. "I thought you would stay."

Warren curbed Moonbeam to a halt and held out his hand. "Never would I leave you, Master Gregory," he said, in a voice much deeper than what Gregory remembered. "Now get on."

With a tug of his hand, he helped Gregory up onto the horse.

"Master Gregory, you might think this is the worst day of your life, but it is not. You stayed in Swinton's tower for a year and lived to tell the tale. That means God has blessed you with a miracle, so be thankful. You have written the chronicle once, which means you can write it again. Until then, we ride like the devil! Swinton has given us a day's head start, but he will hunt us at dawn."

Warren spurred at Moonbeam and shouted, "Yah!" She bolted forth, with the knight, the page, and the priest following her lead.

Gregory looked over his shoulder. A dark pillar of solitude, the rude silhouette of the tower jutted into the blue sky.

A year had been stolen from him, yet the price was right. Twenty pounds and he was alive.

THE
MIRACLE OF
SAINT CUTHBERT

hey crossed Framwellgate Bridge into Durham at midday, fam-
ished and on exhausted horses. Seeing the castle wall and the
tower of the great cathedral, Gregory knew at last he was safe.
The rocky ride from Scotland had left him shaken, and when he dismounted,
his knees went weak. But he collected himself soon enough, and when the
scent of roasting pork wafted his way, he knew it would be a better day than
the one before. The priest dug into his saddlebag, pulled out a small leather
pouch and handed it to Gregory.

"This is from the Earl of Southampton," he said. "You would be wise to
buy yourself a set of clothes, for a wolf's hide and the smell of shit do not
become a man who's worth twenty pounds."

Gregory tucked the pouch away and nodded with appreciation. They led
their horses to the stables, and from there, the priest, the knight, and the
page said their farewells and went their separate ways.

Gregory counted his coins—ten shillings, plenty enough for essentials
and a luxury item. Attired in the foul rags he had worn in the tower, Gregory

cut an odd figure as he moved through the market. He glanced at Warren and smiled as the merchants, perceiving him to be a crude bumpkin, betrayed surprise at his patrician accent and the fine taste in which he selected his boots, tunic, mantle, and cloak. He perused the stalls of the hatters, but Warren put a hand on his shoulder and stopped him.

"But I need a headgear," he said to Warren.

"And you have it," he said, and dug into his shoulder bag and pulled out the beaver skin hat Gregory bought in London, and the under-bonnet Margery made for him in Corby.

Gregory took the items, turned them in his hands, and said to Warren, "How did you manage to keep hold of these?"

"Your captives were superstitious," Warren said. "They thought whoever wore your hat would go insane, so I kept it for you."

"I was afraid you would lose your humanity while riding with Swinton," Gregory said. "I'm glad to know that wasn't the case."

They went to the barber-surgeon, but only after Gregory inquired as to who was the best. Silent Stephen they called him, and he lathered up Gregory's shaggy beard with a soap of mutton fat and potash. He scraped with deft strokes up Gregory's neck and over his jaw and chin. When the loused facial hair was gone, he worked the razor up the back of Gregory's head and high over his ears until all that remained was a short tuft of hair on top—just how Gregory liked it. The barber-surgeon lanced the pulsing, bothersome boil on his back and plucked out the ingrown hair. Silent Stephen's apprentice gave Warren a shave, pulled a large splinter from beneath one of his fingernails, and removed an arrowhead lodged in his thigh from one of his Scotland raids.

They went to a bathhouse and lounged in wooden tubs filled with heated water scented with rose oil. Chamber maids washed their hair, scrubbed their backs and cleaned and trimmed their toe and finger nails. After they finished, servants brought out trays and set them across the tubs. On those trays sat slices of white bread, almonds and prunes, hard goat cheese and sardines, Rhenish wine, and anise comfit. As he crunched on an almond and took a sip of wine, Gregory looked over at Warren. He had grown out his hair, and a servant girl sat at a bench behind him, weaving it into a braid as he reclined in the tub. All the kid in him was gone, replaced with the countenance of a hardened adult. Gregory was saddened the youth in him had vanished, but he could not deny the quality that had replaced it. Husky and assured, and with the speck of regret in his eye, Warren held the demeanor of a lord.

"Are you glad you left Scotland?" Gregory said.

"They have nothing like this up there." Warren gestured at the surroundings and took a bite of cheese. After swallowing, he made a cup of his hand and poured warm water over his forehead.

"I had to leave," he said.

"And why is that?"

"I made a pledge to you," he said. "But I also feared what I might become. I went out on ten raids, I think, and as you can guess, I saw some things of which I will never tell. And I had to do a few things of which I will always seek forgiveness. With Swinton, it was always kill or be killed. You can't think. You just have to do. I got really good at doing. If you noticed, my armor is much better, and I now wield a sword."

"Indeed."

"Those were not gifts. I won those on the battlefield."

"I see, and did you win anything else?"

"My life. Swinton is cruel and is not wholly to be trusted. But he does have a certain sense of honor. When I rode out of his castle, it was because I had earned the right to leave, and he knew it. He said he would give us a day's lead before coming after us, but I don't think he ever did."

"And why is that?"

"Because if he had, he would've run us down."

"Interesting." Gregory rubbed an aching shoulder. "And the little girl I saw you with?"

He laughed. "Youthful sin, Master Gregory."

"What's her name?"

"Fionnaghal," he said, dreamily.

"Did you love her?"

"Yes—but I love England more. My life is not in Scotland. And I asked her, when we first met, if she would come with me when it came time to leave. She said no."

"Is your heart hurting?"

"Yes, but it will mend." He splashed water gently over his shoulders. "Master Gregory, I named my sword after her."

He ate a sardine and washed it down with a quaff of wine. "I believe you have gotten more than you bargained for when you agreed to accompany me on my adventure."

"And I am thankful it is so," Warren said. "So how did you survive in Swinton's tower? I was told many prisoners had died in that very room."

"I don't think I'll ever be able to fully answer the question." He scratched his newly shaven neck. "I know the chronicle had something to do with it. It was always in front of me, so I always knew my life had meaning. Had I known Swinton was going to take it from me, I wouldn't have written it. In that instance, ignorance was good."

"You are smart and always in control. How did it feel when you realized you had been tricked—and by Swinton of all people?"

"I am not yet able to describe how it felt," he said. "Yes, it was terrible, but it is much deeper than that. There is only one thing in this world I have created, and once I had, it was taken from me. It wasn't just that I had been tricked, Warren, but that I had been robbed. But in his haste to embarrass me, Swinton said something he should not have—that the chronicle was on its way to the Bishop of Edinburg. Guess who is going to get a strong letter once I am in London and in full control of my powers?"

Gregory stood up, stark naked and dripping wet. He wagged his finger and in a braying voice of protest, said, "Mark my words, Warren. The chronicle will not remain long in Scotland!"

He stepped out of the tub and wrapped a towel around his waist.

"Master Gregory, I missed you all those months."

"I missed you, too. It means a lot that you are here with me. And that you held onto my hat."

Gregory and Warren entered through the north door of the transept at Durham Cathedral, and found themselves at the back of a large queue of pilgrims. Gregory could not see over the crowd, but a dazzling golden glow hung in the high reaches of the soaring, sculpted vaults of the ceiling, and mid-morning light radiated through the blue and green glass along the east wall of the chapel. As pilgrims said their prayers and made way for those behind them, Gregory and Warren inched closer to the shimmering shrine of St. Cuthbert.

Gregory had been aware of this site for many years, and knew if he left Durham without paying a visit, then he would have remorse. He also wanted to show something special to Warren, who had never heard of the shrine.

"The saint interred behind the high altar had lived in the darkest of days, when Jesus competed with Odin, and when the land was riven by invaders from the frozen north," he had told Warren. "Known in life as a wise man, Cuthbert is known in death as a miracle worker. He is a source of fascination and reverence for many, including kings and queens, bishops and earls, and the countless numbers of the masses. Now it is our turn to pray at the feet of this ancient and noble saint."

With each step the mood grew more solemn, the cascade of light shone brighter, and the divine pull of the saint strengthened. Once within the brilliant amber blush of St. Cuthbert's aura, many pilgrims cried, wiping away tears of faith as their shoulders shook with emotion. The crowd kept moving—weeping, kneeling, praying, and tithing—until Gregory and Warren were up front and in full view of the glorious soul of Durham. On an elevated slab of gilded green marble sat an oaken coffin carved with Saxon runes. Ornately painted cupboards sat on either side of the shrine, crammed with treasure accumulated over the centuries—ingots of gold, piles of silver and all manner of plate, jewelry, a unicorn's horn, carvings of alabaster, statuettes of bronze, a full cloak of mink, an embroidered stole from Byzantium, and endless bolts of silk. Most astounding of all was an egg-shaped emerald, twice the size of a man's head, sitting in the center of the hoard. Soaking up the light and remitting it in a mesmerizing greenish haze, the emerald bathed the shrine with the radiance of St. Cuthbert's sanctity. Gregory felt the impatience of the people behind him, so he stepped to the shrine, kneeled, and said the Paternoster.

Gregory was about to stand up and go on his way, but instead he closed his eyes, put his chin on his clinched hands, and remained kneeling. He thought of everything he'd experienced while in Swinton's tower, and those memories went through him like a churning flood. The confinement and the stench, the sorrow and the fear, the pride that would not die, and the belief that could not be tamed—he had seen himself from the inside out and begged God for more years. Much work needed to be done to become the man he wanted to be, and kneeling there in the gentle hands of St. Cuthbert, he had faith his chance would be allowed.

The reason the saint remained so popular was because he delivered on the promise of miracles. People petitioned St. Cuthbert to ask God to cleanse them of their sins, mend their broken bones, and heal their bleeding wounds. And just moments before Gregory kneeled at the shrine, a man with a bushy, yellowing beard ran joyously from the cathedral.

"The cough that plagued me has been cured."

Another man, a ploughman with leathery skin and a threadbare hat, held up his hands in amazement.

"I came here with one thumb and now I have two," he proclaimed. "St. Cuthbert has done it again!"

As far as Gregory knew, he was in fine health, so he needn't ask for a remedy. But he didn't think only of himself. He begged St. Cuthbert to ask God to look after his friend, Margery Alesworth, and to guard over her fertile fields in Corby.

"If it pleases you, see to it that God keeps her fit and strong, dear saint, for she is one of God's children."

He had a long road home, and if he took all the twists and turns as expected, he would face many dangers. He had his wits and Warren's sword in his favor, but something told Gregory he would need more than that to make it back to London alive. So he hunkered down and continued to pray.

"Blessed St. Cuthbert, in your magnificent presence I have come to seek the meaning of modesty. I am a man of the road and a man of travel, as you once were. I am far from home, and everywhere I look I see strangers. God has put food in my stomach, protected me from harm, and provided fire against the cold. He has guided me on my journey, and though there have been hardships, He has mercifully brought me here, to Durham, to bask in your holiness. I am a selfish man who has yet to break his conceit, so I am not sure if I am worthy of your consideration. But if for some reason I am, I beg you to make my cause yours and to speak my name into God's ear—Gregory du Mont, Gregory of Bordeaux, chronicler from London. I am asking God to give me patience and courage, and to look over me and my friend, Warren Lichfield, as we head south. I am a flawed man, full of pride and quick to preen, yet still I am convinced I'm doing God's work. It is a chronicle I write, a story of us, and in its pages I have found the work of my life. I must see many places and meet many people or this work is no good, and thus, my life is a waste. I humbly beseech you to hear my plea, St. Cuthbert, and to speak with our dear God, for it is only with His blessing that my deeds are possible. Amen."

He opened his eyes and for a long while gazed into the depths of the giant emerald, pulsing with a nourishing light. A sense of peace overcame him as he lost himself in the resplendent heaps of the saint's treasure. A sunray collected in a towering panel of stained glass and filled the shrine with soft shades of orange and ocher. He shivered when he felt a hand on his shoulder. He looked up only to see Warren smiling down at him.

"It's time for us to go, Master Gregory," he said in a hushed tone. "There are many behind you who are waiting."

"Oh... yes."

He stood and took one last look at the shrine and the imposing, rune-inscribed coffin. He hoped St. Cuthbert had listened.

regory needed a horse. He and Warren had gone into Scotland with two of them, Moonbeam and Tamworth, but only Moonbeam made it out. Tamworth was wounded during a raid and put out of his misery. Rather than waste the opportunity for a feast, the Scots roasted Tamworth's flesh and ate him. Moonbeam, pugnacious as ever, would not let anyone ride her, including Swinton, and had bitten and thrown him and two others who tried to mount her. But when Warren climbed into the saddle and whispered her name, she responded with a gentle trot, and Warren rode her ever since. Gregory had every right to reclaim his horse, and Warren had earnestly offered to return her, but how could Gregory accept? To take her now would be to break Warren's heart, and to spoil their friendship, and Gregory knew better than that.

What he needed was a swift palfrey with an ambling gait, but those cost as much as ten pounds. Gregory only had eight shillings. Still, he and Warren went to Durham's horse fair in search of a deal. For Gregory, the pickings appeared slim, and it didn't take long to realize he would have to settle for an old, used rouncey. Warren shared his concern, and the two of them exchanged frowns and shook their heads with disappointment as they made their way through the fair.

Their discontent was interrupted by a commotion up ahead of them, a din of fawning and flattery that could not be ignored. Ever curious, Gregory and Warren made their way toward the crowd encircling one particular horse. Courteously making their way to the front of the crowd, the source of the fuss became obvious—there stood a glorious chestnut courser, a long-boned Arabian colt with a high tail and a black mane, its rump and withers gleaming.

This horse, which seemed to understand and appreciate the adulation, stood calm as the crowd of giddy onlookers swelled. Tethered to a much inferior horse, the Arabian bore no saddle, so the cut of his muscle and balance of his physique were on full, splendid display. He snorted and whinnied with aggression, reminding all who gawked at him that an unquenchable fire burned in his belly.

Gregory glanced up at the owner of the horse, a dandy silk-and-feather nobleman surrounded by his retinue of armed retainers. He held himself aloof and affected a look of disinterest, but Gregory saw it in his eyes—the pride he had in his horse was reckless, and he was infatuated by the crowd's boisterous praise.

A merchant stepped into the circle and said to the nobleman, "In all my life I have not seen such a horse! Surely, my lord, he was foaled in the royal stables!"

The nobleman did not speak. The reply came from his priggish page.

"Indeed, he was," he said. "His name is Black Saddle. He has raced from Canterbury to Cornwall and has yet to be beat. He is the champion of the south and now has come to lay claim to the north. Black Saddle is the fastest horse in the realm, and if there are any here who say otherwise, let them prove their doubt with a running of five furlongs."

The crowd went silent, and just as it seemed no one would accept the challenge, a man spoke up in a steely voice of defiance.

"I find it hard to believe Black Saddle is the fastest horse in the realm when he is not even the fastest horse in Durham."

A gasp arose from the crowd. Gregory looked around and was dumbfounded when he realized the man who spoke was Warren. He turned to him with a glare so molten with disapproval, he expected Warren to see his mistake and back down. Gregory could then apologize for his page's indiscretion and plead for forgiveness from the unknown nobleman who was wealthy enough to own a royal Arabian courser.

But Warren didn't even acknowledge Gregory and his sour expression. He locked eyes with the lord, and the two of them adjudged one another in silence. The page made as if to speak, but the nobleman waved him off.

It was to Gregory's heart-pounding relief that a chivalric smile flashed in his eyes as he said, "Where is your horse?"

"In the stables, and well fed and rested," Warren said.

A groom rushed off and soon returned leading Moonbeam on a short tether. The crowd, whispering and gesturing and craning their necks for a glimpse of the drama, parted as Moonbeam pranced to Warren's side.

"This is my horse," he said and swallowed hard. "And I assure you, she is a spirited mare who will have no fear of your Black Saddle."

As Warren spoke those simple words, Gregory's ire melted away. He stepped back and gave him the field, and in so doing, saw his friend in a new and becoming light. He was no longer the warm-hearted peasant trying to make good. He had already reached that milestone. Warren worked on something much bigger. Though he had not gotten there yet, it was evident he was on his way, and if he had to trample on a nobleman's childish boast to get there, then so be it.

Seasoned by the road and in battle, silvery Moonbeam had proven to be true. Steadfastness and courage showed in her eyes, and in her deep, muscular chest beat a tireless heart. In every move alert and nimble, her compact body betrayed a certainty of tremendous power. She bore a white blaze down her face, four white stockings, and a white whorl on her rump. Her thick, braided mane hung over her graceful neck.

Gregory reminded himself Moonbeam had been hand selected by the Earl of Southampton, and he remembered what the earl had said that day.

"In time this filly will mature, and when she is at the peak of her prime, only a few will be able to run with her."

From the looks of it, that peak was now. A sharp grin came to Gregory's face because he knew Moonbeam could win. For all of Black Saddle's rare beauty and obvious pedigree, Gregory saw in him a young and pampered toy that had probably done nothing but run the five furlongs. Moonbeam, however, had endured wind, snow, ice, and rain, and had forded rivers and climbed mountains. A warhorse with an appetite for daring and peril, Gregory knew Moonbeam could out-tough Black Saddle in a race.

Gregory looked around at the crowd, and in particular at the nobleman. He saw it on their faces—Moonbeam had not failed to impress. Indeed, Durham would have its race, and Gregory hoped to win it before it even started.

He stepped up next to Warren and looked at the page. "Five furlongs? Surely Black Saddle has more in him than a simple dash. How about ten furlongs?"

The page looked to his lord, who shook his head. "We will not do ten."

"And we will not do five," Gregory said. "For the sake of sport, agree to eight furlongs and you will have your race."

The nobleman conferred with his men and for a few moments their discussion grew heated. But they soon settled down and gave a reply.

"The most we will do is seven furlongs," the page said. "And the loser must forfeit his horse to the winner."

Gregory and Warren looked at one another, and though the stakes teetered too high, they quickly reached an agreement.

"We accept those terms," Gregory said. "We will meet you out past the wheat fields tomorrow at dawn."

The news spread fast, and Gregory, Warren, and Moonbeam became the source of much discussion and speculation. Two camps developed—one betting on Moonbeam, the other on Black Saddle. By nature Gregory was not a gambler, but he could not turn his back on this opportunity. He counted his pennies and carefully arranged a series of bets with a group of merchants.

"We will ride out of Durham as lords or walk out as paupers."

In his talks with the townsmen, he learned the nobleman's identity— Lord Baldwin FitzLambert, a wayward, spiteful knight from Essex. Gregory knew if word got out Warren was peasant-born, the race could be called off because a peasant was not allowed to challenge the right and privilege of a man of FitzLambert's quality.

When people asked about him, Gregory kept a straight face and said, "He is a page in the service of the Earl of Southampton. If five years from now you should happen to see Warren, I would venture to guess it would be at his castle near Lichfield."

And so it was set. Lord Baldwin of Essex and his sleek Arabian courser versus Warren of Lichfield and his rugged Spanish mare.

The majority of the town came out for the race, as did many of the pilgrims in Durham for St. Cuthbert's shrine. While many lined the route, most gathered at the finish line. Even as the cathedral bells rang at Lauds, thirsty souls sipped from their cups of ale and nibbled at their cold meat pies. The local nobility attended the event, too, seeing and being seen and parading in their wool and fur. A Franciscan friar milled through the crowd, doling out blessings and reminding people hell awaited those who had no faith. The Bishop of Durham was not present, but some of his deacons—pious, tonsured, and swathed in black—mingled with the nobles. Polite applause and a few raucous cheers sounded as Warren and Baldwin rode out to the grounds. A loop it would be, around the edge of the stubbly, frosted field of winter wheat.

Situated at the front of the crowd, Gregory watched as Warren and Lord Baldwin trotted their steeds into their places.

"Moonbeam, you have always been a great horse, but your finest moment will be on this day." Gregory made the sign of the cross.

Both horses bolted out of the start and in a blink hurtled breakneck along the outskirts of the field. Reaching, stretching, and yearning with a primitive lust for speed and triumph, they gained velocity with each spectacular stride. Breaking through the morn, stoking hope and stealing hearts, those horses split serenity with the quake and thunder of their efforts. And Black Saddle had the better of it. Pulling ahead by three lengths, he settled into the practiced pace of a winter's gale, and, as he'd done many times before, held his lead.

So the race went, furlong after furlong, with Black Saddle unrelenting and Moonbeam working in his spray of dirt and divots.

It appeared the race would remain that way, but Moonbeam veered out and made her move as they surged into the sixth furlong. All her muscles flexed and in one fantastic extension of front legs and back, with just one hoof kissing the turf, she gained a length. Through repeated cycles of stretch and suspension, running rambunctious and free, Moonbeam exploded down the homestretch.

Black Saddle responded with a kick of his own, and in that moment of courage when he strove to hold her off, the darling colt bloomed into an angry stallion. Lord Baldwin looked over his shoulder, and when he saw his opponent closing in, whipped Black Saddle's rump with renewed urgency.

Those at the finish shouted and cheered at the sight of flashing teeth, wild whites of eyes, and fleet hammering hooves. With Warren crouched on her withers and whipping with his willow switch, Moonbeam at last pulled even.

Over the final furlong, the horses dueled shoulder to shoulder, their riders knee to knee. Whipping and shouting and trying to coax their steeds to greatness, Baldwin and Warren struggled for an advantage neither could gain.

Baldwin suddenly swung out with a backhand and caught Warren square on the chin, but he did not budge, and the methodical whipping of his horse's rump did not falter. Baldwin swung out a second time and hit him again, yet still, Warren's efforts did not wane.

When he tried a third time, Warren ducked, Baldwin missed, his arm flew wide and he lost his balance. Before he regained it, Warren threw out his elbow and caught Baldwin flush on the nose, sending him heels over head off his horse. Warren urged Moonbeam onward, and the charging mare answered with one final burst, edging swift and stubborn Black Saddle by a nose.

Gregory, yelling and imploring and praying since the beginning, ran after Warren as he and Moonbeam wound down from the race. And all those who had bet on them came with Gregory so by the time Warren and Moonbeam wheeled around, a happy throng rushed toward them. Splattered with mud and with a bloody lip, Warren held up his fist and grinned. When Gregory arrived, Warren dismounted and pulled him into his arms.

"You did it, my boy, you did it!" Gregory tossed his hat in the air.

"I did, but not without the help of St. Cuthbert." He laughed. "The other day when we prayed at his shrine, I asked him to help us find you a horse. And now you have Black Saddle!"

Gregory clapped Warren over the shoulder. "I'd hoped he listened."

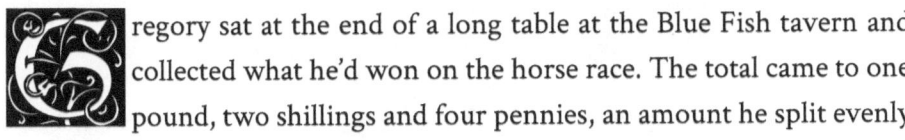regory sat at the end of a long table at the Blue Fish tavern and collected what he'd won on the horse race. The total came to one pound, two shillings and four pennies, an amount he split evenly with Warren. Reluctant to pay, the merchants took their time and fumed with complaints upon arriving at the tavern to give Gregory his due. The accounting took all day, and in the time between the departure of one merchant and the appearance of the next, Gregory sipped on Montauban and worked on his chronicle.

Betting on a race is always about the money. You consider two horses and two men, and place your stake on who you believe is the better of the lot. Simple enough on an ordinary day. But on occasion the true meaning of the wager is unknown, for it is measured not in immediate coin, but in the reach of life and time. In Durham I bet on the victor, and I am anxious to discover exactly what it is I have won.

THE
WHALES
of WHITBY

hey made it known they headed southwest, to Lancaster, and with as much fanfare as they could muster, galloped out through Framwell Gate to complete the pretense. A few hours later they doubled back north in a wide loop around Durham, forded the River Wear, and headed southeast to Yorkshire. Gregory knew better than to trust an aggrieved nobleman, and from what he'd heard before leaving Durham, Lord Baldwin of Essex was livid. Not only had he lost the race and his prize, but more so the great Black Saddle, the means by which he earned his fortune and fame, the way in which he justified his profligate ways.

News of his embarrassing defeat to an unknown page would travel fast, particularly in the south. But if he reclaimed Black Saddle—by force, if necessary—and went on to win another five furlongs and then another, he would erase the ignominy of Durham. Gregory knew he would try, but he couldn't let it happen, and that's why he and Warren trotted their horses down a remote drover's road with nothing to guide them but the light of the moon.

he sea shimmered indigo silver under a bright, low hanging moon. The gentle roar of the waves, the foam on the sand, and a salty wind from far away meant peace in this nook of the realm. The surf raced up the beach and bubbled over the hooves of the horses, then receded, only to come and go again and again. Hypnotic were the rhythm and sounds of the sea, and for a long time Gregory and Warren sat in silence up on their mounts which did not flinch as the cold water teased their shod feet. They soaked up the mystery of the deep, its loud and perpetual churning, its waters full of life, yet its currents so quick to bring death.

Warren gestured toward the east. "Gregory, what is out there?"

"Many things, if I am to believe what I've heard and read, and I do. There is Brittany, Flanders, Normandy, Île de France, Burgundy, and Gascony, where I am from. To the north are the Swedes and Danes. Farther east is the Emperor, and further east still, the Rus. Beyond them is the great Khan, who, they say, rides with a horde so large and terrible no Christian prince can stand against him. To the south is Spain and Rome and the Holy Land, where our once and great king, Richard, did battle with the Saracens. Near there, in Egypt, they say there are pyramids as tall as our cathedrals and a river so wide and deep all of England would sink in it. Still further east there is the empire of the Persians and the Sultan in Delhi, and oceans and cities ten times the size of London."

"That is the east, but what of the west?"

"Outside of Ireland, I do not know what lies to the west of us. A few sailors—Northmen—said they found lands far to the west hundreds of years ago. But no one knows if they told the truth or if it was just something fanciful they wrote in their sagas."

"Do you think there are lands in the west?"

"If there are lands to the east, there have to be lands to the west," Gregory said. "I don't believe we live on the edge of the world, for if there is nothing to the west, then indeed that would be the case. Perhaps one day our people will travel that way, but I shall never board one of their ships."

"And why is that?"

"Because," he said, "I should like to go east, and see the place where the world began."

"Will you ever leave London once you have returned?"

"Oh, I don't know. If I make it home, I will surely want to stay for a while. I miss London. I miss familiar faces and the pace of life. If you have not figured it out, the cities of our realm are small and the people who live in them are smaller still. Only in London do I have the scale I need to live my life. I would be hanging from the gallows soon if I settled down in a town like Lincoln, or die of boredom. But who knows—Paris, Bruges, Rome, or Constantinople—perhaps I will travel again. And what about you, Warren? Is this adventure your first and only, or will you do it again?"

Warren shrugged. "So far, this journey is the greatest moment of my life. I know now I can never go back to what I was. Perhaps Constantinople is too far, but Bruges and Paris sound good."

A huge meteor blazing through the sky cut their conversation short. They gazed with wonder as the orange, tailed ball of fire ripped through the moonlit night. They followed it from left to right and watched as it exploded with a boom and a flash, and then flickered out. In that moment of extravagant light, Gregory saw something out of the corner of his eye, something big, shiny and black, and looking out of place on the beach.

He shook off a shiver of fear as he looked at Warren and pointed to his right. "Did you see something down there a ways?"

"Yes. A ship, perhaps?"

"I don't think it was a ship," he said. "But if it is, I saw no crew."

Gregory saw Warren's eyes light up. He pulled his sword, Fionnaghal, and they raced down the beach. They wheeled their horses to a halt, and with mouths agape, beheld the sight in front of them—whales. Three beached sperm whales had languished on the sand, their toothy mouths gaping with the horror of death.

Warren lit a torch and he and Gregory, exchanging looks of amazement, walked up on top of one of the great creatures.

Gregory knelt down and ran a hand across its smooth skin. "This whale is big enough to have been the one that swallowed Jonah."

He had seen drawings and paintings of whales, and as a child, when he and his family had sailed from Bordeaux to London, he had seen their humps cresting in the Bay of Biscay. But until now, he had never seen them beached. In his unbridled imaginings he had never envisioned something so large, and even in death, of such crude beauty. Nearly four rods in length and black, with epic square heads, teeth the size of a man's hand, and sweeping tails of sheer muscle.

Though the whale he stood on was lifeless, Gregory felt in him the roiling of the sea. How long had it taken to grow so large? How deep did he dive and how far did he swim? Perhaps this whale lived longer and traveled farther than any man in the world. If true, then it was a tragedy it and the others had washed up on this lonely stretch of Yorkshire coast. But Gregory also knew the ways of men, and soon, whatever lord or village claimed this piece of shore would arrive and these whales, majestic when they lived as lords of the deep, would be butchered for oil and meat.

Gregory knew they could have kept on riding. They could have carved out a hunk of flesh, plucked out a souvenir tooth, and been on their way. They could have even taken the tails because they brought good money on the black market in York. But these huge fish promised enormous happenings, and as their finder, Gregory was keen to see what would happen to them.

He asked Warren if they should stay, and the boy enthusiastically agreed that they should.

So it was without misgivings that they roused from their sleep the next morning, curled up next to a dune, and found themselves surrounded by a gang of nervous villagers. Armed with hooks and spears and scaly sea blades, they backed away as Gregory and Warren rose to their feet and dusted sand from their cloaks.

"There is no need for weapons, lads." Gregory held out a hand of caution. "We are not here to take anything from you. Quite the contrary. As you see, we offer you whales."

"From whence did you come?" asked a fisherman with a curling mustache.

"I rode from Durham, where I prayed to St. Cuthbert and asked him for plenty. I arrived last night, when the moon was full and when fire fell through the sky, and behold, a school of fish so big you could never have caught them in your net."

The fisherman looked at the beached giants and then warily back at Gregory. His face puckered with warning, his mustache bristled and he held out his knife. "If this is magic, you man of Durham, you will be gutted and hanged."

Many in the growing crowd behind him nodded with concurrence.

"It is not magic," Gregory said. "It is food to feed your belly, oil to light your home, and bone to carve during those long winter nights when you are drunk and bored and your wife has kicked you out of bed. You need these whales, so don't bother trifling with me."

The fisherman thought about it for a while and sheathed his knife. The others followed his example and the tension eased. Under the splendid spray of a plum dawn, the beach grew loud with shouts and commands and went busy with the fetching of equipment and tools.

At the center of the commotion was the fisherman, standing on top of the biggest of the whales, pointing here and there and fielding all manner of questions. He spoke with authority, and when he asked someone to do something, they did it in silent obedience.

He worked the villagers in steady teams. One peeled back great slabs of pink blubber using hooks and cutting spades, while another piled the hunks of flesh into wagons drawn by stout shire horses. Old ladies gathered the entrails into buckets. Grim men with freshly sharpened blades crawled into the carcass and sliced out thick cuts of meat while others chiseled out teeth from the whale's gaping maw. By midday, the first whale was nothing more than a stain of oil and blood.

Gregory and Warren, sitting on a dune, watched the villagers do their work. While the butchering impressed them, they kept waiting for the villagers to start bickering over who got what and why. But it never happened because their leader, the fisherman, was not just a fisherman.

He was the lord of the manor.

It became clear when he walked back up the spine of the largest remaining whale and planted his green and black banner in its blowhole. Snapping and whipping in the gusting coastal wind, the banner announced those whales belonged to the lord, and if need be, he would kill to keep them. A page handed him his belt and sword, and he girded himself for war.

Gregory and Warren bolted up from their comfortable spots on the dune and looked in the same direction as everyone else. Riders—and many of them—came from the north.

Gregory squinted into the distance, looking at the faces to see if he recognized anyone, particularly Lord Baldwin of Essex. Relieved he was not among them, the sight still troubled Gregory. The men galloping down the beach did not come in peace. They wore armor and carried weapons, and their faces were bent with scowls.

The pair climbed onto their horses as the women and children cowered behind a whale. A plucky band of men and teens stood out in front of them and made a dour show of their spades and long curling knives. The lord jumped down from the whale and took his place in front of his men. The riders reined in their horses and stopped at a safe distance. The lord's banner snapped in the wind and the ocean roared, but no one uttered a word as the two sides considered their chances. At long last the lord spoke, and he did so with a devilish grin. "'Tis a good day to butcher whales, Lord Boulby. I assume you are here to learn a thing or two about cleaning fish."

"Yes, Lord Whitby." The other lord's voice held equal sarcasm. "I canceled my morning boar hunt to be here to watch you work."

"You are welcome to watch, just as long as you remember these are my fish." He wagged his index finger for emphasis.

"Are they?" said Boulby. "This morning I was told they had been moved. I told the messenger it couldn't be, that by God there was no way you would do such a thing. But he insisted, so I decided I should come and see for myself."

Whitby laughed. "Do you see that post?" He pointed to a thick marker protruding from a dune. "And do you see that post?" He pointed to another out in the surf. "Anything behind those posts is mine, and anything on the other side is yours."

Whitby gestured to two of his men, and shortly thereafter they stretched a rope from one post to the next, creating a taut line showing the whales lay close to Boulby's estate, but clearly in Whitby's.

Whitby crossed his arms over his chest and smiled beneath his bushy mustache. "I have a charter from the king giving me the rights to royal fish and shipwrecks that wash up on my shores. These whales are mine. They could just as easily have been yours, because you also have a charter, but on this day they are mine."

Boulby shook his head. "I'm afraid I cannot agree. The person who told me the whales had been moved is a man of utmost integrity. And if he says it is so, then it is so."

Gregory could stay put no longer. Sitting tall and stern in the saddle, he trotted Black Saddle out into the open ground between the two camps. Warren followed him. Both sides looked on with surprise, and some even with awe, at the two strangers and their magnificent mounts.

And Gregory didn't mind being the spectacle.

He knew his black cloak billowed in the wind, the brim of his beaver skin hat threw a shadow over his eyes, and the loyal man beside him was a brave and capable bull. Let them look and gawk and let them think what they will. This was a day to remember, so there is no time for hiding.

He looked down at Lord Whitby and gave a respectful nod, and then turned to Lord Boulby with a frown of contempt. "I tried not to interrupt, but you mentioned something—twice—I wish to rebut."

Boulby cocked his head, raised a suspicious brow, rolled his eyes, and pursed his lips as if he had tasted something bitter. He held that contorted expression for some time, and Gregory guessed that over the years that face, filled with danger and displeasure, had made many a man back down.

But Gregory did not yield.

In his heart hung the lonesome resolve he'd acquired in Swinton's tower, and with a gnash of his teeth, he told Lord Boulby it would take more than his timeworn glare to drive him off the beach this day. In response, Lord Boulby put his hand on the hilt of his sword. "Who in damnation are you?"

"I am Gregory of Bordeaux."

"And what is it you wish to refute?"

"You said someone told you the whales had been moved, and I know that to be a lie," he said. "I am the one who found the whales, and as they sat last night, so they sat this morning when Lord Whitby discovered them."

"Do you call me a liar? For in this part of the realm, a man will die for such a thing."

"No," he said, in a calm and cutting tone. "You have not lied, but your messenger has. Let him come forward now and repeat the claim he made to you this morning. Perhaps then we will get to the bottom of things."

Boulby grimaced and exhaled with a long, angry sigh. He turned to his men for support, but they hung their heads so none could be found. He turned back to Gregory, and in a high voice of frustration, yelled, "Who are you, and why are you here?"

"As I told you earlier, I am Gregory of Bordeaux, and I am here because it is better to butcher whales than it is to butcher men."

"No." Boulby shook his head vehemently. "It is not always true."

Gregory turned to Whitby. "Surely there is a compromise to be made?"

"No. What is mine is mine. Leave this business to us, stranger. You do not know me, and you do not know him. Go on about your way, and soon, or you will find out how cruel all of us can be."

Crestfallen, Gregory looked to Warren.

"As you said in Scotland, Master Gregory, this is not our fight. We are on our way to York. Let's continue on our way."

"Then that is what we shall do."

He looked all around and into many faces to show his chagrin, but his disappointment drew nothing but vacant stares. He and Warren slapped the reins and said, "Yah," to their steeds. Moonbeam and Black Saddle broke from the confrontation and went clean and free down the glistening beach. Over the sound of rumbling hooves, Gregory heard the distant ring of clashing steel and the baleful screams of slaughter, but he did not look over his shoulder.

They rode into Malton just before the gates closed. They took a room at the inn and had a meal of bread, cheese, and pickled pork tongue. Tired as he was, Gregory could not stay away from his chronicle. Driven by the need to replace what Swinton had taken from him, he remained hunched over a piece of parchment long after Warren dozed off to sleep.

Even if the truth is the size of a whale, people will ignore it in the face of self-interest. They want it all, despite knowing if they share their meal, there will still be plenty to eat. When the whale is on the beach and his meat is there for the taking, men would be smart to haggle for a mutual deal. Alas, if the whale has any wisdom to impart, he gives it not to us but to the sea.

A PEACOCK FEATHER IN YORK

Gregory and Warren rode into York through the crenelated barbican at Walmgate Bar. Tired, hungry, and on winded horses, they made haste to the stables. Leaving their mounts in stalls with fresh hay and oats, they went to an inn for bread, fish, and a cup of York's famous ale. As the sun dipped below the western wall, and as the curfew bells rang, they arrived at the Vintner's hall. Gregory introduced himself, explained his London affinity, and was lodged in a loft in a whitewashed timber warehouse on the River Ouse.

Rubbing his eyes and looking out from the warehouse window the next morning, Gregory saw a river choked with single-masted cogs, burly men unloading cargo, and merchants—vigilant from their outposts along the wharves—hawking over their accounts. Tall timber dwellings with slate roofs lined the river on both banks, and the odor of industry thickened the air. Porters scurried about, a mercer argued with a ship's captain, and a horse bucked and brayed as a groom walked it down a plank. Men sang as they worked the holds, and the wharves creaked under the heavy load of commerce.

More cogs arrived as others pulled out, making the river a congested jumble of sterns, prows, and colorful canvas sails. Finally. A real city. This was not London and this was not the Thames, but it was the closest he had seen in over two years. The sight enlivened him.

He looked at Warren, smiled and said, "If Lincoln and Durham dazzled you, I can only guess what you are thinking now."

"There are so many ships." The boy shrugged his shoulders. "Where did they come from?"

"From everywhere. This is York, and she is old and she is proud. Men will fight to earn their spot down on that wharf, and once they are there, they will kill to keep it. When we go to the market, you will see things you have never seen before, and of a quality beyond your expectations. For all your good work, I will buy you something special."

"I should appreciate such a gift. So have you ever been to York?"

"No, but in my wine business, I have met plenty of people who have."

"Now that you are here, how does it compare to London?"

"I have not seen everything yet, but if London is an adult, York is yet a child." He gave a grin and winked.

"Do I hear a bit of self-importance in your assessment?"

Gregory laughed. "You are getting to know me all too well."

They headed into the city on foot. Over a splendid stone bridge they went, down Ousegate to the market for fried pork and dried cherries, and then up Petergate to the great cathedral, York Minster. Still under construction and girdled with timber scaffolding down the length of its grand nave, the cathedral pulsed as the epicenter of an effort so vast and ambitious, Gregory and Warren had to stop and marvel.

Masons high in the scaffolding set beautifully hewn pieces of stone with lime mortar. Artisans chiseled, brutes cut, and a wheel-powered crane hoisted, while the architect pointed here and there at the subordinates scurrying at his command. Promising piles of rough and finished stone, massive beams of heartwood, a web of ropes and pulleys and levers and the horses to make them work—a cloud of dust hung over this scene of precision and toil, and the tap of mallets provided the din. The abundance of thatched hovels, the foundry, the kiln, and the smithy proved the old age of York's commitment. Entire lives had come and gone with the cathedral at its center, and many more would come and go before its consecration. Men and women, worries and wages, elation and despair—a cathedral could have its way with the human soul.

"Come here, lad," Gregory said, speaking to a scrawny kid lugging an adze over his shoulder. Gregory dug into his pouch, pulled out two farthings, and handed them to the boy. "Who is the builder?"

The boy tucked the farthings away. "William, William of Bruges."

"Good enough, lad, now be on your way. Do not tell anyone where you got your coins, and do not spend them in the wrong place."

"So will William of Bruges be mentioned in your chronicle?" Warren asked.

"Of course, but look at all the people who are here, and think of all the ones who came before them and the ones who will come after. Their names might never be known, but it is their blood and their bone that have given life to this heap of stone."

"You are the writer, so you can say what you want," Warren said.

"And I will," Gregory agreed. "I will say William of Bruges had a lot of help and without the anonymous men and women who gave their lives to this endeavor, William would have never had his fame."

They left the cathedral. On their way back into the guts of the city, they stopped at St. Leonard's Hospital, where Gregory donated six pence for the care of the sick and the poor. With no pressing matters at hand and enjoying idle time after a week on the road, they whiled away the day in what proved to be a city heaving with energy.

York prepared for the rumored arrival of King Edward and his army. People and their goods poured in through the city's network of fortified gates. Herds of cows and pigs, all of them destined to be slaughtered and salted for the king's men, clogged the streets as fowl squawked and sagging wagons pulled by oxen and mules wheeled through the narrow lanes. Craftsmen of all kinds crouched over their workbenches, toiling with an urgency only the king's command could bestow. Along with the stench of tanning and the smoke of the forge rose the succulent scent of baking bread and the tenor of ten thousand voices.

Along Mickelgate, men shoveled manure into carts as residents adorned their doors and windowsills with garlands of leaves and wildflowers, creating a dense, festive patchwork of vibrant greens, reds, and heather. An important dignitary representing Guy of Dampierre, the Count of Flanders, arrived on the morrow, and when he did, he would parade down Mickelgate not only with his entourage, but with the Archbishop of York, the mayor, and the town council.

York flexed every sinew of its muscle in preparation for the arrival of the count's emissary, and ultimately, for the arrival of the king. Gregory didn't discount the real air of excitement, but he also sensed a competing emotion, one of dread.

To entertain the king was the greatest of all honors, but he did not visit York for pleasantries. War brewed in Scotland, and the only way King Edward could win the war was if York gave him what he needed. The king came to make sure York supported his side. The only way the city could prove as much was if it gave him enough food, silver, and weaponry to invade north of the border and succeed. York would explode with joy and give its all. Then it would be left with crumbs and empty barrels as the king and his army moved on.

Gregory didn't want to be there by the time the king arrived, for if he was, Moonbeam and Black Saddle would surely be purloined into the royal train. Warren and he did not walk into York, nor would they walk out of it.

Arriving back at the warehouse where they lodged, Gregory was surprised to find a small crowd gathered there. Merchants—he knew by their dress—but as to why they congregated he had not a clue.

As he and Warren approached, one of them looked at him and said, "Are you Gregory of Bordeaux?"

Gregory stopped, glanced at Warren with puzzlement and then looked back at the merchant. "Yes. But I must say I am a stranger in this town so I wonder how you know my name."

"You arrived yesterday evening, did you not?"

"Yes, after a hard ride from Durham."

The gaggle of merchants started to laugh, and one of them said, "Then it *is* him."

"Indeed, it is," said another. "Master Gregory, on behalf of the Honorable and Blessed Guild of Merchants, welcome to York. We have heard of your adventures, and we are honored to have you here."

"You... have heard of me?"

The merchants shook with more laughter.

"I hear you gallop across the realm on a horse as fast as the great north wind," a mercer said.

"They say that your young page is as strong as Goliath and just as mean," a spicer added.

"I understand you told both Lord Tutbury and Lord Newark to eat shit pies," a draper said. "Good show, my boy."

"And who can forget? The man who sacked Skipton was executed at your word," a cordwainer said.

"Best of all, they say you tricked Baldwin of Essex into a race you knew he couldn't win, and you disappeared in the night with his horse and a sack full of loot," a vintner said.

"What about Scotland?" one of them called. "He pissed on a chieftain's boot and lived to tell the tale."

"You fine men have heard many things," Gregory said, "but pray tell— from whom did you hear them?"

"Come now, Master Gregory," one of them said. "We are human beings. We are flawed and greedy and above all, busy learning what others are doing, especially when they are merchants like us. For two years now, news has been arriving in York of your exploits. He is not a nobleman and he is not a priest and he is not an outlaw, they would say, but a vintner from London known as Gregory of Bordeaux. They also say he is a lawyer and he is writing a chronicle for the Earl of Southampton, but he is no mere observer of events. He is as cunning as a fox, as lucky as a fool, speaks with a silver tongue, and holds the baubles of life and death in the palm of his hand. We heard of your arrival this morning, Master Gregory, and have waited here all day."

Gregory and Warren exchanged a long look of raised eyebrows, eventually smiling and nodding their heads.

He gave them a clever grin. "If you know all those things, I presume you know I like almonds, liver paste and white bread, a hunk of hard cheese, a dripping piece of peppered beef, ginger loaf, stewed pears, and a brimming cup of Malbec from Cahors. And that my man, Warren of Lichfield, likes the same."

"Oh, we have heard of your appetite," the mercer said. "And for you, Master Gregory, we have it all in abundance."

They arrived early for a good view. Jostling with strangers, they managed to position themselves in front so when the procession came, it would pass within inches of their feet. A staccato burst of trumpet calls blared from Mickelgate, and a flock of homing pigeons fluttered into the sky. The murmuring of the expectant crowd grew into a boisterous impatience. The biggest bell at Holy Trinity gonged, but its ringing was soon overmatched by the minster's splendid tremor and peal. Like all the others, Gregory and Warren craned their necks for a glimpse of the parade, and soon it appeared from around a crook in the road.

The mayor and the city council—a few of whom Gregory recognized from the feast the night before—and parish priests and noblemen led the way. Accoutered in their finest cloth and jewels, the locals seemed a drab stain compared to what came behind them.

The Count of Flanders's men, on their ambling, snorting black Percherons, clipped and clopped down Mickelgate with haughty assurance, looking grim from beneath the raised visors of their ostrich-plumed helms. Clad in shining mail from head to toe, and with the Count's lion emblazoned on their canvas surcoats, these were knights of the old line, the ones who dared to cross swords with the King of France, the great-grandsons of the lords who had ruled in the Levant. Their glamour took hold and the crowd erupted with euphoria as leaves and petals showered down upon them. Riding in their center was the emissary, Christian of Champagne, a thin, dour cleric in black vestments who did not acknowledge the throng.

The Archbishop of York, seated in an ornate litter surrounded by his deacons, brought up the rear. For just a moment, he leaned his head out and waved to the crowd. A thick ruby ring sparkled in the Yorkshire sun, as did the pearl, sapphires, and gold leaf lining his miter.

As quickly as they had come, they had gone, and the onlookers, enthused by what they'd seen, mingled in a street soiled with Flemish horse droppings.

"If I am correct, the archbishop is the highest rank you have ever seen," Gregory said.

"I am still half blind from the many jewels," Warren replied. "Those knights and their horses and the archbishop—I swear, Master Gregory, he looked into my eyes and smiled!"

"Good," Gregory said. "I am glad you appreciated what you saw. But I want you to remember a couple of things."

"And what is that?"

"Your horse, Moonbeam, is faster than those Flemish steeds. And the archbishop—his name is John le Romeyn—was bastard-born and worked his way up from rather humble beginnings."

"So why do I need to know these things?"

"Because, if you ever think you are far away, perhaps you really are not."

"Do not put foolish thoughts into my head."

"I assure you, my friend, those thoughts are not foolish."

regory and Warren agreed they would stay in York through Shrovetide and leave shortly after the start of Lent. The reception had been too warm and there was too much to gain from York

to leave before it was time. Gregory arranged for Warren to work with the Vintner's Guild down on the wharves, where Gregory hoped he would develop a taste for commerce and the art of making money. Warren had done his duty under the tutelage of a warlord, now it was time to know the taxes, coins, and dickering of commerce.

Gregory, meanwhile, saw in York an important opportunity for his chronicle, as the city's limbs sagged with heavy fruit. For a week, he visited city court. A nobleman fined for killing another man's cow. A widow stripped of her lands. Two ploughmen put in the stocks for beating a monk. A fishmonger declared an outlaw for not appearing on a charge of arson. A baker fined for selling substandard bread. A merchant penalized three ells of wool for fornicating with a nun. And a horse thief sentenced to the gallows at St. Mary's. All of it he had heard before, but he enjoyed being back in court, listening to the arguments of the parties and the pronouncements of law. Each evening he ate with Warren and a few of the merchants at one hall or another. Whether a day of meat or of fish, the food and company delighted him.

Just as he grew complacent with the easy charms of York, word came of stories to be written. He wanted to record all of them, and to talk with all the people who would inhabit those stories, but he knew he could not stay in York forever. Decisions had to be made. He had already seen the city, and had felt York's beating heart when the Count's knights strutted down Mickelgate. He would feel it again during the carnival of Shrovetide, which, he was assured, would be a raucous affair. Reasoning he had the fastest horse in the realm, a few coins in his pouch, salted meat and dried fruit in his pack, and sheaths of parchment and a horn of ink, he decided to take a small tour of the Yorkshire countryside. The names and faces out there, he thought, would not appear in any other chronicle, so he was anxious to put them in his.

Warren was disappointed he was not going, but Gregory told him he needed to make this trip alone, and countered that besides, Warren had much to learn from the merchants. Gregory didn't exactly know why he wanted to go by himself, but he had an image of him and Black Saddle racing across the countryside with fluttering coveys and awed country folk in their wake. And it was with that vision in mind that he climbed up on Black Saddle one dawn, made the sign of the cross, ambled out of the stables, and galloped through the fortified arch at Bootham Bar.

He headed to Thirsk, where, he heard, a ploughman had discovered a hoard of Roman treasure while draining a marsh. The pile of gold and silver coins, jewelry, and tableware had been turned over to Lord Mowbray, who would melt it all down into ingots. Gregory had seen a Roman coin here and there, but never a hoard, so he yearned to see the ancient history before it disappeared into Mowbray's glowing furnace.

With a crisp and clear January day unfolding around him, he asked Black Saddle to give everything he had. The steed responded with a relentless canter through the peaceful emerald vale, and by the time the parish bells rang at None, Gregory and Black Saddle clopped through the market at Thirsk. Gregory gained entry to Mowbray's moated manor by means of a deep bow, words of deference and flattery, and a flash of his letter from the Earl of Southampton.

He sat near the fireplace in the dimly lit hall while monks, working at a great oaken table, dipped each piece of treasure in a urine solution, scrubbed it with a little horse hair brush, and recorded it on a long scroll of calf skin. Coins struck at the imperial mints of Rome and Ravenna, Milan and Trier, and Constantinople. Struck during the reigns of Constantine, Valentinian, and Honorius. Buried for reasons no one would ever know, found by a man who could not write his own name, and melted into oblivion by an old lord who answered to but a few men. Gregory's eyes gleamed when the monks pulled an exquisite gilded spice dispenser from the pile. He watched with wonder as a monk buffed a mesmerizing shine out of the vessel, carved into the shape of a powerful ram.

"Scribe, do you like it?" Lord Mowbray said. "It's a pepper pot."

"Indeed. And oh, how I love pepper."

"Well, would you like to have it?" He gestured toward the piece.

"I'd love to have it, Lord Mowbray, but to my detriment, I'm afraid I cannot accept your offer."

"And why not?"

"Because, if I did then I'd owe you something."

The monks stopped working, breathed a collective gasp, and exchanged wary glances. Lord Mowbray shook with a big belly laugh. "You are a wise man, Gregory of Bordeaux."

And he laughed again.

At seventy-nine, the man known as Boroughbridge was reputedly the oldest person in Yorkshire, and some said even in the realm. A scowling man with an iron will in his prime, he had settled into life as a doddering fool who tended his rose garden, kept bees, and sat for long hours in the shade of a billowing oak. Gregory's associates in York said Boroughbridge, common born to a ploughman and an alewife, had traveled the world. Indeed, he had a scar on his left shoulder where he had been shot with a Mongol arrow during a long ago battle at the edge of Christendom.

Boroughbridge lived near an apple orchard in a handsome farmhouse with a steep thatched roof and stone wainscot, a hearth that never grew cold, and a larder that never went bare. A spotted dog always barked but never did bite. The barn swallows returned each spring and trout leapt in the green pool at the weir. Gregory's friends in York said this old man Boroughbridge, his head bald and his beard bushy, was the grandfather of life. He may be old now, but for most of his life he had been young. Vital. A master of horse and sword with a dove on one shoulder and a crow on the other, the men plied him with song and ale, and the women, noble or not, curtsied and swooned. Merchants in York told Gregory they believed his brood numbered thirty.

He had been born so long ago he had forgotten his birth name, and those who might know it already lay beneath the clovers. So everyone called him Boroughbridge, after the town in which he was born and now lived. Go see him soon, Gregory, his friends said, for the angels remember his real name, and they will be calling it soon. And that's why Gregory found himself heading south out of Thirsk, Black Saddle galloping at the full, on the road to Boroughbridge.

Gregory pleaded with the town burgess to allow him a visit, but the burgess adamantly refused. Boroughbridge was too old and senile, he did not like strangers, and he had been sick of late. But his protestations ceased when Gregory pulled ten pennies from his pouch and presented his letter from Southampton. Soon enough he was in the presence of the venerable man—thin and grey and frail and stooped, hobbling with a cane, slow and trembling, but very much alive. With the help of a servant, he sat in a small chair lined with a bear skin and propped his feet on a cushioned stool. Gregory laid out his parchment and his ink horn, and before beginning, sharpened his quill.

"How did you do it? How have you come to be so old?"

After a long pause in which the winds of time swirled in his bloodshot eyes, Boroughbridge cracked a dirty little smile, scratched the back of his head, and said, "Faith in God, plenty of poached fish—and a succession of wives much younger than I."

He started to chuckle, and then to laugh, and then he fell into a fit of convulsive hilarity, which gave way to coughing and then choking. His face turned red and then blue, and Gregory expected him to fall off his chair and die.

But he recovered, and once the color of his face returned to normal, he smiled. "That's a good recipe, is it not?"

"It *is* a great recipe, my lord, the best I have heard in all my days," Gregory said sincerely.

For the remainder of the week Gregory stayed with Boroughbridge, and day after day he recorded all the details of an extraordinary life that had begun in a one-room hut and would end in this broad-boned country manor. In between was the world, a hungry world that devoured men, yet a maternal one that nurtured souls.

As Gregory was at the door and about to leave, he turned. "My lord, what is your real name?"

Boroughbridge sat there in silence and leaned back in his chair. He looked this way and that, and stared off into the hall's high rafters. For a moment a look of deep sadness creased his face, but then a smile of profound joy showed in his eyes.

"Andrew," he said, and his lip quivered. "Andrew of the fields—I am Andrew Fields!"

"Well, Andrew Fields." Gregory held up his thick roll of parchments. "You will live to be much older than seventy-nine."

Back through Bootham Bar and in York, Gregory stabled Black Saddle, stopped at an inn for a cup of wine, a hardboiled egg, and a hunk of cheese, and then made his way to the wharves. It was late in the day and the haze of twilight hung in the air, yet business along the waterfront bustled. In the hubbub of merchants and laborers, ships, cranes, and loading tackle, Gregory spotted Warren, standing at the foot of a plank leading up to a cog bearing the black and gold standard of Brabant. Warren didn't see him, and Gregory made no attempt to gain his attention. Instead he watched with a prideful smile as Warren, earnest and diligent, counted the barrels being offloaded by the porters. Just as in Scotland, where Warren had blended in with Swinton's raiders, here in York Warren seemed right at place as a merchant's apprentice. It had only been a fortnight, but in that short span it appeared as if Warren had at least embraced the idea of trade. It would take years to gain the experience and toughness needed to deal profitably at the town market and with such hard dealers as the Dutch and the Genoese, but with talent and drive, he also knew, great things were achievable.

"Warren, my boy," he called, once the ship had been unloaded.

Warren turned, waved, smiled, and walked his way. He pulled Gregory into a bear hug. "You are finally back, Master Gregory. Please tell me of your adventure."

"An old man and a pot of Roman treasure. Both of them great stories. But I'm afraid I have bad news for you."

"What?"

"It is Black Saddle."

Warren's face grew grave and he said, "What has happened to him?"

"I worked him hard through the vale."

"And?"

"He is truly a prince of steeds." He kept his tone friendly, cheerful, yet challenging. "And one day, one day soon, he shall end the days of Moonbeam's ascendency."

"We will see, Master Gregory." Warren clapped him over the shoulder. "Let us eat and drink. I want to tell you of what I have learned."

"I would love nothing more."

York relished the arrival of Shrovetide, the three days before the grueling penance of Lent. The six weeks leading up to Easter were a time of fasting and self-denial—no fat, no butter, no cheese, no fowl, no eggs, no beef, and for Gregory, the worst prohibition of all, no pork. Nothing but fish and vegetables for forty days, and wine and ale only in moderation—enough to make people irritable, enough to make them grumble and complain and cheat and squabble and lie, even as they prepared for the solemn celebration of the death and resurrection of Christ.

Indeed, Shrovetide was a time to confess one's sins before the holy rigors of Lent. But it was also a time to eat and drink and openly court gluttony without excuse or qualm. The largest of feasts before the longest of fasts, a session of frivolity that reached its boisterous high on Shrove Tuesday, only to give way to the hushed piety of Ash Wednesday and the forty following days. Gregory had been through plenty of Shrovetides, and like Warren, anticipated what York had in store.

As with everything they had seen and done since their arrival,

Shrovetide did not disappoint. And Gregory decided one of the events would be included in his chronicle. Dozens of boys from the north side competed with dozens of boys from the south side to see who could carry a water-filled cow's bladder through Walmgate Bar. A giant scrum surging back and forth through the city streets ended when a teen, bruised and bleeding yet smiling in triumph, made his way to the top of Walmgate with the bladder tucked under his arm.

More to Gregory's liking were the mystery plays, presented on a procession of wagons, one after the next, and stopping at different stations throughout the city. Gregory and Warren found a good spot on Mickelgate near the bridge at River Ouse and stayed there all day. Gregory employed a boy to run back and forth from a wine stall nearby so whenever their cups went dry, he refilled them with a bright and pleasing Spanish red.

Gregory loved these plays because they told the story of the Bible, but did so with the humor of the common man, not the somber dread of the church. As guildsmen and amateurs performed the plays, Gregory and Warren, and many in the crowd, winced in response to a forgotten line or cringed when an attempt at drama proved comedic. But the plays entertained, and the two of them cheered and laughed and chided, and clapped and sang, along with everyone else.

Gregory drank a cup of wine and then another and another, and swam in the sunny sea of delight as the plays came and went—Creation, Adam and Eve, Noah's Ark, the Red Sea, and Annunciation. The crowd whooped with gusto at the conclusion of the Adoration of the Magi. Herod, an obese huckster outwitted by the wise men, rose to his feet, put his hands on his hips, stuck out his butt, and said, "I sit in Jerusalem jawing on a jar of jelly, while in Bethlehem, brothers bound toward freedom." In the Last Supper, Judas Iscariot, dressed in black with his face painted red, proclaimed in the voice of a coward, "Satan took my soul and gave me silver in return, the Apostles ate the bread that to me tasted bitter."

People laughed as the wagon bearing Doubting Thomas approached. Throughout the play, Thomas, dressed in the silks of an eastern potentate and with a frown drawn on his face, reclined on a luxurious throw of feathered pillows as the other Apostles marveled at Christ's resurrection. After Christ had showed him His wounds, Thomas turned to the crowd and said, "I should rather stick my finger up my nose to the knuckle. Weighing the weeping wounds of Jesus is woe to me." And so it went, with the Ascension and the Descent, and then the Death of Mary.

And that's when Gregory paid extra attention.

The troupe enacting Mary's death was professional, and they rendered the scene in which the apostles gathered at her side with such flair and passion that Gregory, along with many in the crowd, felt a lump in his throat and a tear at his eye. He also experienced the unmistakable heat and jitters of desire. One of the angels, her auburn tresses platted with wildflowers, was the most beautiful woman he had ever seen. When she uttered the words, "Oh, Mary, your halo in heaven is high and hallowed," it was to Gregory a song more sweet and melodious than that of the nightingales. So smitten was he that he left Warren to his own devices and followed the troupe as it went from station to station.

Not wanting to be obvious and shy of his emotions, he stood in the middle of the crowd, not at its front. Still, he kept his eyes on the angel and at the conclusion of each performance, applauded with sincerity. The troupe's tour through the city ended at the market, where they delivered the best rendition to the largest crowd. And then the troupe, its work done for the day, bid farewell to the audience and went to an inn on Stonegate.

Gregory didn't know if he did the right thing, and he felt ashamed of himself, but with the voice of wine murmuring in his head, he followed. Once inside the crowded inn, he saw the members of the troupe, all eight of them, sitting at a candlelit table drinking wine. She must have known he followed, because she caught his eye as he walked through the door. She raised her cup and beckoned him with a smile, and he approached the table. He doffed his beaver skin hat, kicked out his heel, bowed low, and gestured with a graceful, downward sweeping of his arm.

"My lady."

She put her hand over her heart and batted her eye lashes. A blush appeared in her cheeks as her fellow thespians cheered Gregory's gallant arrival.

"And who is this man who flatters me with a courtesy fit for a queen?"

"I am Gregory of Bordeaux," he replied, "and the world is dark compared to the light shining in your eyes. If it pleases you, may I know your name?"

"Alice," she said. "And if it pleases you, will you entertain me on this last day of Shrovetide?"

"Indeed."

He held out his hand and she took it in her satin grasp, and off they went, from tavern to tavern and feast to feast, ebbing and flowing on the currents of wine, skipping and twirling to the sound of pipes and lutes, meandering through the twisting narrow streets, moving with the cadence of a polished poem, and wading deep into the pool of pleasant surprise. A blazing amber dusk spilled through the sky, and with the night came an enchanting front of snow. Wrapped in the thick woolen folds of Gregory's black cloak, they found a lust so vigorous and mutual, they could stay in public no longer.

"I keep a loft down at the wharf," he whispered, and slid his hand into her gown.

"Take me there, Gregory." She kissed his neck.

Gregory awoke the next morning to the dour bells of Ash Wednesday. And Alice was gone. He looked down at his pile of clothes and noticed sitting on top was the eye of a peacock feather—the feather Alice had worn in her braid the night before. He picked it up and marveled at it for a long while. A circus of shimmering blue and green with a bright halo of beige, the peacock feather was a work of art beyond the hands of men.

Gregory put on his undergarments, sat on the edge of the bed, and dug through his pack. He found the silver pendant, in the shape of a rose, he had bought at the market in Durham, and grabbed his beloved beaver skin hat. The fur came from the fjords of Norway, and its deep crown was lined with

red silk spun in the den of Kublai Khan. Finished by the finest hatters in
Flanders, Gregory knew when he flashed his eyes from beneath this brim,
people would know he was a man of means. Few people could afford to own
this hat, and fewer still would wear one. This was his sword and shield, his
statement to the world that he knew and believed in the law of the land. It
would be fitting if Alice's peacock feather embellished his hat, so he fastened
it to the left side with the silver rose. The adornment brought a sad smile to
his face. Alice told him last night was only last night and strange things happened during Shrovetide. She was leaving in the morning with her troupe
and headed to Nottingham for the Feast of the Annunciation. Perhaps they
would see each other again, in London, but if not, they would always have
the fond memory of York.

"You are a beautiful man," she had told him, "and I could gaze forever
into your brown eyes."

He smelled her on him, and the slow moan of her bliss lingered in his ears.

"Alice," he murmured, "when you are done with your wandering, and if
it pleases you, come to me."

t was time to leave. If Gregory ate fish for the next forty days, let
it be on the road, far from York and its many temptations. He
and Warren gathered their belongings and said their farewells.
They had met plenty of people in York, so the act of leaving was not short
and easy. The merchants gathered and met Gregory on the wharf, and while
some of them said Godspeed, others asked him to stay.

Their voices pulled at Gregory's heart. He had written legal documents
for them, witnessed contracts, settled a spat between two spicers, and regaled them with lyrical tales of his time on the road. The merchants had also
accepted Warren into their company and had furnished both of them with
food and lodging. Gregory was a Londoner, and as proud citizens of York,
they should have hated him. But that had not been the case. In York, Gregory

found the close and at times quarrelsome community of merchants to be the kind of community that shaped the man he had become. In them he saw the faces of his past and heard the distant voices of the people who had taught him his trade. On the waterfront at York, he had found his kin.

But the road called to him, and the thought of galloping south with Warren riding at his side was of the utmost appeal. The merchants knew well he would not stay, which is why they handed him a shoulder bag full of letters bound for their associates in Lincoln, Boston, Cambridge, and London. If he would be so kind as to deliver the messages, they assured him, he would be compensated on the back end. Gregory gave a wry smile but did not protest.

Before leaving, the merchants presented him with a gift—a long, double-bladed knife with a cross hilt and a pummel cap of silver. Gregory pulled it out of its handsome leather sheath and held it up to the sunlight—a fine blade with a French inscription, La Bonne Vie. He had to admit this was ten times his old blade, good for little more than sharpening his quills. Still, he kept a face of disinterest.

"What am I to do with such a thing?" He slid it back into its sheath.

"Guard your life with it," said a merchant, who looked at Gregory with a baleful eye.

"Please, Master Gregory," one of them said, "the roads are dangerous, as you know, and the guild would like to honor you with this humble gift. We would be offended if you did not accept it."

"Then consider it done," he said, and with a proper show of decorum, tucked it under his belt. "Now I am finished with these pleasantries. A pipe of Clairac to the first of you to visit me in London, and the best venison and frumenty in the realm. We will go to the tournament at Smithfield and frolic in Southwark. You will forget all about your precious York."

"You will have visitors sooner than you think," one of them said, and they all shared a laugh.

Gregory and Warren mounted and ambled their horses down Mickelgate and out of the city. Before York's skyline disappeared on the horizon, they turned for one last look. A yellowish pall of smoke shrouded the city but could not conceal the ambition of its many steeples and towers. A big bruising city of stone, York would soon be in the hands of the king. He would squeeze it and turn it and wring it and shake it and do his best to wrest every coin from its coffers and every curd from its cupboards. But one thing even the king could not have—York's pride. The city held it so close and in a fist clinched so tight, he could not pry it free. Of that, Gregory was certain.

He must have been beaming because Warren said to him, "I can see it in you, Master Gregory. York treated you well."

"Yes, and you, too."

"It did, but I must ask you. I know how you got your knife, but you have yet to tell me how you came to possess your peacock feather."

"Warren, my boy, there are many things about York of which I will tell, but the story behind this peacock feather will not be one of them," he said, and a delicious grin came to his face.

They rode south, finding hospitality at Conisbrough Castle. They remained there for a week. Each day Warren and the householders trained with lances at the quintain. Gregory had no interest in the tiltyard. Instead he stayed put, and behind the great hall, in a quiet little whitewashed cottage near the bake house and the brewery, he worked on his chronicle.

In a city as big and ancient as York, there are many places where which to drink a dram of virtue. I quenched my thirst and found joy at the bottom of the cup. Indeed, in York did I learn to smile again.

No Mind for Contrivances

our wine, rancid fish, and stale bread. No musician strummed on his lute and no logs crackled in the fireplace. The Bishop of Lincoln, a man known for his hospitality, also excelled at being rude. Gregory came to Lincoln to deliver letters to the merchants. But he also went there to pay a special thanks to the bishop, who had helped pay his ransom, and to discuss the circumstances of the death of his bastard son, Marcus of Burwell Priory. This would be a difficult conversation, for his testimony had sent Marcus to the gallows.

He wanted to say, "Your bastard son died like a bastard, and it is best he is gone," but he knew it wouldn't be so easy. Judging by the way the table was set, Gregory guessed it would be more arduous than he had imagined.

After making him wait for an hour, the bishop entered the hall. Gregory rose and made as if to bow, but the bishop waved him off. He took his seat, and moments later a servant brought out a bowl of steaming fish stew and placed it in front of the bishop.

He swallowed a spoonful, took a quaff of wine, and looked at Gregory with a phony expression of welcome. "What, Master Gregory, you are not hungry this evening?"

"I am starving, but not for rotten fish and moldy bread, and if I drank this wine, I would soon spew it back out. No, I will be content to watch you eat."

And watch he did as the bishop licked his fingers, smacked his lips, and worked his way through four courses, including peppered cod, saffron sturgeon, and a dessert of plum fritters dipped in honey. He picked a piece of fish from his teeth, dipped his hands in a bowl of water, and dried them off with a towel. Then he took a drink of wine so long and hard Gregory saw his Adam's apple move up and down. He slammed the cup on the table and motioned for the servant to pour more. Gregory knew this was the prelude to the drama about to unfold, so he braced himself, but for what he knew not.

"Gregory, as the Bishop of Lincoln, I receive many letters," he said. "I receive so many I cannot even read them all. But the important ones, like the one you wrote to me in Scotland asking for your ransom, never escape my attention. So imagine my surprise when a fortnight ago I received a letter from the Bishop of Edinburg. Do you have any idea as to why I would receive a letter from him, when in fact we have not had diplomatic relations in five years?"

Gregory cupped his forehead in the palm of his hand and sighed. "Lord Bishop, I apologize."

"He chided me for fathering Marcus of Burwell Priory, who, as you know, hanged in Lancaster for an assortment of heinous crimes. The bishop said he read in a chronicle, written by a man named Gregory of Bordeaux, that Marcus is believed to be my bastard son. Tell me, Gregory, did you write such a thing? And if so, why?"

Confronted with the questions, a gush of memories overcame Gregory. Swinton's tower, the rat, the frigid, haunted drafts, and the overflowing bucket of excrement in that lonely room where his sanity nearly died. He thought he would never come out of the tower. His life was not in his flesh and bones, but in the parchments and the quill. What people thought of him meant nothing, only that they would read and appreciate the stories he told. Gazing into the bishop's angry eyes, and growing nauseated with panic, he no longer felt that way. He wanted to erase what he'd written and start again, but he knew it was too late.

> *A bastard son is unpredictable, especially when he knows his father abandoned him. All his life he tries to prove himself worthy, driven by the hope he will one day find the love denied him at birth. In the quest to prove to the father that the fruit of his loins had not spoiled, a bastard can say and do spectacular things. Some succeed where others do not. One such son was Marcus of Burwell Priory. He fashioned himself a savior, but became a criminal and died on the gibbet. Thus was the folly of his pursuit. Marcus of Burwell never knew who his father was, but the Bishop of Lincoln most certainly did.*

"Yes, lord bishop, I wrote it." He shook his head in despair. "But I was held captive at the time and had no mind for contrivances."

"No mind for contrivances?"

"If I should have died in Swinton's tower, at least I would have told the truth. That I lived is no reason for a change of heart. Yet I apologize, for if you are being chided by the Bishop of Edinburg, then you will surely be chided by others."

"Gregory, I helped pay your ransom. You would have remained, and died, in Scotland without my silver. I counted on your discretion, but in hindsight, I shouldn't have."

"You told me your secret, lord bishop, but you did not ask me to keep it. You asked me to do the right thing."

"And was it right to soil my name?"

"Was it right of you to break the promise of your holy orders? Lord Bishop, you must have wanted this to get out. Why else would you have come to me, a friend, but a chronicler, as well? You tell your secret to a man who makes his living with ink and quill? You would have done better confessing to someone who was deaf, blind, and dumb."

"Gregory, when I first met you, you were a snot-nosed brat still hiding behind your mother. We all knew you were smart and you would make something of yourself, but now you are a wealthy merchant and lawyer, and you work for the Earl of Southampton. I wonder if you have become bloated on your achievements. There are so many things you could've written about Marcus, and I think your arrogance caused you to link his name to mine."

"Lord Bishop, I disagree. Your name is tied to his because you are his father, and if Marcus had turned out to be a great man, our present conversation, I believe, would be much different."

"You have caused me much embarrassment, Gregory, and if that is all that comes of this then you should be content we are no longer friends and that I should no longer care when your life is in danger. But if things go bad for me at Westminster—or in Rome—then I will do everything in my power to do to your reputation what you have done to mine. And believe me, if your quill is sharp, mine is sharper."

Gregory left the bishop's chambers shaken. It was one thing to make an enemy of a backwater nobleman like the new Lord Corby, but quite another to make an enemy of a friend who was the Bishop of Lincoln. If the chronicle were true, then it would live forever. But until now, Gregory hadn't thought much about the lives, including his own, that must be sacrificed for the truth. He wrote so many things while up in Swinton's tower. His time there was a blur of ink and burning candles, of crashing waves and calling gulls. He couldn't remember exactly what all he'd written.

How much of himself had he revealed? Alas, everything. And how much had he said about others?

Enough to get him killed.

He scurried through the streets back to the inn, from time to time taking a nervous look over his shoulder. He burst into the room where Warren sat at a table, crouched over a piece of parchment with a quill in his hand. He looked up with a grin, said, "Look, Master Gregory," and held up the parchment with his name, Warren of Lichfield, written on it dozens of times. Gregory had taught him the letters, and Warren wrote them over and over so he would know his name by rote.

At any other time Gregory would have congratulated him on reaching such an important milestone—the magic of a written name—and would have encouraged him to learn more. It hurt him to shrug off Warren's moment of triumph, look at him with a frown, and say, "Gather your things, for we are leaving right now." But say it he did, and Warren's crestfallen response wounded him.

"What is the—"

"There is no time for chatter, Warren! Do as I say and gather your things."

In haste they packed their bags. Just as they readied to head down the stairs to the first floor and out the front door, Gregory stopped and grabbed Warren by the elbow. For a long moment they stood there, at the top of the steps, motionless and silent. A dark and dreadful thought made his stomach turn, and his breath grew short as the cold, warty hand of fear clutched at his throat.

He gestured for quiet with an index finger to his lips and led Warren back into the room. He pointed to the window. Gregory shimmied through the sill, leapt to the ground, and Warren soon followed. They grabbed their belongings and walked toward the stables, acting as if they didn't have a care in the world. Before rounding a corner, Gregory glanced back in the direction from whence they had come. To his horror, he watched as a group of armed men barged into the inn. Then came a scream and the rumble and clatter of overturned tables and broken chairs.

He and Warren dashed to the stables, and to Gregory's disbelieving relief, there stood Black Saddle and Moonbeam, in their stalls and munching on oats. They had no time for tack and saddle, so they mounted their horses bareback. The steeds snorted and whinnied, and with the kick of hooves and the whisk of tails, Black Saddle and Moonbeam erupted from the stables. They banked through the market at Bailgate with such violence people dropped their things and scattered. Charging down the great High Street they went, with Gregory and Warren working their heels.

From Bailgate, Gregory heard someone yelling, *"The gates! The gates! Close the gates!"* Watchmen turned a huge gear, and with the yawn of timber and the rattling of chains, the towering oaken doors slowly started to close. The Bishop of Lincoln had sprung his trap, yet Gregory flashed a grim smile. Warren gave his command to Moonbeam—*yop-yop*—and Gregory hissed through his teeth to Black Saddle. The horses yearned anew, plying their talents in each aggressive stride, racing nose for nose to the gate. By the time it shut with a thud, they were a full twelve rods beyond the city wall and bounding down the road to Boston.

They rode until they could ride no longer. The horses had plenty left in them, but without saddles, Gregory and Warren grew raw from being jolted and jarred. They had turned off the main road long ago and followed a series of boar trails into a moonlit glen. And it was there they at last found rest for their aching bones. The spring night was warm, so they built no fire. As they made camp, the horses grazed on grass grown lush from a recent rain. Gregory felt a stab of pain, groaned, and put a hand on his hip as he sat on his outstretched cloak. He leaned back on his pack and looked into the sky. A dense belt of stars, twinkling in a smear of gold and blue, dipped into the night. A sense of peace arose in him as he gazed into the constellation. He clasped his hands over his stomach, closed his eyes, and fell asleep.

He awoke the next morning to the comforting scents of smoke and bacon. Wiping the sleep from his eyes, he noticed Warren squatting by the fire and turning the bacon on a makeshift spit.

"Good morning, Master Gregory."

"Is that bacon?"

"Yes, a big hunk of it."

"Where did you get it?"

"York."

"But it is still Lent, Warren. Bacon is forbidden."

"I know, but don't be so pious. This morning we will break our fast like lords, and if you do not tell anyone, I certainly will not."

Gregory thought about complaining, but the bacon got the better of his scruples. He and Warren devoured it, and when they finished, Warren pulled something from his pack and gave a big country grin.

"What is that?"

"It is cheese," the boy said, pulling it from a small linen bag.

"And where did you get it?"

"York."

"But it is Lent, Warren. Cheese is forbidden."

Warren shook his head and laughed as he pulled out his knife, shaved off the husk, and sliced the hunk into two equal pieces. They looked at one another with happy eyes as they made quick work of it. Gregory would ask for forgiveness later, but for now he enjoyed the sin.

Stiff and chafed from yesterday's ride, neither Gregory nor Warren had the fortitude to mount their steeds. They walked them through the glen and into the forest, and found a stream they followed east. They stopped at a waterfall, bathed in its cool waters, and sunned themselves on rocks until they dried, red and glowing with the sun. They made camp, built a fire, and cooked the trout Warren caught with a baited hook he'd made from a few links of his mail. They drank the last drops of wine from their skins and nurtured the fire as they talked. Warren asked Gregory about what happened in Lincoln, and Gregory told him of his meeting with the bishop. Gregory expressed to him his fears and rattled off the names of the enemies he'd made since leaving London—Tutbury, Stafford, le Gaunter, Corby, Swinton, Baldwin of Essex, and now the Bishop of Lincoln—and said there could be more as the chronicle came to light.

"A great man has great enemies," Warren said. "Isn't that what they say?"

"Yes, but I am not great. I am a merchant, and my enemies are much more powerful than I."

"That is true—for now. Master Gregory, they knew you in York before you had ever even been there. And by the time you arrived in Lincoln, the bishop had already heard tell of your chronicle. I know what is happening to you. You are achieving fame."

"Fame?"

"Yes. To me you are Master Gregory, but to the world you are Gregory of Bordeaux—a man who must be reckoned with."

A
PROMISE
IN BOSTON

oston wasn't much of a town. A protective ditch but no city wall, a few parish churches but no grand cathedral. Unlike York and Durham, Boston had no monuments or shrines or Roman ruins or a revered place in the annals of the realm. Just a jumble of shops and warehouses crowded around the port along the River Witham. A new town, it cared for only one thing, the wool trade. Situated near the North Sea, Boston had boomed to the point a representative of the Hansa, a powerful trade syndicate based in the imperial city of Lübeck, kept a residence there. Fortunes came and went each day, and as a Boston burgess, you pissed silver, shit gold, and shed tears of sapphire.

Gregory traveled here to see Geoffrey Wool and Lady Anne, the lovebirds from Lichfield. Anxious to see them because they had helped pay his ransom, Gregory needed to give thanks with a proper visit. In York he had also heard Anne had given birth to an heir and again grew heavy with child. Having attended their wedding, he wanted to see what the union had yielded.

After they stabled their horses and found lodging at an inn, Gregory sent word he was in town. Soon thereafter a messenger returned with an invite to come and stay at the Wool family's townhome overlooking the port.

Gregory responded to the invite with a smile, turned to Warren, and as he pulled a handful of coins from his pouch, said, "Take this and buy something nice to wear."

Warren looked a bit puzzled but took the money and headed to the market nonetheless. When he returned, he carried with him a green tunic, a blue mantle, a wool cap with a goose feather, and pointed leather shoes.

"Perfect, my boy," Gregory said once Warren had washed his face and had gotten up into his new gear. He looked just as Gregory had hoped—like a rugged dandy with a faint hue of intellect about him, like a man who could turn a phrase, a coin, or a sword.

"And what of you, Master Gregory?"

"Oh, I will go as I am." Which was to say he'd go in his black, travel-worn cloak and robe, his dusty Cordovan boots with the nub spurs still attached, and his beaver and peacock hat. He wanted Geoffrey to see in him the road, while in Warren he would see refinement.

Bearded, plump, and draped in wool and fur with accents of precious metal, Geoffrey walked out from behind a large table where his associates sat to his left and right and corralled Gregory with a hug before kissing him on both cheeks.

"Look at you—eagle-eyed and thin as a reed," Geoffrey said. "The road has been good to you, eh?"

"In places," he said. "And in others, not so much." He looked at Geoffrey's paunch and back into his eyes, then winked. "You appear to be growing into your role here in Boston."

"I have grown too much." He patted his belly. "But what can I say? My ships keep coming in."

"And God willing, may it always be the case."

"And who is this you have brought with you?"

"Take another look and you will not have to ask again."

So Geoffrey did, and a twinkle of curiosity showed in his eyes. "Is that—is that you, Warren?"

"Yes, Geoffrey." He gave a deferential bow.

"You are—"

"No longer a ploughman," he said, in a deep, courteous tone.

"I heard you had traveled with Master Gregory, but I wasn't sure of whatever became of you," he said, looking him up and down. "But now I know. You have become a man, and it is evident you have seen many things since leaving home."

"Yes, but there is much more, so I ride with Gregory still," Warren said.

Gregory stood to the side and said not a word, but inwardly he felt jubilant as the two embraced and fell into rapid conversation. Geoffrey Wool, the golden boy, and Warren, the ploughman, grown into the men they had hoped to be. One with chances given, the other with chances seized. Gregory remembered it all too well. When the fighting at Lichfield was at its thickest, Geoffrey and Warren had been side by side at the front of the line. And when it looked as if Lord Tutbury would have Geoffrey's life, Warren saved the day. The wedding took place the next morning, and Geoffrey had his beautiful bride and her dowry of ships and piers. Now blessed with an heir and perhaps a second for good measure, Geoffrey was on his way to becoming a merchant prince. The deciding factor had been Warren's courage and his trusty billhook.

Gregory watched closely to determine if the excitement of the reunion was mutual and genuine. He looked for a touch of pompousness in Geoffrey and a dash of subservience in Warren. Gregory detected neither. These two men of Lichfield were glad to see each other, and when their laughter echoed in the hall, all was well in Boston.

"This man—" Geoffrey pointed at Warren as he faced his associates "—saved my life when it seemed all was lost. He is a good man from my hometown, and I am proud to have him here with me today. Raise your cups in honor of my friend, Warren of Lichfield."

The burgesses, in their discreet and decorous way, raised their cups and drank. A servant approached and pushed a cup of wine into Gregory's hand. He took a long sip of a big, ripe Malbec from Cahors, one of the finest wines he had tasted in years. He raised his cup with the others in honor of Warren.

e watched them sail away. Geoffrey traveled to Bruges to consummate a deal with the burgesses there, and Warren went along as part of his entourage. They begged Gregory to go, and though sailing and the sea coursed in his blood, he told them no.

"I have been to Bruges many times," he had told them. "It would be best if you go and see it for yourselves. I will write and wait for your return."

The ship, its red and white sail filled with wind, glided over the placid river and out of view. If all went as planned, they would return in two months. But the sea never offered guarantees. Just because a boat left port did not mean it would return. Though the mariners knew the shipping lanes and channels, the sea always yielded sad stories. So with a solemn hand and a forced smile, he waved goodbye.

Yet Gregory was excited, too. Geoffrey went to powerful spice traders in Bruges, men who could connect him with the riches flowing out of the Mediterranean. With wise words and agreeable terms, Geoffrey would return to Boston with clout immeasurable. And though Warren would not participate in the negotiations, he was in Geoffrey's train, and that meant status. The things he would do and see along the canals of Bruges would change and enhance his life, and once he returned, he could look at someone and say, "I have been to Bruges and have seen the silver flow. I have heard the peal from the great belfry, a fine and splendid thing."

Much had been made of Gregory returning to London so he could hand over his writings to the monks who would make of it an illuminated manuscript, and indeed, that was the mission. But Gregory also had an eye for arriving home with a polished up-and-comer. In addition to everything else, he surmised Bruges would do the trick for Warren. The trip just had to go as planned. Gregory prayed for favorable winds, fruitful negotiations, and a safe return. He made the sign of the cross and said, "Amen."

As Gregory watched the ship pull out of port, he did not stand there as the upstart chronicler known as Gregory of Bordeaux. He had stashed his black cloak and beaver skin hat deep in one of Geoffrey's warehouses. Instead he wore the garb of a household servant—pointed shoes, a russet robe with a rough belt, and a red hooded mantle—and answered to a name he knew almost as well as his own, Jean du Mont. He would go hither, thither, and yon on foot and in silence. It was known in Boston that Gregory of Bordeaux and his stallion, Black Saddle, had boarded the ship sailing to Bruges with Geoffrey Wool. He would not return with Geoffrey as he had important business in Ghent, Paris, and Champagne. No one knew when he would return or what port he would arrive in when he did. If you had business with Gregory of Bordeaux, it would have to wait, because he had left the realm. Gregory chuckled to himself as he walked back to Geoffrey's townhouse. Sooner or later someone would poke a hole in the story of his departure, but when they did, he hoped it would be too late.

When he'd first arrived in Boston, Gregory had hoped to bask in the wit and beauty of Lady Anne. Fond of pomp and pageantry, in her festive hall Gregory could at least pretend for a time to be a courtier. But alas, she was back in Lichfield with Geoffrey's family for the birth of her second child, and Geoffrey had set sail to Bruges to seal his riches. Entertainment had given way to family and money, which Gregory well understood. Still, a household without its lord and lady was a dreary place, and for a day, Gregory cursed himself for having not sailed with the others. But his doldrums didn't last long. Before he left, Geoffrey had procured a stack of parchments and enough ink and quills to last Gregory for a deep spell of writing. He had a full hogshead of Malbec from Cahors, was lodged in the quaint guesthouse on the banks of the river, and had access to the kitchen, where a terse Burgundian cook roasted meats and stirred sauces. Lent was over so he could eat flesh again. Even though he was incognito and without his friends, Gregory had to admit life was not so bad.

Heartened by a morsel of fresh cod, a bite of pungent goat cheese, and a buttered apple pastry, Gregory headed down to the cavernous timber-and-thatch enclosure where Geoffrey and Lady Anne's largest ship was being built. An oaken cog at over four rods in length, it would hold one hundred fifty tons of cargo and would race from Boston to Spain on the calmest waters, or dip and rise through the fiercest Baltic swells. A single mast, a stern rudder, and raised castles at both ends, this was the ship that would one day deliver the Golden Fleece. Or so Geoffrey believed.

Gregory entered the enclosure, taking pains to be discreet so as not to disturb the men busy with their axes and adzes and hammers and saws. As he breathed in the comforting aroma of sawn oak and beech, a man glanced up at him with a frown. With a confident nod and a respectful wave, Gregory put him at ease and he returned to work. Gregory found a perch on a pile of scrap wood and surveyed the scene. Atop a framework of supports sat an elegant, bulging curve of beveled strakes sweeping up from the keel, stem to stern. Iron rivets and rove and caulking of horse hair and tar, a vertebrate of keelson, timbers and hammered wooden pegs, and a smooth golden hull of strength and balance. Unfinished, but already thirsty for the sea.

This ship had made a hole in the forest and had wounded its verdant soul. Imbued with the life of what died to make it so, this ship would face the frigid waves alone, with the fate of men in its hold as it veered past the treacherous shoals. When the time came, Gregory wanted to be on this ship, standing on the stern castle with wind whipping through his hair, the sail billowing.

He snapped out of his reverie to notice a group of men pulling a plank from a cauldron-powered steam box. Moving quickly toward the ship, they laid the plank across the uppermost strake on the starboard side, and with their collective strength and precision, bent the hot plank into place and held it there with clamps. They did it with another plank, fitting it next to the first, and thus laid a strake from stem to stern. Gregory had never watched a ship being built. That they brought him pipes of wine was good enough, and as long as that was the case, he was satisfied. But he found himself spell-bound by the way the shipwright and his men used artistry and force to piece together such an intricate, magnificent puzzle.

For the first week he'd go to the site, take his usual place on the pile of scrap, and watch in silence. But the shipwright finally confronted him and Gregory had to explain himself. Fluent in English, French, and Latin, and the bastardized amalgam thereof, Gregory also knew Dutch, so he spoke with the shipwright, a leathery blond from Antwerp.

"I am an associate of your employer, Geoffrey Wool," Gregory said. "You do not know me and might not think much of what you see, but I assure you, if your work is good, I can perhaps recommend your services to others."

"Then you are welcome here," the shipwright said. "I am van Scheldt, and I am not known for my good graces. Stay out of my way, but watch closely, and you will learn much."

Gregory kept a cold face, but inside he laughed because in the past he had told many people much the same thing. He understood that kind of language, and a man who spoke it was the kind of man Gregory respected. A shipwright, after all, was a craftsman of the top tier, and without them, there would be no wine in England. Indeed, Gregory would not only watch and listen to van Scheldt, but would write of him and write well.

And so it went with Gregory falling into the routine of going to the shipyard each morning to watch them lay in a strake or fasten a rib or set a through beam. When the men broke for dinner, he would leave them be and set his curiosity to something else. He watched the farmers in the fields, the tapestry women in their vaulted stone workshop, the dog trainers and the barrel makers and the potters at their wheels, the weavers, the cordwainers, and the stinking duty of the dyers—all manner of the city's travail.

We always wear our best garments and turn out in droves for processions, tournaments, and fairs. But the guts of living are in the mundane, in the drudgery and reward of repetition and improvement. There is no tourna-

ment without toil, and no pageant without perseverance. We celebrate the
saints with our festivals and feasts, and so it should be for they have shown
us the way. But we must also celebrate what's achieved by our hands. God
created the world, but it is we who cut and lay the stone.

Gregory had every intention of sitting at his desk and writing about the
ship and to portray the ordinary moments of Boston life. But a curious thing
happened. When he set his quill to the parchment as if to write, he started to
draw instead. A smooth upward loop and then another below it. For a long,
still moment in which a new flower bloomed in his heart, Gregory looked
at what he had done and admitted to himself he was perplexed. But it came
to him soon enough. The curving lines, touching as they did at each end,
resembled the shape of the ship.

His mouth agape with wonderment, he drew another line and many more
to represent the strakes. Then he drew a man with a mallet in his hand, and
though it did not resemble him, Gregory knew it was the shipwright, van
Scheldt. He drew two more men sawing timber, another holding an adze, and
yet another crouched over a piece of wood with a hammer and chisel. Even
though he was alone, he felt a tinge of embarrassment over the poor quality of
the drawing. The ship was too small and the men too big. No one was recog-
nizable. His first piece of art was a flat mess of perspective and proportion.

He held up the parchment and made as if to tear it in half, but just before
he did, he thought better of it and laid it back down. He got up from his
desk and stretched. With his forearms propped on the sill, he looked out the
window at the skiffs and barges gliding up and down the river. A broiling
sun burned high in the summer sky and the distant clouds out over the sea
churned east. Gregory found elation in such a simple scene. He made the
sign of the cross and thanked God he still lived and had command of his fac-
ulties. He turned to the desk and took account of what was at hand—enough
ink and parchments to record history. So he returned to the desk, dipped the
quill in the well, and drew with fury and abandon, the sharpened tip of the
goose feather racing across the parchment with a sharp scratching sound.

Page after page, memory after memory until days turned into weeks and weeks into months. Only breaking for sleep, food, and the garderobe, Gregory burned down the candles as he had in Swinton's tower. He reached deep into the dark night of his past to find things once cherished that had been taken away—his mother, Herleve, knitting next to the fire. His father, Henri, counting the casks of wine. His favorite teacher, Master Thomas, holding a book and a scroll.

He drew a portrait of a woman in a veil. The sun shone on her shoulders, the wheat stood tall in the fields, and gentle woodland creatures gathered at her feet. In one hand she held a bouquet of flowers and in the other a ring of keys. Benevolence and authority. This was not Alice, but Margery. She had come out of him to show herself on his parchment and to take her place in his life. Once the parchment dried, he kissed it and put it away. This time, only death would come between him and what he had created.

arren and Geoffrey returned. They arrived with the tide in a ship laden with the bounty of Bruges. Along with a few household servants, Gregory scurried down to the port and watched as the cog towed into its berth. Gregory kept an even countenance even though he was enthused. He knew the sights and sounds of Bruges would sculpt the very core of Warren's humanity, and he wanted to see how the journey showed in his bearing.

Toting a large sack over his shoulder with one hand and leading Moonbeam on a tether with the other, Warren came down the gangplank first. He laughed and looked over his shoulder at the man-at-arms behind him. By the way they communicated with each other, Gregory knew they had already become fast friends. Even a short channel crossing could have that effect on people, and Gregory watched them celebrate their return by clapping one another over the shoulder and grinning.

Next off the ship stepped Geoffrey, crowned in a blue silk hat and draped in a luxuriant red robe and a blue mantle trimmed with deer fur. He held the hem of his robe up over his ankles to make sure he did not trip and moved slowly down the gangplank. His servants hastened to assist him, and in this way he returned to Boston in a conspicuous show of ascension.

Gregory could tell Geoffrey's mood was good, which meant the trip had gone well—he and his cartel had been authorized to trade directly with the Hansa. Gregory shared in this triumph. Before Geoffrey set sail, Gregory had written him a letter of recommendation. As a member of the London guilds and as the scion of a family that had traded wine for a century, Gregory du Mont was known in Bruges, and to the Hansa, and to have his letter in hand when looking to make a deal meant you stood in good stead.

Others must have read Geoffrey's mood, because merchants appeared at the wharf and in short order formed a small crowd of supporters kissing him on the cheek, patting him on the back, and some bowing. Mingling in the crowd with confidence and humor was Warren. Gregory smiled when he noticed the glint of silver around his neck and the glimmer of gold in his eye. Gregory wanted to head down and join the welcome party, but if he did, Warren might give him a bear hug and blurt out, "Master Gregory, it is good to see you again!" And though Gregory's disguise was thin, he still wore it. So he just stood there, at the top of the walkway leading down to the port, dressed as a servant and bearing a yoke and buckets for show.

To Gregory's dread, he was not the only one watching from afar. He spotted a lone horseman, his clothing and gear covered in dust, who seemed interested in Geoffrey's arrival. The horseman looked on with more than casual attention at the scene unfolding on the wharf, and from the look on his face, Gregory knew he pondered something of importance. Gregory dug into his memories and searched for this man, but try as he did, neither name nor association came to mind.

He walked toward him, and when just a few feet away, he said, "That is a beautiful ship, is it not, my lord?"

The rider looked down at him with disdain and said, "It is not the ship I'm interested in, servant boy, but who is on it. Tell me, do you know?"

"That, my lord, is Geoffrey Wool, a powerful merchant, and he has just returned from Bruges. Is that who you seek?"

"No, an associate of his." He put a hand on the pummel of his sword. "A liar. A libeler, a debtor, a coward, a betrayer, a butt-fucking whoreson who will have his teeth pulled and be gelded when he's captured. He is a horse thief, and his name is Gregory of Bordeaux."

"Oh," said Gregory. "I have heard tell of him. He fled on Geoffrey's ship to Bruges, and then, they say, to Champagne and beyond. If I am right, the Bishop of Lincoln wishes to bring him to justice."

A dark smile spread over the rider's face. "The Bishop of Lincoln? He is hardly the only one."

regory hated to do it. The hall was full of such merriment. Geoffrey and his associates sang, Warren and his friend bragged, and the servants cavorted through their duties. For the sake of sport, Gregory said nothing of his encounter with the mysterious rider. Instead, he sipped his wine, put on a smile, and listened as Warren told him of all he had seen and done during his trip to Bruges. A skirmish with pirates, a tailwind during a storm, a dash to Ghent bearing a message, Arabs and Jews, and business and leisure on the busy canals.

To see Gregory was to see a man of content. And he was. Truly heartened by the return of his friends, his joy was sincere. Still, deep inside, he was rattled. He had just learned from an armed stranger he was wanted for stealing a horse, and worse, he would be disfigured if apprehended. Sharing news of that nature would kill this moment, and Gregory could not bring himself to do so. He would wait until the morrow and let them have this night. He held out his cup and did not pull it back until it brimmed. And he cheered with the rest of them when Warren climbed on top of the head table and did the Scottish kick step as the bagpipes chanted and droned.

When the next afternoon came and he was alone with Geoffrey and

Warren, Gregory told all. Warren made as if to speak, but Geoffrey stopped him with a stay of his hand. He gave Gregory a resolute stare, sighed for emphasis, and paced across the hall.

As he warmed his hands at the fire, he gave Gregory a second look and said, "Gregory, go home. If you ride hard and the roads are good, you can make London in three days. There you will have the guild, your associates at King's Bench, and the protection of Southampton. I have been married for two years, and you have been out and about since before then. Don't you think it's time to bring this part of your life to a close?"

"No." Gregory paced to the opposite end of the hall. "For a year, I was told when and where to shit. Through the course of this blazing summer I hid like a rat in your guesthouse while wearing another man's clothes. I know you mean well, but my journey is not over, and I am the only one who can determine when it is."

"But you are an important man, too important to be killed out in some backward village—by a flea-bitten nobleman, at that—when in fact your only business there is your curiosity," he said. "You have matters to attend to in London, and there are people there who love you, and they have waited long enough. Besides, you have done well by Southampton. I'm sure he will be more than pleased with the stories in your chronicle."

"I cannot please Southampton until I please myself. And as of yet, I am not pleased. I do not know what it is, Geoffrey, but there is something else I need to see."

"Which means there is something else you need to write," Geoffrey said. "I understand. You want to leave something to posterity. I want the same thing, but instead of writing a manuscript, I have an heir."

"Thank you for making the point for me," Gregory said. "I may never have this opportunity again, and despite being a hunted man, I will not kowtow to my enemies. For if I do, then I would have taken their standards as my own. And if that happens, then I am a fraud. Believe me. If it is true I speak ill of others—and in all honesty, I have—it is also true I will speak ill of myself, if warranted."

"No," Geoffrey said. "We will not let you hate yourself. You will ride out of Boston with my full blessing and support. And you Warren, what do you say?"

"I have ridden with Master Gregory for all this time, and it is his road if he wants it. If there is a man foolish enough to try and take his teeth and his balls, then that man will not live long."

Encouraged by what he heard, Gregory returned to the guesthouse and sat at his desk. He wrote two letters, one destined for York and the other for London. Since these letters meant the difference between life and death, he chose his words wisely and took pains to give easy instructions. As he sealed them with red wax, he sneered.

Indeed shall his enemies feel the full might of the guild.

He packed his belongings, most of all his voluminous parchments, which he rolled up and slid into a cylindrical case of boiled leather. He put on his breeches and his black robe, adjusting it so it hung to right below his knees, and tightened his belt. Sitting on the edge of his bed, he pulled on his cordovan boots and strapped on his brass nub spurs. He stood and shoved La Bonne Vie snug at his hip and draped an intricate silver and emerald chain around his neck. In a billowing wave of wool, he whipped his hooded black cloak over his shoulders and cinched it with a silver brooch. He pulled on his cordovan gloves and pushed his beaver and peacock hat deep over his brow—high enough up so he could see, but low enough down so when his eyes flashed from beneath the brim, he might strike fear in the hearts of those who opposed him. He tucked his parchments under his arm, slung his pack over his shoulder, and with his letters at the ready, headed toward the stables.

When he arrived at the paddock, Warren waited. Mounted on Moon-beam, he wore mail, a black surcoat, and black cape. On his head was a mail coif and over it an open-faced conical helm with a nose guard, adorned with a plume of greased crow feathers. Armed with a sword, knife, and axe, and with a shield slung over his back, Warren was the blooded brute from Scotland, the grim guarantee Gregory would not be easy prey. They traded long looks without saying a word. They shared so much, and both had done their part to build the brotherhood. They did not want to lose it anytime soon, and the understanding between them was clear—now was the time to ride, and to perhaps even kill.

"The road is yours, Master Gregory, so when it comes time to take it, ask not permission and have no regrets," he said. "I am at your command, and I did not sharpen my weapons for naught."

"And I have sharpened my weapons, too." Gregory held up his letters. "Let nothing happen to me, and I will do the same for you."

A stable boy came out with Black Saddle fully rigged and looking well fed, rested, and ready to run. With immense satisfaction, Gregory climbed into the stirrups and settled into his seat atop the fastest courser in England. Black Saddle snorted and twitched his ears. As he strutted nervously in a circle, Gregory felt his anxious power.

He leaned down, patted him on the neck and whispered into his ear. "They say you are a champion, so prove it to be true."

Black Saddle whinnied and reared, and then trotted the length of the stables, holding his head high and tossing his mane. Gregory glanced over his shoulder with a sharp look, and Warren gave a respectful nod. Then Geoffrey and the messengers arrived.

"This goes to London," Gregory said to one of the messengers, and gave him a letter. "And this goes to York," he said to the other. "Ride as if the devil is at your heels, and don't look back even after you've arrived. If at the Stourbridge Fair I see what I need to see, then you can each demand a mark from me when next we meet."

As the messengers rode out, Gregory looked down at Geoffrey. "Do you have it?"

"Yes." From under his arm, the other man pulled an ell of red felt and handed it up to Gregory. He unraveled it and wrapped it around his neck like a scarf, making sure to hide it beneath his robe.

"And Gregory, I want you to have this," Geoffrey said, and pushed something else into his hand.

Gregory looked at it and shook his head with disbelief. A gold Bezant. From the coin's inscriptions, Gregory knew it had been minted in the reign of the second Emperor Basil, long since dead but remembered as one of the greatest of the Byzantines. This coin, a hunk of gold from the wealthiest city in the world, could melt the heart of a normal man and make a great one say maybe, or perhaps even yes, when he otherwise would say no.

"This is a lot to bestow." Gregory gave the coin to Warren for safe keeping.

"But you might need it," Geoffrey said, in a knowing voice. "So you are headed to the Stourbridge Fair?"

"Yes, eventually," Gregory said. "I hear an elephant from the king's menagerie will be there, and a three-headed lady, and a cow that sings the Song of Rolland."

"Curiosities," Geoffrey said. "I'm sure you are going for more than that."

"We shall see. When we meet again, I want to sail on your new ship. The hull, I believe, will be swift and strong."

Geoffrey smiled. They exchanged heartened farewells and repeated assurances to see one another again. The pleasantries done, Gregory and Warren pulled out of Boston into the dead of night, as the crickets chirped and as the Greyfriars chanted Nocturns.

PRINCESS
GWENLLIAN
OF WALES

ust as it seemed they had reached the end of the world, the path opened up to a rickety village stretching out on either side of a leaning stone church. Sempringham, a drab place of labor, obedience, and chastity, was at the end of an overgrown road, down a valley, over a hill, beyond the glen, across the creek, and through the woods. A true backwater mired in a century long since passed, Sempringham had neither charm nor beauty. But a famous person lived there. Princess Gwenllian, the only daughter of the last Prince of Wales, Llywelyn ap Gruffudd, had been brought to Sempringham Priory when but a babe, shortly after her father's execution, and had been confined there all her life. Gregory had heard of her while in Boston, and though he knew it improbable, he went to Sempringham for a chance to see the princess, and to describe the last drop of royal Welsh blood before it dripped into the soil and disappeared forever.

Dressed in their boots and their black and mounted on gleaming steeds, Gregory and Warren noticed frightened stares and nasty glances from the bumpkins who called this place home. Everything shut down, and the street emptied as people scurried to their homes and slammed the doors behind them. Gregory surveyed the scene in one direction while Warren surveyed it in the other. Nothing suggested enemies lurked, so they dismounted and led their horses to the public trough.

As the horses drank, and as Gregory and Warren watched the town recoil from them, a monk in a black cassock approached. He seemed cautious, but unlike the others, not consumed with fear. The prior, Gregory guessed, and in light of the town's disquiet, he knew he needed to make a good impression.

He doffed his hat and made a courteous bow.

"Judging by the sincere piety of this place, I assume I have arrived in Sempringham?" Gregory said.

"Yes," the monk said. "And who is it who has come to such a humble place on such a majestic horse, unannounced, and with a man-at-arms?"

Gregory had never backed down from speaking his own name, but if word had spread he was a horse thief, then he could be strung up by anyone, at any time, from any tree, without fear of repercussion. The townspeople now hiding in their homes could just as easily pour out and surround him. The thought gave him pause, and for a moment he considered climbing back up on his horse and leaving Sempringham. But Gregory doubted word had made it down this bramble-strewn rabbit trail, at least not yet.

He looked deep into the monk's eyes, and with an edgy confidence said, "I am Gregory of Bordeaux, and I am here to speak with the prior—Prior Wynchecombe, I believe."

"I am Prior Wynchecombe, but I usually don't have business with strangers."

"My apologies, but I am not just any stranger." He handed over his frayed letter of recommendation from the Earl of Southampton.

"Ah, you are a chronicler," he said as he looked up from the letter and handed it back to Gregory.

"Yes, and I have collected stories from London to Scotland and back," he said. "There are many magnificent things outside the comfort of our homes, Prior Wynchecombe, but there are other things that make you glad you have a swift horse."

"I can only imagine," the prior said, "though you will not need a fast horse here. We are simple creatures of God, tied to the land, our ploughs, and prayer. But tell me, what brings you to this place. After all you have seen, what can possibly interest you in Sempringham?"

"If I have heard the truth, then Princess Gwenllian of Wales is here. And if you arrange a meeting between us, then I will give you a gold Bezant."

"You have a Bezant?" Prior Wynchecombe's eyes grew bright.

"Yes, but it is not in my pouch, but in his," he said, and gestured toward Warren. Prior Wynchecombe looked at him with a squint. Warren returned his expectant look with a cold, dead gaze.

The prior looked back at Gregory and said, "This is too much for me to consider just yet, and before anything can happen, I would have to speak with the prioress, Elise, who as you know, holds as much authority as I in this order of Gilbertines."

"I understand the protocol," Gregory said. "When your negotiations are done, I will be here awaiting the verdict."

The prior went into the church and closed the doors behind him. Warren looked restless, and Gregory understood why. Here at remote Sempringham they were vulnerable. Not that they hadn't been before, but the danger they faced in the past had mostly been random. Under those circumstances they were confident because both of them knew they either had enough wits or enough horsepower to make sure they got their way. But now Gregory was a target and people looked for him, so it was quite plausible a trap, much bigger than their resources could allay, had been set. Not a good way to travel, and not a good way to collect stories for a chronicle, either. So this place, Sempringham—basic, impoverished, humble Sempringham—exuded an aura of danger when just a year ago they would have ridden through, even spent the night, with nary a concern.

Gregory could not keep Geoffrey's warning out of his head. "But you are an important man, Gregory, too important to be killed out in some backward village—by a flea-bitten nobleman, at that—when in fact your only business there is your curiosity."

Too true. For a moment he felt like a fool. But in the short conversation between him and the prior, Gregory had peered into the man's soul, overturning the rocks at the bottom of the stream, and rolling back the fallen limbs in the forest. He searched for what the prior knew and the secrets he hid. Gregory had found nothing, yet the enduring trust in his own intuition escaped him. The prior was much older, with a grey tonsure and deep wrinkles as proof of his wisdom.

Perhaps he was strong enough to conceal the truth from Gregory's prying eyes. Perhaps he was not talking to the prioress, but to the men who were here to arrest him.

Gregory remounted Black Saddle. Warren did the same with Moonbeam, and there they sat, as midday turned into afternoon and a cold drizzle came in on the wind. Warren had turned his horse around so he could keep watch over the village, while Gregory remained facing the church and its oaken doors. His mood improved when Prior Wynchecombe emerged from the church, alone, and with the air of a man who had no tricks to play.

"I am sorry to tell you this, Gregory, but the prioress wants nothing to do with you and your gold Bezant. Princess Gwenllian is never to be before the eyes of a man. That is why the king put her here. I know that is not the answer you wanted, but it is the answer I give."

"And it is the answer I must accept," Gregory said. "If the prioress can turn down the lure of a gold Bezant, then she truly is a child of God."

Gregory and Warren took a rutted road south, and soon trotted their horses through a wasteland of sedge and fen, where screams went unheard, where lives sunk in the slough, and where the dead of night was an endless black. Had Gregory a new parchment, one adorned with the notes of his meeting with Princess Gwenllian, he wouldn't so much mind. He accepted danger and inconvenience as the price for getting what he wanted. But he had left empty-handed. Surprised the gold Bezant had not been enough to open the lock at Sempringham, he questioned his decision to try and bribe a prior. So Gregory sulked and fussed with himself as he guided Black Saddle down the trail through the moor, its marshes and peat bogs on either side.

Warren led the way, and in the wake of Moonbeam's precise steps, Gregory felt sure they would make it without incident to the other side. Then Warren pulled in the reins and Moonbeam stopped in her tracks. Gregory and Black Saddle did the same. Warren pulled back his hood and cocked his head so his ear faced forward.

A few moments later he turned to Gregory, and with a baleful crease in his brow, said, "Riders are headed our way, Master Gregory, and if they are foes, and we fight on this soggy land, we will die today in this wretched swamp."

"Then let us go back to Sempringham," he said, "and hope they admit us to the church."

They doubled back on their tracks and made speed. Whoever trailed them did the same thing, and the sound of their horses grew louder as they gained on Gregory and Warren. After a nervous and exhausting hour of navigating the treacherous path, they emerged from the marsh to solid ground. They kicked with their spurs, and in but a few strides their steeds hurtled at full gallop back to Sempringham.

As they wheeled their horses into the green in front of the church, in the high voice of alarm, Gregory yelled out, "Prior Wynchecombe!"

After what seemed like a long, cold year, the prior appeared at the church door, flanked by a few of his canons and lay brothers, and said, "What is it that bothers you, Gregory? You left in peace but have returned in great distress."

"There are riders on the way, and their intentions are not good. I know you will not allow me to speak with the princess, but now I ask you, will you take the gold Bezant in exchange for shelter in your church? This is a yes or no question, and I need an answer now."

Warren dug into his pouch, pulled out the coin, and held it at just the right angle so, in spite of the drizzle, it caught a ray of sunlight and glowed with imperial splendor. Gregory saw the gold dancing in his eyes, and knew the second time around Prior Wynchecombe would not resist.

"Yes," he said, to Gregory's relief. "Come inside, and wait out the danger behind these old and impregnable walls."

Gregory had hoped to enter the church before the riders behind them arrived. But just as he goaded his horse forward, they rumbled around the corner of the church. Gregory looked at them, and their leader looked at him. Recognition dawned with a gush of bile and anxiety. Here in front of him, and closing fast, was Lord Miles le Gaunter of Newark, the slouching boor who had tried to extort him of his horses a couple of years ago.

Le Gaunter pulled his sword and cocked it over his head as an expectant grin showed in his under bite. In the fleeting moment before the blade fell, Gregory spurred Black Saddle, and the steed lurched through the church door. The canons slammed it shut and slid the iron crossbar into place. It took a while for Gregory's eyes to grow accustomed to the dark interior of the church, its walls lined with rush lights, its altar set with flickering candles. Warren and Moonbeam pulled alongside his left, and in front of him stood Prior Wynchecombe and his tonsured canons. Gregory nodded and Warren handed him the gold Bezant. He gave it to the prior, who took it a bit more willingly than Gregory would have wanted and tucked it away.

"Who are those men?" the prior asked.

"My enemies, for sure, and I did not get inside soon enough, so they know I am here."

"And why are they your enemies?"

"They say I am a horse thief, but that is a lie. But even if it were true, I invoke the right of sanctuary, and ask you to shelter my man and me until more suitable arrangements can be made."

"That is your right, and I shall honor your right as best I can."

Then from outside came the voice of le Gaunter. *"Prior Wynchecombe, open the door, now, and hand over the horse thief known as Gregory of Bordeaux. He is wanted in three counties. You do no honor to your name or to your priory by holding him here."*

Prior Wynchecombe and Gregory walked up the steep spiral steps to the top of the bell tower, and from there, Gregory had a full view of the dregs who had come for him—le Gaunter and four others, one of whom he recognized as a deacon in the service of the Bishop of Lincoln. Still mounted on their horses, they crowded near the front door, a cluster of mail, weapons, and cloaks. A posse in the service of falsehood, a gang of fools with not a smile among them. Le Gaunter and the others looked up.

And that's when Gregory felt the dread. He had forgotten how enormous and stoop-shouldered le Gaunter was, and how his teeth jutted like fangs from his moist, fleshy under bite. Le Gaunter and his men had come to capture him and send him to the netherworld without benefit of his rites. Gregory didn't want things to end like that.

But looking down on them, with nothing but the thin promise of the prior in his favor, he didn't see how things would end any other way. He cringed as he remembered what he had written about le Gaunter while confined in Swinton's Tower. At the time, he had laughed. Now he realized he had written his own death warrant.

> *He has the face of a rodent, the body of a pig, the legs of an ostrich, and the mind of a worm. If he wasn't such a curiosity, he would indeed be worthless. In all my travels, I have encountered no man as cheap and ignorant as Lord Miles le Gaunter of Newark. My guess is when he dies, they will not know what to do with him. He is not a man, but a beast, and he has not a soul, but an aching desire to fornicate with himself, to sire youngsters more ignorant than he.*

Gregory assumed le Gaunter had seen the fear in his eyes, because a slow sneer of malevolence crept into the corner of his mouth and a wash of confidence showed in his bearing. Gregory knew he should keep quiet, but this was le Gaunter.

In spite of his predicament, Gregory would never give him anything other than contempt. "It seems as if my chronicle has somehow gotten out in front of me. I hope your priest read what I wrote about you."

"He did," le Gaunter said, "and I have since killed two men who laughed about it."

"I must tell you, when I wrote it, I at first tried to think of something good to say about you," he said. "I sat for a full two days, but nothing came to mind."

"But tell me," he said. "When you wrote it, you didn't think you'd see me here, did you?"

"No, but had I known, it still would have been written. I just would have come to Sempringham with a war band of my own, instead of arriving alone."

"You have at least one man with you, and if he is who I think he is, then he is not enough," le Gaunter said. "Prior Wynchecombe! Gregory of Bordeaux was charged with horse thievery at the court in Lincoln. He was summoned to give his pledge and to deny the charge but did not show, so a jury of the finest men in the shire declared him an outlaw! It is his right to claim sanctuary, but it is my duty to apprehend him. If you continue to harbor this man, then I will do what I must to keep the oaths I have sworn to men much more powerful than yourself. Turn him out, or I will destroy the mill, burn the village, and batter down this door. I will drag you out by your collar and make you watch as I fuck the princess you keep in your church. Now do we have a deal, Prior Wynchecombe, or do I send my man to go and crack the millstone?"

The prior turned to Gregory and in a sighing, deflated voice, said, "I will have to talk with the prioress."

They walked back down the steps of the bell tower. When they reached the ground floor, Prioress Elise, stern, standing akimbo and austere in her white veil and black cassock, waited, as did the monks and nuns gathered behind her. The prior's shoulders slumped and he looked to the floor as he stepped into the aura of her displeasure. Gregory felt like doing the same, but instead he kept his shoulders straight and his chin high, and withstood her full reproach. She looked him up and down, made the sign of the cross, and stared into his eyes until he felt low and ashamed. Gregory knew he could not assail her conviction, and no amount of money or wit or status would sway her. He stood and waited in silence, resigned to the reality that his fate rested in her hands.

"Prioress," one of the monks said, as he gestured toward Gregory, "Prior Wynchecombe has accepted a gold coin in exchange for housing this outlaw. Do not let the prior lie to you, because I saw him take it just moments ago."

"Is that true?" the prioress said.

The prior, downcast and embarrassed, nodded his head.

"Give it back." she demanded. "That is the devil's gold. Give it back!"

Prior Wynchecombe pulled it out of a fold in his cassock and handed it to Gregory.

"Now turn them out," she said without blinking, and without taking her eyes off Gregory. "We do not harbor outlaws at Sempringham, nor do we associate with men who use payoffs to make their way in this world. Open the door and leave them in God's hands."

Gregory did not have time to entertain his despair. He knew her command was final and that it would soon be obeyed. He climbed up on Black Saddle and wheeled him around to where he was knee to knee with Warren facing the door. He pulled his blade, *La Bonne Vie,* and with it made the sign of the cross. He asked God to watch over him and Warren and to deliver them to victory or to safety, whichever was easiest or whichever came first. And please, dear God, do not let Warren forget what he learned in Scotland.

Gregory went hot and trembling, a ringing pounded in his ears. The horses whinnied and snorted as the monks placed their hands on the crossbar.

"Open the door, you piss-gurgling dogs, and behold the hell you have unleashed," bellowed Warren. He yanked Fionnaghal from its sheath and hunkered behind his shield.

With a pious heave, the door flew open. Warren sallied out, drove Moonbeam into striking distance, and then came the crack and thud of weapons on his shield. He stood in his stirrups and closed with three men, hacking to his left and then to his right, Fionnaghal singing the war song as he cleaved into the mail and bones of those unlucky enough to have found him.

Sickened yet emboldened by the abrupt crudity of Warren's assault, Gregory rode around the mêlée to confront Lord le Gaunter. Gregory saw he was startled upon realizing Warren made short work of his men, and in le Gaunter's moment of pause, Gregory tried to lay him low. With his knife high over his head, he stabbed down with all his might to plunge the weapon into le Gaunter's neck. But Gregory was a clumsy warrior, and the dagger glanced harmless and lame off of his helm.

Then it was le Gaunter's turn to join the fight. As a grunt disgorged from the deep of his innards, he countered with a stroke that would split Gregory from crown to crevice, and make of his life a bag of foul guts. As the sword arced down to the place where sorrow dwelled, Gregory heard the bells and tasted the wine and saw his place in the continuum of time. If his strength had failed him when he'd tried to take le Gaunter's life, it arrived in full at this moment to preserve his own. He held *La Bonne Vie* between himself and where the sword would come. It landed with a sharp metallic ring. A jolt went through his arm, which quivered under the magnificent weight he held, just this one time, in an instant of triumph, when a merchant bested a lord.

Le Gaunter's sword caught in the corner of the knife's blade and cross-guard and came to within a nose of Gregory's face. Their eyes met. Gregory smelled the ale on his breath and saw the rotted canine hooking out from his under bite. And for some time they remained locked, blade on blade, le Gaunter trying to prevail, and Gregory knowing he wouldn't.

A shadow of fear fell over le Gaunter's face as he took notice of what happened around him. One of his men, his shoulder gashed and leaking, fell from his horse, while another shrieked in agony as he held the gushing stump where a hand used to be. The third took flight with the bishop's deacon, as Warren, reins in one hand and sword in the other, set his sights on le Gaunter.

Le Gaunter disengaged with Gregory, pulled out on his horse, circled around to the far side of the green, and collected himself. Gregory, drained by the energy it had taken to thwart the death blow, rode in behind Warren.

"The last thing you will know about me is I rode with Swinton the Red, and he taught me how to kill a man," Warren said to le Gaunter. "Perhaps you did not know it earlier in the day, but now is the time for the truth. You came here to die."

Moonbeam careered into full gallop, racing across the green in a spray of turf. Warren's black cape whipped out from his shoulders and Fionnaghal gleamed bloody in the amber twilight. Le Gaunter waited, his weapon cocked and ready, as Warren approached his right. But in just a blink before their swords crossed, Moonbeam, with a tremendous flexing of her muscles and all her hooves churning, veered so Warren's attack came at le Gaunter's left. The switch came so swift and superb, le Gaunter had no time to react. There he sat, poised to strike at nothing, while Warren found a target he could not miss. He reached across his body, and as Moonbeam made her pass, laid out Fionnaghal. Off came le Gaunter's head. It spun cleanly through the air and rolled for a full rod before coming to rest with the eyes wide open. Warren banked Moonbeam to a halt and looked at Gregory, who saw in his face no conceit or churlish satisfaction at what he had just done. But there appeared a natural, earnest danger about him that, along with his subtle smarts, made Warren look full and important, and, Gregory thought, even noble.

Gregory looked at le Gaunter's headless corpse, and then at his men, slumped, dying, and clutching at their wounds. Warren made them pay the price, the price of the chronicle—blood for ink, flesh for parchments, and breath for words. A steep bill, thought Gregory, and yet more accounts needed to be closed.

Before riding out, he took a last look at the church and noticed Prioress Elise glaring down at him from the bell tower. Next to her stood one of the nuns—plump-faced, pockmarked, cross-eyed, bucktoothed, as homely as a dandelion without its blow ball, as ugly as the weed choking the rose. Princess Gwenllian of Wales, on display as a final gesture of rebuke. Gregory had gotten what he'd come for, a glimpse of royalty, but had imperiled innocent Sempringham in the pursuit of his selfish ends. It was a tale he had to put in his chronicle because it was true. He shook his head and made the sign of the cross.

Their torches lit and crackling, he and Warren headed south, to Margery, down the twisting, treacherous path through the moors.

THE NEW
LORD CORBY'S
FEAST

Gregory and Warren rode into Corby in a cloud of dust. People peered out from behind the shutters of their thatched homes, but nobody came out to greet them in the place where they once held esteem. The village near a stand of beech, south of the foxgloves and north of the bluebells, cowered in the hush of a sin. The stink of death lingered ripe in the early autumn air, and a murder of crows, perched along the ridge of a steep roof, croaked and chattered. Gregory and Warren trotted their horses over to Margery's stone farmhouse. They exchanged looks of gloom before dismounting. A parchment, as rude and foreboding as a royal summons, had been nailed to the front door. Gregory yanked it off, holding it at the top and the bottom.

Scrawled in the vernacular was a copy of something he had written while imprisoned in Swinton's tower. A piece from his memoire, a private passage meant only for his eyes. But here it dangled on public display in Corby, nailed to Margery Alesworth's door in an act of crude revenge. Only a snippet of his memoire, a tiny bit of an otherwise sprawling treatise on the world. But a dagger does not have to be long to pierce the heart. A wound kissed with poison will never heal. And such was the case that day with Gregory, when he came face to face with innocent words that had managed to kill.

She is the sun piercing the clouds on a somber day. She is the field yielding bounty when all others fail. In her heart rises the bread of love, and in her mind turn the gears of the wheels rolling over fear. The dew on the grass is bright in the morning light but is pale compared to her tear falling honest in the night. The doe in the glen and the hawk in the tree, the rose in the wind and the blue of the sea, dusk on the hill and dawn in the vale, the wheat growing gold and the laughter of tales, wind in the leaves and rain on the thatch, truth in sheaves and wits to match. Margery's song I will sing as I go, over mountains and rivers and deep through the snow.

He stood there for a long while, awash with a torrent of memories, holding the parchment with two trembling hands. He thought of tearing it into pieces. But he folded the poem and slid it into the breast pocket of his robe, carrying it close to his heart. He looked at the door and gave Warren a grim nod. Warren kicked it open. A revolting stench, bloated with evil, billowed out the door. Gregory bent over, put his hand on the doorsill to keep from falling, and wretched out a vile jet of melancholy.

After collecting himself, he pulled his cloak over his face and entered the house. What he saw made him stop and utter a prayer. Margery, naked and hanging by a rope from a rafter, a fat grey rat sitting on her shoulder. He shooed away the rodent, climbed up on a chair, and with *La Bonne Vie*, cut through the noose and lowered her body to the floor. He found a blanket in the disarray of her looted home and laid it over her discolored corpse. Then he cried. Down on one knee and with his face in his hand, he cried with the conviction of a man who feels blame, of a man who accepts the completeness of loss, and of a man who swallows a morsel of light knowing it will never shine again.

He wiped the snot from his nose and the spittle from his chin and took a moment to compose his injured soul. Looking back out the door he saw

Black Saddle standing next to Warren and Moonbeam. He could leave and forget this cursed place. Say a prayer, cross his heart, and ride out, never looking back.

But Gregory could not commit such a heartless deed.

He went to the home's south wall, and from memory found the sliding stone. He pulled it out and stuck his hand into the space inside the wall, and to his great surprise, the trove had not been burgled. Gregory pulled out Margery's most prized possessions—a canvas sack filled with silver and gold, a brass pendant in the shape of an eagle, an ivory comb with inlay of pearl, a silver necklace with a ruby, and most importantly, all of her records and deeds.

He would pledge her wealth in exchange for prayers at the parish church of St. Martin in London. With the deeds he would hold onto her name and glean from them her year and place of birth, the names of her parents, her loves, and create for her a place of honor in his chronicle. But that was work for the future, and he would do it with the stroke of his quill.

At the moment, though, he had work to do of a different kind.

He stashed Margery's belongings in his saddlebag, told Warren he would soon return, and went to the barn behind her house. He found what he needed, a pick and shovel, and as he hoisted the tools up over his shoulder, he heard the first sounds of life in this town.

He ran back to Warren, who pointed toward the market. There on the road leading through town was the new Lord Corby and a host of mounted men on either side of him. Gregory swallowed hard and in a flash of regret, remembered what he had written about him in the chronicle.

Everything about Lord Corby is pusillanimous. If he were a star, he could not be seen in the night sky. If he were a rock, he would be a pebble. If he were vegetal, he would be nettle. If he were water, he would be a puddle. If he were winter, he would be the snow that quickly melts away. If he were wheat, he would be the chaff. If life is a dog, then he is the flea, and if he is the flea, then let him be scratched away from the testicles of this world and forgotten for all time.

Corby's face flickered with a rotten grin, and he made a caustic gesture of hospitality by opening his arms and placing one hand over his heart. His gaze met Gregory's. The enmity between them flowed deep and wide, and roiled, bubbled, and spat as does the river down in the chasm of hell.

Lord Corby leaned back in his saddle, put his hands over his stomach, and shook with a belly laugh. "I hoped you would come. When I heard you went to Sempringham, I knew you would. I wanted to make sure everything was ready for your arrival. So now that you're here, Gregory of Bordeaux, welcome to Corby."

"I did not come here for you. You are not worth my time, and your hospitality I do not accept. I came for Margery, and, I realize, to right your wrong."

"I see you have a pick and a shovel," he said. "Have you dug a grave before, Bordeaux?"

"No, but now I must."

"So the first grave you dig in your piss-pot life will be in *my* village?"

"Yes."

"Will you put it in your chronicle?"

"Most certainly, and I will also mention the circumstances. If you thought I had impugned your name before, then you will be astounded by what I say of you once I am back at my desk in London."

Corby laughed again. "I wish you could see yourself, Bordeaux. The powerful scribe with his feared, venomous quill is now a gravedigger in my little corner of Lincolnshire. Your pride brought you to me, and it is your pride I counted on."

"Let me dig this grave, Lord Corby. If it is the only kind act within your power, let me dig this grave."

"Oh, I will grant your wish," he said. "And when you are done, we will make good sport of you. Men from three counties are already on their way, Bordeaux, and we will hunt you down, like the horse thief you are, and teach you the lessons you need to learn."

"There is nothing I can learn from you, Lord Corby. You are ignorant and you are a fool. Education, you see, is beyond your means."

Gregory took off his cloak and his hat, rolled up the sleeves of his robe and went to digging in the hard patch of ground in front of Margery's home. Soon into it he knew he would break his back and rub his hands raw. He looked into the sky and thanked God it was not yet midday. He had plenty of hours before nightfall, and faced with this task, he knew he would need them all.

Lord Corby had not lied. Group by group and alone they arrived all day, riding into town as special guests at a grand social event. Cavorting, jesting, drinking, and feasting in the market square, the old lads of the shire geared up for a fond memory. Corby, dressed in blue worsted wool trimmed with sheared marten fur, fluttered at the center of this gathering, flashing his handsome smile and laughing as he twisted the ends of his waxed mustache.

The moment Gregory started the grave, Corby ordered his household to set up a banquet right in the middle of town, complete with tables pushed end to end, and benches and servants, and a boar roasting on a spit. He and the nobles who came to support him grew boisterous and lewd, and their entertainment, besides their own gluttony, was Gregory, sweating, panting, and fretting as he dug Margery's grave.

"Bordeaux," one of them called. "You do know once you have buried your whore in that grave, all of us will piss on it, don't you?"

Still another said, "Bordeaux, when you are done with the first one, dig another, for that is where we will stuff you at the end of it all."

And yet another nobleman, after a long drink of ale, burped and said, "A dead man digs a grave for a dead woman, and they will fuck in their muddy hole and conceive dead babies."

Good fun, and a communal affair, as some of the villagers stood off to the side and chuckled at the harassment. Gregory heard it all and all of it hurt, but he reacted to none of it. He kept stabbing at the earth, pausing only to collect his breath and to wipe his brow, and hour by hour, a grave took shape.

Warren didn't help with the digging. He kept watch, stern and unmoving, atop Moonbeam. He had used his sword to draw a wide circle around the gravesite, the implication being that anyone who came within the circle would have to deal with him.

And while Lord Corby and his associates enjoyed their loathsome celebration, and while they would not hesitate when it came time to murder, they themselves did not want to risk Warren's weaponry. Gregory assumed they knew what he had done a few days ago at Sempringham to Lord le Gaunter and his men.

Though the invitation for single combat stood, none of them were brave enough to accept what Warren offered. Instead they passed their time with drink, yet Gregory knew at some point one of the youngest among them, encouraged by the wine and the goading of his peers, would come, and then another and another, and Warren would be overrun. With that in mind, Gregory dug with fervor knowing the window of dignity Warren had opened would soon enough close.

Gregory worked with diligence, and the farce of the situation faded. He felt the villagers taking notice. He did, after all, bury a leading member of their community, a Christian woman who had committed no crime. With each spade of dirt, he heard them speak their regrets, and as the grave went deeper and deeper, and as Gregory stood inside the hole and shoveled down, he would catch their eyes and let them know with a squint they were cowards.

His shaming caused a few village teens to come with shovels and help. The parish priest shuffled out, and as he wrestled with his remorse, blessed the ground and made the sign of the cross. Perhaps unconventional, but Margery at last received a proper funeral. Her body, wrapped in a rough woolen blanket, was brought out by the elders, sprinkled with holy water, and placed in the ground as the priest read psalms from the Office of the Dead. Gregory and his helpers shoveled the dirt back into the hole, and after a day of labor, Margery rested in consecrated ground. The villagers crowded around the grave and wept, not just for their fallen friend, Gregory guessed, but for themselves. Corby was now in the hands of its lord, and with Margery out of the way, they would be next.

The priest offered Gregory a cup of ale. He drank it down. He wiped his mouth with the back of his forearm, and gave the cup back to the priest. A boy handed him his cloak, and with a billowing wave of wool, he whipped it over his shoulders and cinched it with his silver and sapphire brooch. He donned his under-bonnet, then his beaver and peacock hat, and pushed it deep down over his brow. He climbed up onto Black Saddle, clutched the reins, and made ready for the gallop. He glared at Lord Corby, drunk and sucking at the pit of his mirth.

Gregory raised an index finger as if to speak, but what came next was so unexpected and extreme, he and everyone else did nothing but watch in wonderment.

Warren trotted Moonbeam into the den of Lord Corby's banquet. The merriment stopped, and what had been a raucous show of privilege and power became a halting gala of silence. So close was Warren, any of them could have grabbed a knife and gone at him, but instead they watched to see what the young warlord would do. He gave a guttural command, and with two strides and a stupendous trick of exertion, Moonbeam leapt onto the table.

The silvery mare high-stepped all the way down and back, knocking over cups and goblets and squishing trenchers of food as she went. The click and clack of her shoes proved her precision, and she snorted and whinnied in giving voice to her daring might. Warren stood her right in front of Corby, who looked up at them with a mix of amazement and fear.

Showing the dark, eternal hatred the ploughman has for the lord, Warren flashed his teeth and stared down at Corby. "Margery was my friend, and you are not allowed to laugh at Master Gregory."

He uttered another command. Moonbeam kicked out with a rear hoof and flattened Lord Corby's face. As he slumped, she kicked again and broke his head into many pieces. The villagers gasped, one of the lords vomited, a dog barked, and the squirrels scurried up the trees. Birds took to flight, a cold wind circled in the market square, and the flame at the spit licked higher and higher.

Gregory, his mouth agape, felt a deep sorrow. He now knew without a doubt a fiend lurked within Warren, something Gregory had never wanted to see. But here it shone, bright and tough and full of vigor, the armament of the chronicle.

Warren looked into the distance toward Corby's moated manor. On the horizon appeared a new gang of riders, at full speed they came and in great numbers. Moonbeam leapt back down to the ground, found her stride, and sped out of town. As she and Warren shot past, Gregory remained. He watched and waited as the nobles gathered themselves, and as the band of riders approached. As he'd expected, the lead man, under the spray of a blue plume, was none other than Lord Baldwin of Essex. His arrival meant Gregory could at last bait the trap. With his thumb and index finger, he pulled the brim of his hat down even lower so an umbra of menace slanted across his sparkling eyes.

To the nobles he said, "Tell Lord Baldwin I am bound for the Stourbridge Fair to see the three-headed lady and to hear a cow sing the Song of Rolland. And while I am there, I will contest his claim and clear my name. Please, do tell Lord Baldwin."

He wheeled Black Saddle around, laid in with his spurs, and bolted out of Corby.

THE MERCHANT
ARMY
OF STOURBRIDGE

utside the village of Brigstock, Gregory and Warren pulled in behind a thick hedge along a brackish pond, and with their steeds standing ankle deep in leech-infested water, waited for the men who hunted them. They heard them romping down the road. Then they saw them, a swarm of angry hornets, pouring into the town. They heard them kick in doors and pull down stalls, yelling and imploring the town's inhabitants to hand over the doomed and cowardly waif, Gregory of Bordeaux.

But the villagers said the fugitive had not been there. They knew neither his name nor the nature of his alleged crimes, and nor did they care.

Lord Baldwin called all the townsmen liars and cursed them to hell. Then for spite, he torched the town. As he and his men rode away, and as flames and ash curled into the sky, Gregory shook his head. He had seen too many villages burn.

They trotted in behind Lord Baldwin's retinue, making sure to keep themselves at a safe distance, just out of sight. They traveled that way for two days, with Warren inspecting horse droppings and the remnants of camp fires to determine the proximity of the enemy. Gregory knew Lord Baldwin would figure it out sooner or later, and when he did, he would set an ambush. But by the time that happened, Gregory hoped, he and Warren would be on the Roman road to Stourbridge, and Moonbeam and Black Saddle would have the puissance to get them there.

At the end of the second day, they did what they had always done—they followed game trails deep into the wastelands, using the sun and then the stars to find their way, crisscrossing the fens, leaping over creeks, skirting ridges and descending bowls, trampling and pulling back the tangle of the wilderness. They emerged in a remote and ramshackle hamlet. There the ignorant and inbred looked at them in awe, the cats hissed and arched their backs, and the children hid and looked out from behind the protective thighs of their mothers. Then they would camp, and no one from the hamlet would bother them because they were unsettled by what they had seen. The militant horses. Warren's sword. The hint of calamity in his eye and the dreadful plume of crow feathers. Gregory's black cloak, his brimmed hat casting wicked shadows across his face, the twinkling of his brooch and jewels. Appearing as they often did, from seemingly out of nowhere and with the sun and the moon showing simultaneously in the sky, they always got the locals to murmuring.

This day was no different. As they settled into a night of rest just beyond the rows of rye, the bumpkins pointed and stared. Paying them no mind, Warren squatted next to the kindling, showering it with sparks from his flint and steel. He cupped his hands around his mouth and blew out a soft jet of air. The kindling caught, and a puff of smoke and fire promised comfort in the hours ahead.

"Blood has been spilled of late." Warren fed the flame with twigs. "And all of it in the name of the chronicle."

"Yes," Gregory said. "Much of it is written in ink, but some of it now is written in blood."

He rummaged through his bag of hard victuals. "Which do you prefer?"

"Ink." Gregory took off his hat, ran a hand through his tuft of hair, and scratched the back of his head. "But what I have learned, unfortunately, is sometimes ink begets blood. Why do you ask?"

"You did not think it would go this far," Warren said. "Now that it has, I know you have questioned yourself. But I know the story just as well as you. There is no blood on your hands, Master Gregory, only the blame of others. This I know. Still, one thing puzzles me. What is going to happen at the Stourbridge Fair? And don't tell me about a three-headed lady and a singing cow. This is the largest fair in all of Christendom. What is going to happen there?"

"I cannot tell you, dear Warren, because I do not know. But if I have my way, there will at least be a few friends waiting on us when we arrive."

"But why Stourbridge and not London?"

"Because it's easier to get to," he said, and the ghost of a smile flickered in the firelight.

hey rode through the morning mist to Huntingdon, a new town easily forgotten but for a wide timber bridge over the River Great Ouse. Gregory and Warren needed this bridge. On the other side ran the Roman road leading southeast to Cambridge and the annual orgy of food, frolic, and fancy it hosted—the Stourbridge Fair. Gregory looked at his calendar that morning and knew this was the first day of the event. They did not have time to search for a ford or another bridge. They had to cross there and make haste.

Gregory dismounted, crept down the side of one of the many timber-framed buildings along the waterfront, and peered around the corner. What he saw surprised him. A seething, cursing crowd on the north side of the bridge wanted to cross to the south side, but town officials and their men-at-arms had formed a cordon and held them back in a scrum of angst and impatience. The source of the disturbance was a huge wagon, its cargo high and tilting, with a blown front axle sitting in the middle of the bridge.

The wagon was of such size it could not be gotten around, and the flustered wheelwright, enduring the jeers heaped on him by the crowd, tried to make the repair there on the spot.

What chaos, but within a maelstrom can be found an opportunity. People crossed the river in all types of vessels, and with the curl of his brow and a gleam in his eye, he noticed two barges, vacant but for their crews, idle on the shore. Gregory ran down to the quay where the barges docked.

"Are you for hire, waterman?" he said to the man who looked to be the owner. "I am in urgent need of a crossing and have no time to spare."

The waterman held out his hands, shrugged and said, "Had you asked earlier, I would have said yes, but just before you arrived, Lord Baldwin of Essex reserved them, and it is for him and his men these barges will cross. They are in the stables preparing their horses and will be here soon. I cannot afford to keep a man like him waiting."

"True," said Gregory. "But nor can you afford to say no to a man like me. You see, I am the sworn man of the Earl of Southampton, who himself rode with the king to fight our enemies in Scotland. If the king is the wolf, then the earl is the teeth. And Lord Baldwin of Essex, well, he is the tick on the tail. So who do you choose, waterman, those who bite, or those who don't?"

In the silent moment between the waterman and him, Gregory summoned all of his sorrow and all of his joy, his fatigue and his heartbreak and his triumphs and desires. He felt the heat and the cold, and tasted the dust and saw the flurries of snow. Sunsets danced in his eyes and the many dawns swelled in his heart. Timber and thatch and stone and steel, the sinew of the world. He heard the sweetness of songbirds and the baleful caw of crows, and the pounding of hooves and the clank of harness and mail. Many names of people, cities, and towns, some still standing, others just embers or in the ground. All of these things came through Gregory and he mustered them into a stare that showed as an ugly threat, one he hoped the waterman understood and could not withstand. Gregory put a slow hand on the hilt of La Bonne Vie, and with the other hand, dug into his pouch with patience and pulled out the gold Bezant, turning it so its sumptuous light caught the waterman's eye.

Death or riches. The choice is usually easy, and God please make it so, for today I am not bluffing.

"I will ferry you to the other side," he said at last.

"You have chosen well."

He snapped his fingers over his head and in a flash Warren came out from hiding, mounted on Moonbeam and leading Black Saddle by a tether. They stepped onto the barge. The waterman and his crew pushed off with their great poles and the barge floated out over the River Great Ouse.

Halfway through their passage, Lord Baldwin and his men galloped to the quay. Baldwin's bearded face purpled with rage, and spit spewed from his mouth as he pointed and yelled at his retainers. Some of them poured onto the second barge and implored the crew to row and row hard. Lord Baldwin and the others turned and went back toward the bridge, smashing through the crowd and using the flat sides of their blades to beat back those in their way.

They broke through the cordon and rode up to the stalled wagon. One of Baldwin's men threw the wheelwright off the bridge, another climbed into the driver's seat and cracked the whip over the backs of its team of oxen. With the front axle dragging across the bridge, and the leaning cargo now falling into the river, the wagon moved.

Lord Baldwin screamed, "Go, go, go!" and pulled right in behind it with his men. On the river, Gregory's barge came closer to the shore with each pull of the oars, while the other barge, weighed down by many men and horses, lagged.

With a collective grunt and an immense jolt of power, the oxen lurched forward with the wrecked wagon in tow. At about the same time that the oxen emerged on the other side of the bridge, the barge slid ashore. Gregory handed the gold Bezant to the waterman, and he and Warren pressed with their spurs. Baldwin and his men teemed over the bridge just moments after Gregory and Warren galloped by. Warren kept riding, but Gregory wheeled Black Saddle around.

As his enemies bore down on him, he shook his fist, and called, "Perhaps tomorrow, Lord Baldwin, but not today!"

They weathered the first leg of the chase, when Lord Baldwin and his retinue galloped fresh and full. They had come close, so close they had drawn their swords, stood in their stirrups, and proclaimed it time to pay the penalty. But they had not come close enough, and once they had winded themselves and had fallen off the pace, Moonbeam and Black Saddle settled into a grueling canter only the finest of steeds could maintain. Mile after mile it went, with Gregory and Warren clopping down the road and their pursuers doing the same about twenty lengths behind.

Gregory rode nervous, with constant glances over the shoulder, anxiety over the condition of the horses, and bothersome guesswork as to when the men would come again. But he felt a glimmer of optimism, because he knew Black Saddle well, and the rhythm of his hooves proved the stallion had plenty left in him. He knew Moonbeam even better, and to see her broad chest heaving smooth and strong, he doubted she could ever be caught. They just had to keep up the frantic pace, and victory would be theirs.

From the excitement in Lord Baldwin's retinue, Gregory knew they wound up their horses for another run. He and Warren followed suit. With a kick of their spurs, their steeds accelerated midway between a canter and a gallop and poised themselves to charge, do or die, all the way to the fair.

But Gregory and Warren had come late with their response, and Baldwin and his men had stolen five lengths and strove for more. And like an arrow taking flight from its string, a single rider broke from the pack, on a horse much like Black Saddle. He came barreling down the road with such momentum, he doubtless would overcome them. Crouched over his mount's withers and slapping its rump with the flat side of his sword, the rider drove forward, pulling in behind Gregory and positioning himself for the kill.

Warren slid out his axe. Even in the heat and jostle of speed, he took the time to find just the right heft on the handle, and once he had, he swung the axe in a side-sweeping, backhanded motion and let go of it with the snap of his wrist. The axe left his hand and spun toward the oncoming rider, who ducked and cut his horse hard to the right to avoid being hit. Full on the hoof, the maneuver was too much and the horse's legs came out from under it. He and the rider tumbled across the road.

The threat, however, continued. Looking over his shoulder, Gregory saw Baldwin still gained on them, and in a horrific moment of doubt, he thought they might be captured. Their horses had plenty left in them, but perhaps Baldwin's had more.

Three lengths. Then two. Then one, and swords came out.

Baldwin's men, grinning and howling, pulled alongside them.

Gregory and Warren looked at each other and exchanged solemn nods.

"Yop yop," Warren uttered.

Gregory hissed through his teeth.

The earth shook, autumn leaves fell from the trees, and then the world went silent. In that moment, when time turned only for two, Moonbeam and Black Saddle burst with the light of life, and with every ounce of their valiant power, surged away from the men who sought their masters. Beyond a gallop they went, yearning, striving, desperate for heroics, nose for nose with wind in their manes, racing into a story forever to be told. Gregory looked down and could have sworn their hooves did not touch the ground, gliding as they did over the rough and pitted road.

He glanced over his shoulder to find Baldwin and his men still riding hard, but falling ten lengths behind. When Gregory looked back at the road, his heart swelled. On the horizon loomed the skyline of Cambridge, and off to the side, the sprawling makeshift jumble of the Stourbridge Fair.

Keeping the fantastic pace, the horses weaved through the people, veered past the wagons, and leapt over the junk clogging the Stourbridge road. Gregory and Warren urged them without mercy, and as the horses ran yet faster, and as they cut and hurtled through the moving labyrinth of humanity, people gawked at the spectacle sweeping by them.

Gregory dug into his robe and yanked out the ell of red felt given to him by Geoffrey. He held it above his head. It caught in the wind and trailed behind him like a war pennon as Black Saddle blazed down the main thoroughfare.

A thousand throats sounded a booming cheer, and in many places, Gregory saw scarlet flickers.

He and Warren broke around a corner, past the spicers and the alewives, the grocers and the drapers, and the hatters and the shoemakers. Past all of them, up on a hill outside the fair, just beyond the stink of the latrine and the waft of baking bread, a knot of men rallied around a bright red banner. As Gregory and Warren galloped toward them, the men arrayed their weaponry and greeted them with a deafening salute.

Gregory doffed his hat, reared Black Saddle, and then rode him prancing down the line, his hooves and knees popping in a haughty show of pedigree. Gregory circled back and joined Warren at the center. From left to right, he observed this collection of men. Sons and fathers, masters and apprentices, horsemen, archers, and an ugly clutch of criminal spearmen. And yet more fellows ran to the banner, swelling the ranks with their grips and irons. Patchwork and threadbare, with many too young and many too old, and with rusty mail and borrowed arms, this assembly was the brazen work of amateurs. But there it stood, flinty and inspired, The Merchant Army of Stourbridge.

"The day will be ours, lads," Gregory called, and donned his hat.

Gregory watched Lord Baldwin and his men rush out from the fair and start up the hillside. A grim smile came to his face, and his army jeered, when Lord Baldwin's train pulled to a stop. Gregory, feeling the power and pressure of three hundred men at his back, stared across the field at Lord Baldwin. Though he commanded a much smaller force, his was of prized stallions, seasoned killers, and polished steel. Gregory knew if they attacked, they could possibly win.

He had done much this day, and still it might not be enough.

With this many men trapped in this circumstance, patience would give way to the shrill call of conflict. These two forces would collide. God and the devil would have their allotment of souls, and the crows would grow fat on the flesh of the vanquished. Gregory did not want that to happen. He wanted to win by the threat of force, not the use of it. Only one man really needed comeuppance, and it was Lord Baldwin. There was a way to flush him out of his retinue and, once by himself, lay him low and disperse his forces. To do so, Gregory would have to risk the life of the man he had grown to love, but such was the will of war.

"Warren?"

"Yes, Master Gregory?"

"Go get Lord Baldwin and bring him to me."

"Yes, Master Gregory," he said, and swallowed hard.

Warren rode out into the area between the two camps. Once in clear view of all, he coaxed Moonbeam into a series of swaggering, hoof-shuffling circles. He drew Fionnaghal and twirled it twice before holding it over his head. The wind ruffled his black cape, the plume of crow feathers dipped and danced, and he glowered out from the space between the top of his shield and the rim of his helmet.

"Lord Baldwin, come and be first," he called. "The time for the tally is at hand, and I want your name at the top of my list."

Stuck in the mire of his cowardice, Lord Baldwin did not respond. Instead, he conversed with his page, shaking his head and gesturing with his hands. Warren, alone and formidable in the lull of reckoning, waited as his challenge went unmet. A rising thunder of hooves broke the calm, and everyone on the hill looked at what headed their way—a glinting phalanx of mounted warriors tearing across the turf at daring speed.

Gregory made the sign of the cross. His army buckled and breathed a collective gasp of fear. Even Warren and Moonbeam flinched at the sight. As they drew near, Gregory saw on these horsemen a gloss of grit and grime, of grease and death. They banked into the open land between the opposing sides and with splendid horsemanship, circled around Warren and wheeled to a halt facing Gregory's line.

These men followed a terrible lord, his custom armor and embroidered green cloak punctuated by gilt silver spurs, a collar of sable, and a single golden feather sprouting from his helm. His visor was up so Gregory saw his ruddy cheeks and the dour privilege in his alert brown eyes. A mix of assurance and recklessness, he bore the vigor of a man barely out of his teens.

But if he had just grown into his kit, the same was not true of his men. Much older, with stubble and beards, and scars and gauntlets, and long unwritten lists of men who had perished at their hands. At each end of their line were Welsh archers with their magnificent long bows. Even the priest looked as if he could murder. And sizing up their lean coursers, Gregory realized perhaps Black Saddle was not the fastest horse in the realm.

Though Gregory did not see what happened behind him, he felt it. His merchant army, so dearly made and so recently confident, neared the brink of desertion. Such was the glamour this lord and his men conveyed, and under the searing light of their presence, Gregory knew he too would soon wilt.

The lord said not a word but peered into Gregory's eyes, sharing with him the peril of the moment. Looking out from beneath the brim of his beaver and peacock hat, Gregory managed to hold his gaze. As he searched the soul of this young baron, he found in him a newness that belied his ancient blood. Of the horse and the sword, but also of the quill and the manuscript. If a road led out of this world and into the next, this lord was already on it, galloping faster than the others and showing the way. The expression on the nobleman's face, framed in mail and the accoutrements of command, showed he was both ruthless and enlightened to his core. An abiding fierceness flashed through him as he pulled a square of red silk from beneath his etched chest plate and held it high above his head. A wet and triumphal roar belched out of the army's maw. And it was then Gregory nearly fainted because the truth in the time finally dawned.

Richard Beaufort, the Earl of Southampton, had arrived.

"It has been nearly three years, Bordeaux," he said. "When we first met you were a conceited lawyer content to count his pennies, and now you are at the head of your own army. I must say, the chronicle has been good to you."

"It has, my lord, but only because of your steadfast support."

"You have summoned me, Bordeaux," he said. "What is it you ask of me?"

"Lord Baldwin of Essex, my lord, and others, have slandered my name and have accused me of being a horse thief when I am not. I ask you to discredit the falsehoods my enemies willingly purport."

"And are those your enemies?" he said, gesturing toward the horsemen across the field.

"Yes," said Gregory. "And Lord Baldwin is among them."

"Do you know what Lord Baldwin is?"

"No, my lord. Please tell me."

"He is a man who will learn contrition, and he will learn it the hard way."

Southampton motioned with a hand and called out a series of commands, and in a blink, ten of his men galloped toward Lord Baldwin and his cringing retainers. They pulled him from his horse and drug him back across the field. By the time they dumped him in a heap in front of Gregory, Lord Baldwin was a trembling mess. He looked up at the men who would decide his fate. His eyes were those of a beggar.

"Do you see this horse?" Southampton gestured toward Black Saddle.

"Yes, my lord," Lord Baldwin said.

"And whose horse is that?"

"The horse is Black Saddle, and it is the right and fair property of Gregory du Mont, also known as Gregory of Bordeaux. His horse was won clean and outright at a race in Durham, a race in which I cheated and in which Warren of Lichfield bested me. Here in front of the witnesses of Stourbridge, I renounce any and all false claims I have made."

Southampton glanced at Gregory. "Does this please you?"

"Yes, my lord, it pleases me."

Southampton gave another command in a voice conveying his brutality. The biggest and burliest of his men climbed down off his horse, strode over to Lord Baldwin, and grabbed him by the collar. With his enormous, iron-clad fist, he socked him so hard his face went lopsided and remained that way. Lord Baldwin fell to the ground, holding his shattered jaw, heaving with a crooked pain that would remain until his dying day.

"Now that is the face of a man who dared to speak ill of my scribe," Southampton said. "Now be gone, you dog-ass of a man, and pray you do not soon see me at the gates of your castle."

Lord Baldwin collected his broken life and slunk away, and as he did, he looked over his shoulder one last time and made eye contact with Gregory. He wanted to say something. He wanted to turn the dagger by putting something in Lord Baldwin's ear he would always hear and hate. But Gregory thought better of it and said nothing, and left Baldwin alone with his sorrow.

"You know I was in Scotland—at Falkirk with the king," Southampton said.

"I did not know for sure, but I figured you would be," Gregory said.

"An interesting thing happened during the battle."

"What was that, my lord?"

"I had the honor of meeting your old friend, Swinton the Red. He was no match for me. Try as he did to kill me, I got him down from his pony, put my boot to his neck and my sword to within a lash of his eye. And I said to him, 'I think you have something that belongs to me. It is a chronicle written by my esteemed scribe, Gregory of Bordeaux. If you give it to me, I will spare your life.'"

"And what came of that?"

"See it with your own eyes."

The priest drew near. From a saddlebag he pulled a waxed leather satchel and handed it to Gregory. He undid the buckle and opened it. There they were, the original parchments from Swinton's tower. His mouth agape, he thumbed through the pages, dense with Latin, French, and the English vernacular, and felt the chronicle breathe. He looked up at the earl as if to make a grandiloquent statement of gratitude and appreciation, but Southampton waved him off.

"My priest has been reading the chronicle to me," he said. "While I have enjoyed all of it, there is one part I would like to hear out of your mouth. Go ahead. I have marked it for you."

Gregory noticed a tassel hanging from one of the pages and turned to it. When he realized what the passage was, his heart sank. Meddling in the affairs of men high above him had never been his intent, but while in Swinton's tower writing for his life, nothing, it seemed, was off limits. Gregory cleared his throat, summoned his gumption, and in a refined tenor, read from the chronicle.

Idle and resistant to new ideas, a baron can rot on his own vine and still
believe he is happy. Such is the shortfall of the peerage, and it is what I hope
the earl can overcome. He is young, so there is no telling what kind of man
he will become. But if he remembers to use his pruning shears, he can cull
dead leaves and bring light to green fruit. A great lord should use his posi-
tion for the betterment of the world, not just the betterment of his interests.
All the realm will watch to see what Southampton does with his life. I trust
it will be the right thing.

Gregory looked up from the parchment and into the eyes of the earl.

"That is why I am here today. Have two copies made, with gold leaf and the brightest paints, and have the originals returned to me."

"Yes, my lord," Gregory said. He closed the satchel and tucked it under his arm.

"I'm sure you know Lord Tutbury was recently disinherited," said the earl. "It was your account of the events at Lichfield that led to the forfeiture, and don't you know, you have produced the perfect candidate to fill the open slot. If Warren rides with me now, I can install him at Tutbury and make of him a lord. But he will have to fight for it because even as we speak, Earl Stafford is collecting his forces and will oppose us."

Gregory looked to Warren. "Do you want to be a lord?"

"Yes, Master Gregory. I should like to hold the manor at Tutbury and have the earl as my liege."

"Then it is time to say farewell," Gregory said.

He looked away for a moment, and watched a gliding buzzard circling high in the distance. He remembered when Warren's life changed for good. Hugging his parents, wiping away a tear, and telling his younger brother and sister he would return one day. Such tenderness rarely visits, and when it does, only upon deserving people. Gregory took off his hat, clutched it over his heart, and turned in his saddle so he faced Warren.

"I am alive but by your loyalty and courage," he said. "Your account is always good with me, Warren, and until I take my last breath, I will be honored to name you among the best of my friends and family."

"You believed in me from the beginning, Master Gregory. I promise I will learn to read and write and keep the count, and when I come upon a problem I cannot solve, I shall think of you and find the answer. And if trouble ever finds you, let me know. We will ride again, and we will win again."

"Let us perhaps catch our breath first."

Southampton bellowed at his horseman and they went taut on the hoof. With Warren and Moonbeam among them, they pulled out over the turf to Staffordshire. Gregory watched them, gallant and glinting and giving chase to their era, until they disappeared into the horizon. He made the sign of the cross and asked God to look over Warren as he competed for his title. Sitting at the head of an army, he felt alone, sad, empty, and drained. Black Saddle's ears twitched and he gave a soothing neigh.

"Yes, my boy, you will make quick work of the road to London," he said. "My hands are tired, my ass is chapped, and my stomach is growling. At last, dear Black Saddle, it is time to go home."

EPILOGUE

CAHORS AND RHENISH

He stayed on the field long after Warren and Southampton had gone and took the time to at least try and thank each man who had come to his defense. Gregory noted as many names as possible and got the headcount. Six archers, twenty-five horsemen, two hundred eighty-five footmen, and the earl and his forty-two retainers had assembled that day. Many of the men had been hired and were thus temporary soldiers of fortune there for the coin and nothing more. But Gregory had the honor of speaking with the apprentices and masters and all manner of craftsmen and traders who had risked their careers and lives in defense of his name. Even a nobleman had entered the ranks—Pierre D'Iberville, the squire he had met at Sudeley Castle who had become a knight and now had a squire of his own.

Before dashing off to Tutbury, the earl had flipped Gregory a pouch heavy with silver, and with a stern glance had said, "Buy every hogshead of ale and every pipe of wine you can and share it with the men who came here for you. Get drunk with them and laugh with them, and in a year, you will be a legend."

And so he did. Despite his aching bones and his longing for London, he remained at the Stourbridge Fair until it closed. He went to see the three-headed lady, and her show bedazzled him. With one mouth she swallowed swords, with another she blew fire, and with the third, she put in an egg and pulled out a chirping chick—all while standing on stilts on top of a barrel. Gregory gave her a penny. He listened to the cow's rendition of the Song of Rolland, and sang along as stanza by stanza the hero's epic unfolded. He patted the cow on the rump and gave its owner a penny. When the fair ended, he joined a caravan for the slow yet safe and comfortable journey home.

His heart jittered when he saw the skyline of London, its steeples and spires stained with soot, its walls and towers casting shadows across the suburbs. On the wind came the distinct stench that could only leak and waft from the great sphincter of a city with the appetite of London's. Gregory waved to his companions as he shed the caravan and galloped to the city alone. He passed through the arch at Bishopsgate, and with Black Saddle prancing, turned right at Tower Street and then left down the little nook near the River Thames to Royal Street. Boys who recognized him had run ahead so as he made his way through town, people looked and pointed and in some instances called his name.

"There goes Gregory of Bordeaux."

"Master Gregory left as a lawyer and has returned as a lord!"

In response, he sometimes tugged at the brim of his beaver and peacock hat, or nodded and flashed a respectful smile. As he neared his destination, his presence created more commotion. People stopped working and quit their haggling and gossiping and all the mundane things people do on an otherwise ordinary day.

By the time he reached his wine shop, dozens of people followed him, and as many more awaited his arrival. It touched him that those who had seen him off were among those who welcomed him back. Alan Spicer, Joan the Widow, and the four Williams—William Purchase, William Pepper, William Stokes, and William Hawkins. Standing at the center of this crowd was Gregory's cousin, Jean du Mont, the man who had made all of it possible, and the man who in time would learn in full how the chronicle had changed Gregory.

"You are home, dear cousin." He bowed.

Gregory swallowed back his emotions, and after composing himself, gave a weary smile. In a voice that nearly cracked, he said, "I want a pipe of ripe Malbec from Cahors and a pipe of crisp Rhenish from the vineyards of the Holy Roman Emperor."

"You have arrived at the wine shop of Gregory of Bordeaux," his cousin said. "And indeed, my lord, we have it in plenty."

native Texan, Richard Massey lived in New England, the Midwest, and the Deep South before settling in Northwest Arkansas in 2007. A career reporter with over a decade of experience, he has written everything from fluff features to hardcore crime stories. While he's been to just about every juke house on the Mississippi Delta, he also appreciates the Rembrandt collection at the Metropolitan Museum of Art in New York. Mr. Massey has a bachelor's degree in history from Ohio State University, and a master's degree in journalism from Ole Miss.

www.ingramcontent.com/pod-product-compliance
Lightning Source LLC
Chambersburg PA
CBHW031949240626
47153CB00003B/921